Praise

'*Brightfall* is beautiful insi...
and filled with bittersw...
read, perfect for readers of Juliet Marillier. I loved it'
Stephanie Burgis, author of *Snowspelled*
and *Masks and Shadows*

'An immensely satisfying read with its unexpected and
unique twist on the legend of Sherwood Forest, Robin and
his men, and the brave, determined, resilient Marian'
Kate Elliott, author of *King's Dragon*

'[A] brave retelling'
Daily Mail

'Boldly envisioned and beautifully told'
Sebastien de Castell, author of the Greatcoats quartet

'Putting a contemporary twist on a centuries old myth,
Brightfall breathes new life into the tale of Robin Hood –
bringing Marian to the fore and plunging her into a
mystery that threatens the lives of all she loves'
The Bookbag

'A genuinely new take on the Robin Hood tales ... A
treat for those who like their myths with extra magic'
The Times

BRIGHTFALL

JAIME LEE MOYER

Jo Fletcher
BOOKS

First published in Great Britain in 2019
This edition published in 2020 by

Jo Fletcher Books
an imprint of Quercus Editions Ltd
Carmelite House
50 Victoria Embankment
London EC4Y 0DZ

An Hachette UK company

A CIP catalogue record for this book is available
from the British Library

PB ISBN 978 1 78747 922 7
EB ISBN 978 1 78747 919 7

10 9 8 7 6 5 4 3 2 1

Typeset by CC Book Production
Printed and bound in Great Britain by Clays Ltd, Elcograf S.p.A.

Papers used by Quercus are from well-managed forests and other responsible sources.

For my favourite hedgewitch, Kat Allen, who gave me a magic word that showed me a forest green in the light of a rising moon.

Chapter 1

And if Robin should be cast
Sudden from his turfed grave,
And if Marian should have
Once again her forest days,
She would weep, and he would
craze . . .

JOHN KEATS

In the middle of the greenwood stood an oak, broad as it was tall, with roots the Fae believed wrapped around the heart of the world. People on the farms outside Sherwood still told tales about that tree; most called it Robin's Oak. Few spinning tales about Robin and Marian's adventures knew I shared a cottage there with my children. Much as it pained Robin to claim Kate and Robbie, they were his children too. Only a few close friends and the monks in St Mary's knew he'd left us on our own almost twelve years ago.

Not many ventured this far into Sherwood. Trees were widely spaced near our house, the ground running more to glades and

1

meadows dotted with the oldest oak and rowan. King John's foresters and woodcutters might stop by to share a meal, or women from Nottingham come seeking small vials of the philtres and elixirs that only I knew the making of, but other visitors were rare. Seeing Brother Timothy striding down the dusty, seldom-used path that led to Nottingham was a welcome surprise. Tim was a member of Abbot Tuck's order and an old friend, though I hadn't seen him in a year or more.

I continued dipping water from a bucket onto the mint growing near the door and waited for him. The bow and quiver slung over his shoulder looked out of place with the wooden crucifix bouncing on his chest and the awkward way he carried them as much as shouted that they didn't belong to him.

A gift for Robbie, from his father. I hoped that Robin had remembered Kate as well this time.

Timothy raised a hand in greeting and called out, 'Blessed day to you, Lady Marian.'

The fourth son of a noble house, he'd taken vows as a boy, yet he still held to courtly ways and granted me titles I'd lost long ago. I waved back and hurried to meet him at the edge of the path. His fringe of hair was whiter than the last time I'd seen him, making him look old enough to be my father. Age had settled deeper around his eyes, but his cheery smile still belonged to a young man.

'Ah, Tim, the title came with the marriage. I gave up being Lady Marian when Robin put me aside.' I stood on tiptoe to kiss his cheek. 'You're the only one who still greets me that way.'

'Don't expect me to approve Robin's folly,' Tim said. 'You know neither Tuck nor I agreed with his reasons for asking to annul the marriage. Cardinal Liam was wrong to grant Robin's request.'

'Old hurts and sorrows are best forgotten, Tim. And it's all long in the past now. So, tell me why you've come and if you'll be able to stay for supper.' I pointed at the bow and quiver. 'And forgive me, but unless Robin remembered a gift for Kate this time, I'm going to ask you leave the bow right here.'

He reached into the oft-mended purse at his belt and pulled out a small packet, nicely wrapped in a scrap of yellow linen and tied with a blue ribbon. Yellow was Kate's favourite colour, but remembering that was more like Tim than her father.

'A silver locket, and with a penny tucked inside. I made it plain to Robin I wouldn't carry gifts for only one of his children,' he said. 'Come and sit in the sun with me, Marian. We need to talk.'

I slipped the locket into my apron pocket and took his arm for the short walk to the cottage. He leaned the bow against the wall, emptied the remaining water in the bucket onto the flowers under the window and upended it so I could sit with the sun warming my shoulders. He lowered himself to the step, his back to the runes painted on the oak door.

Tim stared off towards the path. His long silence was making me uneasy, but finally he sighed and looked straight at me, sorrow and pity filling his eyes, and a strange reluctance.

I shivered, convinced a shade had touched my face and left the cold of the grave behind.

'Marian . . .' He cleared his throat. 'There's no easy way to say this. Will's dead.'

I stared, thinking I'd misunderstood. Foolish thoughts skittered about in my head, thoughts that led anywhere but to never seeing Will again; never hearing his laugh, or feeling his warmth next to me.

Tim touched my shoulder, making me jump. He smelled of

greasy wool, tallow smoke and too much time spent indoors. Odd things to notice, normal things, that kept me from hunching over my knees and wailing. 'Did you hear me, sweet lady? Will's dead.'

'I – I heard.' I stared into his kind blue eyes and I saw he believed what he'd said. 'But it's not true, Tim, it can't be. It's a mistake or . . . or another man died and they mistook him for Will. He's not dead. Please tell me he's not.'

He crouched in front of me, putting us eye to eye. 'There's no mistake, Marian. The messenger who arrived at the abbey and gave Robin the news wore the earl's crest. I read the message myself. Will died while visiting his father.'

Dead was only a word, nothing more, but that word held so much sorrow. I screwed my eyes tight shut, unable to stand the pity in Tim's face a moment longer. A vision of Will Scarlet as I'd last seen him taunted me: him grinning as he reached for me, his hair tousled from sleep, blue eyes sparkling in early morning light.

Will's ghost was standing at Tim's shoulder when I opened my eyes. Knotting my hands in my apron was all that kept me from reaching for him.

'How long ago?'

'Less than a fortnight. Will had put the finishing touches to the earl's trade agreements the day before. He'd planned on leaving for home within the week.' He glanced away, then squeezed my shoulder before standing. 'I wanted you to hear the news from a friend.'

Kate and Robbie needed to be told, as gently as I could manage. Unlike his older brother, Will hadn't hesitated to be a father to my children. We'd been together more than seven years. Robbie and Kate loved him nearly as much as I did.

'That was more than kind, Tim,' I said. 'Did the message say what happened, or how . . . how he died?'

Tim sat on the step, looking defeated in a way I'd never seen in him before. 'Will went riding just after mid-morning and the stablemaster saw him return late that afternoon. The groom who stabled his horse told the earl that Will was laughing and joking, just like always. He greeted those he passed as he went upstairs to his rooms to change before the evening meal, as was his wont. But Will never came downstairs. May God have mercy on his soul and forgive William his sins.'

Touches of grey may have frosted Will's temples, but he was only a year or two older than me. Healthy men didn't spend the day riding and return home to die before supper. 'I . . . I don't understand. What killed him?'

'I wish I could tell you, but I don't know. No one knows.' Tim clutched his cross with both hands. 'The earl's own physician said there weren't any wounds or signs of an injury and he told Will's father that even the most quick-acting poison would leave traces – retching or foaming at the mouth, an odour that clings to the body or bleeding under the skin. And any poison that kills that quickly causes unendurable pain. None of the upstairs servants heard Will cry out, not even once.'

Tim was toying with his cross and avoiding looking at me: he had more to say, but needed to work up the courage. I'd known him well for almost twenty years. I could give him the peace to find the words.

He didn't make me wait long. 'The housemaid who went into his rooms to lay the fire found Will sitting in a chair . . . holding a scroll in his hand. He'd turned the chair to the window, maybe to catch the light. His eyes were open wide and he was staring at a mirror on the wall.' Timothy looked down the lane again and frowned. 'He was dead, his skin already cold when the girl raised the alarm. The earl and Robin both accepted his death as the will of God. I have a harder time laying his passing at the Lord's feet.'

'Do you have someone else to blame?' A name: I wanted a name, someone worthy of wrath and vengeance; someone to whom I could return all this pain.

Tim crossed himself and sighed. 'Will isn't the first to die, Marian. We've had word of others dying, men who were friends to us all. At first we thought their passing was natural, either from age or illness, then when we began to hear the stories of how they died, Abbot Tuck sent me to beg your aid. He hopes you can find the reason behind what's happened and put a stop to it.'

'Me?' I wrapped my arms over my chest and held myself tightly, afraid of how much more grief Tim meant to set at my feet. 'Why would Tuck send you to me?'

'He thinks witchcraft might be involved. A curse.' He fidgeted, obviously uncomfortable. 'Tuck is sure we need a witch to unravel it all.'

I shook my head 'I've never denied being a witch, Tim, and you're not going to hurt my feelings by calling me such.'

My mother had raised me in the old ways, as her mother had raised her, and her gram before that. She'd taught me herb-craft and lore, healing and midwifery, and to respect the Fae while staying wary, and when I had learned all she could teach me, Mam had found someone who could teach me more.

No longer able to keep still, I stood and paced in tight circles. A breeze ruffled the plants in my garden, stole the scent of rosemary for its own and carried it away. 'Tell me who's dead. Then tell me what Tuck needs me to do.'

Tim shut his eyes, as if reciting the names of our dead friends would be easier if he couldn't see my face. 'Alan died sitting alone in a tavern, staring out of a window. Midge went out to water the animals before starting the day's work in the mill. His wife found him dead next to the horse trough. Gilbert White Hand and Gamelyn died in late spring. The man who brought us the news said they'd set Gamelyn's wagon up for the market in Sheffield, but he didn't know how they died.'

He stopped talking, but the sorrow on his face told me he wasn't yet finished naming those we'd lost. I touched his shoulder. 'You've at least one more name to give me, Tim. I need to know everything if I'm to be of any help.'

Tim kept staring at the dirt between his dusty boots, his hands wrapped tightly around his cross. He finally looked up. 'Ethan – John's little boy. He died a month ago.'

'Oh stars, no . . .' All the rest were grown men, friends since our outlaw years in Sherwood. I could imagine someone seeking revenge on any one of them for some slight, or a deed performed in the name of our cause, but not all of them, not for things that had happened so far in the past they'd blurred and all but faded from my memory.

And Ethan? My heart refused to believe he was gone. He was only six, an innocent little boy with no stains on his past. His death wounded me as much as Will's.

I moved away from Tim and looked with other sight into places most didn't believe in. My garden and the surrounding forest were bright with butterflies and blossoms, full of life. No shadows intruded, no taint of death reached for those I loved.

Not yet.

A red vixen raced out of the trees, the rag poppet Kate normally carried everywhere hanging from her mouth. The little fox dived behind Tim's legs and wiggled into her den under the step.

Kate charged out of the forest an instant later, her skirts lifted above her knees so she could run and a storm brewing on her face. 'Bridget! Bring her back or you'll be sorry!'

Robbie, my own innocent, was labouring to keep up with his sister. Blackberries bounced out of the overflowing willow basket he was clutching in both hands, leaving a trail of glossy blue-black fruit snaking behind him.

Kate ignored Tim as she slid to a halt next to the step. Her braid, the same reddish brown as Robin's, was half-undone, strands of hair stuck to her dirt-smudged face. Fresh mud clung to her apron and I spied leafy sprigs, gnarly roots and flower-heads peeking out of the pockets. She stomped a bare foot on the step and glared at the den opening. 'You're not funny, Bridget. Give her back, right now!'

Tim stood and moved a few paces away from the step, hiding his smile behind his hand, struggling not to laugh.

Robbie had slowed to a walk when he'd spotted the monk in front of our door and stood there, hesitating, until I held out a hand to him. He was too old at eleven to hide behind my skirts, but not too old to shy away from the arm I laid on his shoulders. He watched Tim warily.

'Bridget, come out here,' I said. 'Don't make me call you twice.'

The hole under the step wasn't the only way in and out of the vixen's den. Her head popped out of an entrance hidden in the shadow of the woodpile, tongue lolling, laughing at her own cleverness.

'Give Kate her doll. Then make yourself useful and fetch a couple of hares for the stew – and big full-grown bucks this time, not any of those scrawny younglings you left on the step yesterday. Hurry yourself along.'

She whined and shimmied backwards. Kate's poppet was clutched in her mouth when she reappeared. Bridget made a show of carrying the rag doll to Kate – but dropped it just out of reach, then yipped and danced to the side, daring Kate to chase her.

'Enough!' I pointed towards the trees behind the cottage. 'If you want supper, do as you're told.'

With another low whine, Bridget loped into the forest. Of course she was more than capable of catching her own supper, but she'd bring back the rabbits I'd asked for first.

Kate picked up her poppet, dusting it off and checking to see if the vixen had done any harm. Bridget never did damage her toy, but my daughter wouldn't leave that to chance.

'Will you stay to supper, Tim? We have plenty to share.'

Tim rested a hand on Kate's head. She peered up at him and smiled. 'Another day, Marian. I promised Tuck I'd return to the abbey tonight. A word with you before I go?'

'Robbie, take the blackberries inside, please. Kate will help you sort out the best ones for tarts, but don't eat any more right now,' I said. 'Save room for supper. Go on now, I'll be in to help soon.'

He looked up at me, blackberry juice on his chin and big brown eyes full of innocence. I smoothed a hand over his dark hair, remembering how I'd lain awake at night feeling two babes tumble and roll inside me, imagining twins would be exactly alike. But Kate had all my fire and fight, while Robbie had my curiosity and need to know.

Once they'd gone inside, I walked with Tim to the edge of the path. My hands shook, the thought of telling Kate and Robbie that Will would never return to us almost more than I could bear. We'd never said vows nor felt the need for Church blessings, but Will had been part of our lives since they were very small. Breaking their hearts would cause mine to bleed anew.

Tim kissed me on the forehead, offering both comfort and a blessing. 'How soon will you be able to come to Nottingham? Tuck needs your knowledge and skill. Others in the Church might not agree, but not all things in the world can be handled with prayer.'

He didn't need to say that Robin was one of those; I already knew that.

'Tell Tuck I'll meet him at The Lark and Wren in three days. Once I speak to him, I'll know better what I need to do. No scrap of gossip about how our friends died is too small. Make sure he knows.'

Tim fingered his cross again, a nervous habit he'd acquired since I'd seen him last. 'What will you do for the next three days?'

'Find a way to ward my children against Ethan's fate. I can't leave them unprotected and trust that whoever took John and Emma's son won't look in their direction. I can't be that careless with their lives. And I need time to mourn with my children before facing more troubles. Tuck will understand.'

'I'll tell him.' Tim made the sign of the cross over me. 'May God watch over all of you and keep you safe.'

Thickening shadows stretched away from the rowan trees to darken the path. As I watched Tim being swallowed by distance and nightfall, my thoughts were full of the last time I saw Will walk away. A lifetime wouldn't be nearly long enough to mourn Will Scarlet. I'd wanted to spend the rest of my days with him.

Bridget's yips called me back to myself. I wiped my eyes on the corner of my apron and turned towards the cottage, determined to get through supper before breaking the news to Kate and Robbie. Will's smiling ghost stood on the path, arms outstretched.

'Please don't haunt me, Will.' His ghost drifted closer, but I backed away. 'Please. I don't have the strength to send you away.'

The shade faded, thinning into the twilight until I couldn't say if I'd really seen him. I hurried to the cottage, tears in my eyes and all the things needing to be done before I left for Nottingham whirling in my head.

Protecting my children wasn't a simple thing and asking for help to keep them safe was a risk I couldn't avoid, but I needed to prepare carefully before sending out a call. One misstep could mean summoning disaster down on all our heads. That truly frightened me, but the uncertainty scared me more.

I didn't know what I'd do if I called and none of the Fae answered.

Chapter 2

Merry, merry England has kissed the lips of June:
All the wings of fairyland were here beneath the moon,
Like a flight of rose-leaves fluttering in a mist
Of opal and ruby and pearl and amethyst.

ALFRED NOYES

I left the cottage with night well underway, the moon already high in a sky full of stars. Bridget was lying in front of the door, a sharp-toothed guardian in addition to the shimmering wards I'd laid around the cottage. Robbie and Kate slept deeply, bad dreams and grief held at bay for the moment by a packet of herbs under each pillow and a protective circle drawn around their bed. I'd never shielded them from life before; guilt and the knowledge there'd be a price later left a sour taste on my tongue.

But that was my only choice, to ward Kate and Robbie as best I could and leave Bridget to watch over them. I didn't want them waking to find me gone, or fearing I wouldn't return.

Five days before the full moon and for a full five days afterwards, Sherwood's clearings and meadows were brightly lit.

Dewdrops on every flower and blade of grass were transformed into softly glowing orbs, earth-bound moon-twins reflecting light and soaking in power. For these few nights, creatures that thrived on darkness and foul deeds were banished to the densest parts of the forest; the new moon was their time.

Roaming Sherwood at night was never safe for mortals, so I welcomed the small protections moonglow brought. Power hummed in the air, building towards its peak four nights from now. Every hedgewitch and herbwife, even unschooled in true craft, recognised the power of the moon as women's magic and used it to full advantage. I planned to help protect myself from the Fae with it, but first I had to call them to a ring.

Faerie rings have never been rooted in one place. The Fae move them with the seasons, abandon those defiled by the king's foresters, or even stop using a ring because they grew bored with the view. They'd taken to hiding their rings deeper in Sherwood, away from common folk and the bustle of towns, but I still heard tales of young maids on far-flung farms being beguiled to leave their beds and dance under the full moon. Some, who found special favour with a Fae Lord, never returned home, while others reappeared months later, their bellies swollen with half-Fae babes and memories of the revels they'd willingly joined shining in their eyes.

Gossips used such tales to cast doubt on anyone who showed signs of having other sight or of being skilled in craft. Stories concocted to explain my gifts claimed my mother had been one of those maids, that I was the price she paid for the touch of a Fae Lord's hand. All I knew was that my father loved her till the end of his days. He loved me as well, and if I wasn't his true child, it was never spoken of.

The particular ring I sought was built from tall standing stones rooted deep in an earthen mound and spelled to turn away anyone without at least a touch of sight, or the few mortals called to dance. This ring never moved. None of the Fae would ever say, but I suspected the mound concealed a way Underhill.

Tall grey stones were glowing with an inner light when I arrived, shining across the clearing like a welcome candle in a window. The Fae wanted their light to draw moths to their flame, but I wasn't fool enough to step between the stones and into their power. Summoning them from outside would work just as well, and hold more than enough danger. I dared much by disturbing the High Lords and Ladies.

Salt for the first protective circle sank into the grass, only a slight shimmer showing where it lay when I stepped inside and woke the protections. Next, pebbles for the inner ring, charmed to keep me inside and safe from beguilement, disappeared in the same way. I closed the second circle, wove my will around the power of the moon and cast the spell to see who would answer my summons.

Air sprites were the first to appear, gossamer creatures who swirled like wisps of smoke, high keening voices echoing off the stones as they circled above my head. The whirlwind they stirred up whipped my hair into my eyes before they tired of the game. Water sprites arrived next in churning clouds of mist, weaving in and out of the standing stones the way a cat seeking cream greets a milkmaid. They curled around my protections, looking for a break in salt or pebbles. Moisture beaded on my face before they gave up and I wiped my eyes clear on a sleeve.

I saw the glitter of Fire sprites before they left the cover of the trees, buzzing sparks rushing loud as a swarm of angry bees protecting a hive. They circled me – once, twice, a third time – seeking a way through my protections, before settling atop the tall stones.

More of the lesser Fae came in response to my call: lobs and brounys, goblins, bugbear and piskies, all settling in to wait at the foot of the stones for the Fae Lords and Ladies to appear, clinging to the shadows as was their nature.

The glow from the stones pulsed, brightening in the time it took to blink dazzle from my eyes. Out of the space between shadow and light stepped the High Lords and Ladies of the Fae. I'd hoped for one or two to answer my call, not a crowd large enough to fill King John's audience hall. Their attendants trailed behind them: full humans who were allowed to stay until they grew too old or fell out of fashion, Demisang who favoured their Fae heritage, full-blood Fae of lower rank and status.

All the Lords and Ladies and their court gathered a few paces away. The entire assemblage was dressed for a revel. Those of lesser rank eyed me openly, whispering behind fans and feather masks that did little to hide flattened noses and cat-shaped eyes or far from human-looking faces. The least powerful of the court carried the blood of hobs, goblins, brounys, bugbear and greenmen in their veins, but those with enough power used glamour to disguise their faces and hid among the humans and Demisang.

The highest-ranking Lords and Ladies had no need of disguise; their beauty was the source of all the stories told about the Fae. Like mortals, some were pale, with golden hair, or tawny-haired with deep brown skin, and every shade between. Often those of the highest rank were the darkest, something men forgot at their peril. Even in the light of the standing stones, the High Lords and Ladies illuminated the night with their power.

Two of the Fae moved away from the court to stand at the edge of my salt ring. Their clothing marked them as a matched pair even before I saw the way he held her arm to steady her, and the swell of her belly. Scars covered most of this Lord's bare chest and his upper arms, signs of the highest rank and status. Black linen breeches embroidered with silver thread hugged his hips like a second skin and embroidered hose were tucked into shining black leather boots that clung tightly to well-formed calves.

I'd heard stories from my gram about Fae Lords battling each other for rank and favour, contesting with wooden staves and silver knives, sometimes to the death. Each victory was marked by the winner cutting runes into his own skin, patterns that sealed the power he'd stripped from the loser inside him, making the magic his own. Gram said it was a private thing among the Fae and she didn't know how it came about, but I'd do best to be especially wary of Lords with a great number of scars.

This Lord pulled off his feathered mask and paced a slow circuit around the circle I'd made, reaching out and trying to pierce the protections. Sparks danced around his fingertips, causing him to laugh. My wards held against his testing. He stopped squarely in front of me, arms crossed over his chest. I met his amused gaze, pretending to be unafraid and hoping he couldn't see how I trembled.

The Lady stepped up next to him. Her black gown, also heavily embroidered in silver, was cinched tight around her hips with a wide girdle of black leather. She was heavy with child, obviously near her time, and wanted the court to know. Russet hair hung loose around her shoulders, framing her face. Clear green eyes watched me, as if judging my worth.

'The stories I've heard about you are true, witchling. Sending out such a calling takes a great deal of skill.' She looked back at the throng of Fae gathered and smiled. 'Many have come in answer. Let us hear the boon you wish from us, but be sure you understand that listening doesn't bind any of us to granting your request. I am willing to listen because of favours you've done for the Folk in the past.'

Gram had taught me that it was best to bite my tongue when dealing with the Fae and not give a quick answer. Favours were at the heart of my being so bold, why I dared call on them without knowing the Lord and Lady's true names. Long before Kate and Robbie were born, I'd started taking in frail Demisang babes left on my doorstep or abandoned in the nave of Tuck's church. The reason these babes came to me – the mother had died in childbirth, or the human family wanted no part in the raising of a Fae Lord's child – didn't matter. All of Sherwood knew I'd do my best for them.

Once the little ones were growing strong and healthy, I found ways to return them to their father's kin. Favours indeed. The Fae treasured all their children, full-blood or half.

'I do have a boon to ask. Dear friends and . . . and the man I loved have died. If what I've been told is true, they were murdered by a spell or a curse. I've no reason to doubt the story, or the person telling it.' I held tight to my apron, bunching the fabric in my hands and squeezing until it hurt. Pain would give me something to focus on aside from fear. 'I can't know if my children are in danger from the curse that killed Will and the others. I came to ask for a way to protect them until I can trace the spell-casting to the source.'

One of the Demisang girls, a pretty thing with sparrow-brown hair and slanted sage-green eyes, stepped out of the crowd to stand beside the Fae Lord. She rested a hand on his shoulder and leaned against him, a familiarity that drew a frown from the Lady. 'Even given that your lover died from this so-called curse, why would your children need our protection, witch? Surely no one wishes the two of them harm?'

'I can't know that!'

The Fae Lord scowled and I softened my tone. 'A child is already dead. Ethan was only six, too young to do much more than carry kindling for his mother or help his father feed the stock, but being a child didn't shield him from this curse, or from dying. My twins are eleven, not much older. I've no reason to think they're any safer.'

The Lady touched a hand to her belly. Her court had been muttering in the background, but they quieted as she spoke. 'You knew this dead child?'

'I was the midwife at Ethan's birth,' I said. 'He carried my breath inside him when he gave his first cry. I knew him.'

Ethan had been born blue and still with the cord wrapped twice around his neck. John and Emma had tried not to panic, but tears were sliding down John's face as he watched me trying to breathe life into his son.

The Demisang exchanged glances with the tall Fae Lord, trailing a hand down his arm before she stepped towards me. She smiled and I no longer thought her pretty. 'Sounds to me like just knowing you is ill luck, witch. More the pity for your young ones.'

'Maddie! Enough.' The standing stones pulsed in time with the angry tapping of the Lady's silk fan against her palm. 'Back to your place. You will not speak again until I give you leave.'

The Demisang's smile vanished. The use of her common name was a sign of how displeased the Lady was with her. A partial name wasn't enough to bind the girl if she took care, but it was still enough for enemies to use against her. Whispers among the court began again, more than one pair of eyes taking the measure of the girl, weighing what this loss of favour might mean. Some of the Demisang women eyed the Fae Lord instead, making their own plans.

Maddie curtsied; her face flushed and voice quivering. 'Your pardon, Mother. I thought toying with the witchling would amuse you.'

Now I saw the likeness between them in the curve of the girl's chin and the shape of her eyes, something I'd never have looked for if Maddie hadn't spoken. It set me to wondering how the Lady of the Fae came to bear a half-human child, and why, now that she was grown, that child was working so hard to steal away her mother's Consort. Only a full Fae child could be heir.

The Lady snapped the fan sharply against her hand. 'I said enough. Do as you were told.'

Maddie spun on her heel and pushed through the crowd of Fae and Demisang, though few gave way for her. The games of power among the Fae were more tangled than any in King John's court. I wanted no part of them.

'I will grant your boon, witchling.' The Lady rested a hand on her belly again. 'One child is lost already and I'd not see more come to harm. Step out of your circle. You have my guarantee of safe passage.'

She looked me in the eye, calm and steady, with no hint of guile. She wouldn't break her word once given. I nudged the circle of pebbles apart and smudged the salt with the toe of my boot. Power flowed into the night, swirling on the wind back into the forest. Fire sprites lifted off the top of the standing stones to give chase, bright sparks racing to gather what they could before the power spread thin and vanished.

An amulet dangled from a thin cord hung around the Lady's neck, the small silver circle almost lost in the embroidery on her gown. She pulled the cord over her head and cupping the amulet in her hands, warmed the silver with her breath. A faint glow leaked from between her fingers for an instant, then vanished.

Magic burned cold against my skin as the Lady draped the cord over my head and hung the silver disc around my neck. 'Take this, witchling, and hide it in your house. You have my pledge the charm will conceal your children from any who wish them harm.' She glanced over her shoulder at the assembled Fae and touched my cheek. Her voice dropped to a whisper. 'Find this killer of children, Marian Annalise. When you do, I'll know. Now go home.'

She stepped back and light flared from the stones, blinding me. When my vision cleared, I was alone.

A soft sigh of wind through the trees accompanied me home. The night was quiet, too still, as if all of Sherwood drowsed under the moon's spell, but my fears had vanished with the Fae Lady's touch – a warning I should have heeded.

Other nights and another time, I might have, but tonight I hurried along the tree-lined paths, anxious to put the Lady's protections in place while Kate and Robbie still slept. It wasn't until I saw my cottage with shimmering wards unbroken and Bridget trotting up to greet me that I remembered.

The Lady had known my name. She'd spoken it aloud and not bound me, nor bartered for payment. Her aid came with a price, that much was certain, past favours aside.

I hoped her price was one I could pay.

Chapter 3

Morning came too quickly after my spell-casting the night before, but as dawn touched the sky I set to work. I'd much to do before meeting Tuck in two days, and all the normal chores besides.

I sent Bridget off with a message to one of the few people I trusted to mind Kate and Robbie. Beth, a herbwife with more skill than most, had helped me nurse my mother through her last days. She knew all the best places to find mushrooms and roots and those plants I couldn't coax to grow in my own garden. Kate loved the old woman, trailing after her and filling her apron pockets with leaves, blossoms and berries and all the bounty of the forest. Beth's patience in answering Robbie's endless questions had made him just as fond of her. My children would be well cared for, leaving me carrying one less worry.

They helped me fill the water butt after the midday meal. Robbie, struggling to lug the sloshing buckets from the stream, was much too quiet and solemn, while Kate wore her temper on her sleeve, unleashing anger on her brother for being clumsy or slow. Each was mourning Will in their own way, the one with silence, the other striking out at anyone who came near, but that didn't make clinging to my patience easier as they quarrelled. I was fighting my own battle with grief.

Bridget returned, and knowing Beth wouldn't be far behind, I left Kate to wait for her and took Robbie with me to tend the dragon. He skipped ahead, more than happy to escape his sister's temper, but glanced back frequently to make sure I still followed.

Cornflowers and ox-eye daisies nodded in the sun, lulled by the lazy drone of bees and the warmth of a midsummer afternoon, and the air was heavy with the scent of meadowsweet. Clouds of yarrow, clusters of scabious and heartsease and tall spikes of faerie-bells dreamed at the feet of my oak's younger brothers.

In the centre of the flower-studded meadow, the dragon slumbered.

Layers of glamour hid his true nature from those without other sight or magic of their own. Woodcutters or foresters who chanced upon him would see a large lump of grey rock mottled with lichen, a favoured resting place of rooks and sparrows. Sharp, broken edges revealed quartz that glittered blade-bright in the sun, discouraging climbing, allowing the ancient guardian of Sherwood to bake his bones in the sun and nap unmolested.

Robbie ran off to hunt grasshoppers at the edge of the trees, still close but out of the way. Other sight revealed the dragon as he was, coiled like a cat in front of the hearth. I set my basket of tinctures and salves near his head and prodded one massive leg with my toe. 'Marlow, wake up. I've come to dress your wound.'

An amber eye blinked open, the milk-blue inner lid sliding away to uncover a dark pupil bigger than Robbie's head. Marlow peered at me, still fuzzy with sleep. 'Ah, it isn't a dream, you are here. Step back, fair witch. I've no wish to harm you with my thrashing.'

Glamour fell away, layers flaking off his hide and raining onto the grass, a shimmering summer snow that instantly melted. Dull grey rock became polished silver skin and lichen stains markings of pale platinum. He'd never told me what the markings meant, though I'd asked often enough when I was younger. Knife-edged quartz wavered and settled into rows of curved scales able to stand against the iron weapons wielded by man.

Marlow wore his armour with more grace than any knight of King John's court or Richard's motley army of Crusaders before them. Those scales were his strength and his shield against those who'd seek him out and attempt to do him or the greenwood harm. Tales of the challenges he'd weathered were told by the fireside on cold winter nights, the stories about him passed into legend. Few now remembered the dragon was Sherwood Forest's real guardian, and its heart.

Nor did they remember men first coming to this land, when Marlow and his brothers had welcomed them. In this time, with John Lackland on the throne, dragons were feared as mindless beasts, vermin who thought of nothing but filling their enormous bellies, and the king was determined to rid England of the scourge. Any who dared show themselves, from timid firedrakes to the giant guardians of the land, were hunted down with iron.

With the death of each wyrm, magic faded from the minds of men, replaced by what they called 'reason'. I feared what would become of the world when the last dragon passed.

I'd never before known him to look outside the forest for trouble, but Marlow had dropped all his glamours to poach King John's horses, and he'd done so in full view of the castle walls. Armoured he might be, and a creature of magic, but the royal archers and crossbowmen were no fools: they'd aimed for his wings.

Marlow unfurled his left wing so I could tend to the holes torn in the taut silver membrane. The iron heads had burned as they'd passed through, reacting with his magic. The holes had continued to spread, swiftly eating through his wing and causing him great pain, until I managed to put a stop to the iron poisoning. If I hadn't found him the day he'd fallen from the sky, the taint would have spread to his blood, killing him as surely as a lance through the heart.

I smeared the raw edges of the wounds with salves made of barley seed and rue, muttering spells to knit the delicate silver-leaf membranes together again. He bore my treatment without complaint, only the twitch of an ear or the slight tremor in his wing letting me know when I'd touched a tender spot. The constant hungry growl of his stomach reminded me that he hadn't eaten in days. I'd use a bit of magic to lure five or six of King John's deer into the meadow when I left, an act that would cost me little and would mean a great deal to him. The wounds were healing, but the first chill of winter would be upon us before he was able to fly again.

He flexed the wing and grimaced, if such an expression could be said to grace a dragon's pointed snout. His mouth wasn't made for speech, what with tusk-like teeth protruding on both sides and a tongue split like a grass snake's, but his words filled my head nonetheless.

'As always, you have my thanks and my gratitude.' Marlow folded his wings tight to his side and rested his head on his outstretched front legs. One amber eye peered at me. 'The wing mends a bit more each time you work your craft.'

I patted his soft jowls, much the way I'd pat a horse. His flanks were high as my head and covered with sharp-edged scales and I didn't fancy cutting my hand to ribbons by attempting to stroke him there. 'And the price you pay is that I scold you each time. I hope you've learned your lesson, foul beast. Tempting fate that way was madness.'

Marlow sighed and the thin inner lid slid over his eye, clouding the amber. 'I was angry. Forty wolves died because the pack took one foal from the castle herd. It was an unfair accounting for such a small damage. You're right to scold me. Not waiting for nightfall was reckless. I'll not make that mistake again.'

I'd been just shy of six the first time I wandered into Marlow's meadow, as fearless about exploring Sherwood as Kate was now. Gram had told me stories about the protector of the greenwood and her tales left me eager to find him and completely unafraid once I did. I told him my name, still too young to know I'd handed him power over me, and asked to be his friend.

Bemused by the tiny child plucking daisies under his nose, Marlow gave me both the gift of his own name and his protection. He took me in as if I were a stray puppy, teaching me more about magic and lore than my mother ever could – indeed, more than any witch or wizard in Lincolnshire. The guardian of Sherwood made sure my craft grew true and strong. My childhood passed

27

happily in his company and I never noticed or mourned the lack of siblings or playmates.

I'd gone to the dragon for comfort when my mother died, and again when my father breathed his last. Will's death was a different sorrow, deeper, threatening to drown me, and made far worse for knowing he wasn't the only one. I needed Marlow's comfort again, and his counsel. As a little girl I'd known how to ask, but grown and with babes of my own, I couldn't find the words.

Marlow tipped his head and watched Robbie stalking a squirrel. 'What's happened since your last visit, little witch? The boy is so swaddled in wards he shines in other sight.' He turned those looming eyes back to me, seeking the full truth from me, nothing less. 'Tell me why the witch of Sherwood and her son need Fae protections against death.'

'A curse, Marlow, one that has already taken far too many from me. I don't know how to unravel the spell, or who set it on us. I couldn't risk losing my children too.'

He went back to watching Robbie play, perhaps sensing I'd talk more freely without his measuring gaze weighing me down. I told him of Tim's visit, of all the friends I'd lost and of being desperate enough to seek help from a Lady of the Fae. An ear twitched as I explained how I was to meet Tuck in Nottingham. My voice broke describing Will's death, choking on tears that were never far away. I told the dragon all I knew, and hoped he'd know more.

Marlow quivered when I'd finished, a single ripple that started at his head and travelled to the tip of his tail, the only outward sign he'd heard my words. 'Tuck waited over-long to seek your help. Did the monk tell you why?'

'Tuck got word of the deaths at different times, months apart. Sad news travels slowly among men.' I wiped my eyes on a sleeve. 'He didn't see a pattern until Ethan and Will died so close together. I can't place all the blame on him. He's a good man who rarely deals with magic.'

Marlow growled softly, startling flocks of songbirds in the oaks and elms ringing the meadow. They rose up in chittering clouds and streaked away. 'Yet he willingly lays the burden on your shoulders and sends you into battle. This isn't the first time a man has put you in harm's way.'

I almost held my tongue, unwilling to quarrel with him, but in the end, I couldn't let it pass. 'Will's death made it my battle and my burden. I wouldn't have anyone else fight for me, even if I could.' I brushed my hands down the front of my apron, trying to wipe away the feel of fear itching on my palms. Peeling away the skin would do more good. 'And I can't be sure that I'm not already in harm's way, or that Robbie and Kate aren't in danger. I won't sit idly by and hope no one else dies.'

He stretched his long neck up and up until he was peering down at me with both enormous eyes. Twice before he'd looked at me this way: at six, when I'd feared nothing, and later, after I'd met Robin. The old tales say a dragon's eyes see into your heart, take your measure and know the whole of who you are. Meeting Marlow's gaze now, I thought there must be some truth in that.

'So you would do this thing alone, brave witch?' He lowered his head, but not before I'd marked the quirk to his jowls, what passed for a smile among dragons.

'I have no choice. Who else would find justice for Will and Ethan, or any of the others?' I hugged my arms across my chest, taken by a sudden chill on this warm afternoon. 'Who else can?

A great deal of craft is needed to weave a spell that can kill a man without leaving a mark. I'll need all my skill to undo it.'

'You were wise to seek protection for your young ones. The stench of anger and revenge clings to all you've told me. Your friends were good men, undeserving of such a passage to the next life.' The tip of his enormous tongue brushed my cheek, startling me. 'Your Will Scarlet was the best of them, for making you happy, if for nothing else. I can't feel your pain, Marian, nor can I take it from you. Doing so is beyond the power of an old and regretful dragon, even if he wishes it were otherwise.'

My voice refused to work, and I'd have likely choked on the words if I'd tried to speak, so instead I nodded and began to gather up my jars and crocks, packing them back in the basket. Stars and sparkles danced on each of them, the result of viewing the world through a curtain of tears.

He'd used my name for the first time since I'd pledged myself to Robin at the age of twenty. Blinded by the passion I'd felt and the blur of living eighteen years since, I'd missed how Marlow had turned away from me then – I'd missed it until he turned back to me and I felt the world shift into place again.

Robbie called from the edge of the meadow, 'Mam, I'm going to the pond. I'll be home by dark.'

Fear was sudden and sharp and unlike me, but my hissing breath and a half step taken towards Robbie let Marlow know that allowing my son to wander out of sight frightened me.

'Let the boy go, Marian. You've protected him the best you can,' he said, his voice so quiet only I could hear. 'You can't tie Robbie to your side, nor make your fears a part of him. I'd know if death walked within Sherwood's bounds. No harm will come to your children, on that you have my promise.'

Marlow had never lied to me.

The smile I gave my son attempted to hide how my heart was lodged in my throat, choking me. I waved as Robbie ran into the forest.

'Can you help me find this spellcaster?' I asked. 'Or tell me where to start?'

The dragon's eyes blinked closed, and his sigh set the meadow flowers bobbing. 'I will do my best, but what I can accomplish is limited while I'm tethered to the ground. Meet with Tuck as you planned. Find a common thread in the way Will and the others died, if you can. I will help unravel this weaving for you, but we need a place to begin.'

'A place to begin. Sounds simple enough.' I doubted finding the right thread would be simple, but once I did, Marlow would make good on his promise. No power could withstand dragon magic, not even the mightiest Fae Lord or Lady. I gathered up my basket and patted his jowls in farewell. 'Beth is coming to stay with Kate and Robbie while I'm gone. I'll ask her to check your wing if I'm not back in a day or two. She can rub salve on the wounds and scold you as well as I can.'

He coiled up tight and began to pull glamour around himself. 'Does the old herbwife have the sight to find me?'

'Kate will lead Beth here. She'll have no trouble seeing you.' His stomach growled loudly, reminding me. 'Don't go to sleep just yet. I'll send some supper your way before I go.'

'You have my thanks, as always.' His amber eye appeared in the side of the pitted, lichen-stained rock. 'Safe journey, sweet Marian. Guard yourself well.'

'I will, old wyrm.' I hurried away, weaving spells to lure a dozen of King John's deer to the meadow. Poaching them to feed the dragon didn't give me an instant's guilt. Truth be told, Marlow had more right to the harts roaming the greenwood than the man pretending ownership of all the creatures in Sherwood.

Marlow's words buzzed in my head all the way home. A place to begin was all we needed. Such a simple thought to fill me with such dread.

Chapter 4

'Oh mother, mother, make my bed
Make it soft and narrow
Sweet William died, for love of me,
And I shall die of sorrow.'
17TH CENTURY ENGLISH BALLAD

Market days always filled the streets of Nottingham to bursting. Every cottager, farmer and yeoman's family rose before dawn to make the journey, wagons and carts piled with whatever they could spare to sell. Crated ducks and chickens squawked each time wheels hit a rut, setting the birds to bouncing and tilting. Small sons and daughters carefully balanced baskets of eggs or crocks of wild honey. Onions and cabbages filled one cart, another held waxed rounds of cheese. Women brought fine-spun threads, yarns made from strong local wool and cloth they'd woven from flax or linen, knowing they'd find a ready market with Nottingham's seamstresses and lace-makers.

I kept my head down and walked on the rutted edge of the road, basket in hand, just another woman among the many entering

Nottingham's gates. Once, I was well known here, but I'd seldom ventured to the city since Robbie and Kate were born. My old friends were now scattered across Lincolnshire and the Ridings. Those townsfolk who knew me by sight dwindled every year, but not being readily recognised suited my mood and my purposes.

The Lark and Wren was a smaller inn, set away from the bustle of the market square, frequented by merchants and minor officials from the castle. Malcolm, the innkeeper, was a pious man, one of the few people in Nottingham I'd known since my days with Robin. He didn't allow men with a reputation for picking pockets into the common room. The first time he caught a stranger lifting another man's purse, Malcolm hustled the thief away to confess his sins to one of Tuck's priests. Very few came back a second time.

Widows of soldiers who'd died in the Crusades and wives who didn't yet know their husbands' fate found safety working here. The innkeeper treated his serving girls well, protecting them from drunks or any man who sought more than a smile and a kind word. Malcolm made the journey to my cottage from time to time, bringing lengths of fine linen or soft wool to exchange for potions to heal childhood ills or calm a fever. He had two sons of his own and much as he might grumble about little ones always being underfoot, the widows kept their children with them. He'd never turned away a mother and child in need.

Many day-time patrons were older men of means, long married and with families. Meeting a mistress here, spending a few hours together, allowed them to feel younger, and to a man, they pretended their wives didn't know. Taking a meal with Tuck in the common room wouldn't look out of place or draw stares in a city where priests kept mistresses as often as wealthy merchants.

Candles and the fitful light of a dying fire rendered the common room more shadow and vague shapes than anything I could see clearly with sun-dazzled sight. I slid to one side as the door shut, my back to the wall until my eyes could adjust and lumps became solitary men bent over plates and tankards or a woman pressed so tightly against a companion they appeared to be one person. The closed-in odour of mutton stew, tallow candles and beer was very strong, especially after so long in the open air of Sherwood.

Tuck raised a hand in greeting from his seat at a small table against the far wall and I threaded my way towards him, choosing a path that would keep me out of reach of any questing hands, if not free of curious stares. Malcolm looked up from a pile of platters and saw me, pausing a moment in surprise before he nodded his own greeting. He scowled at the watchers and they turned away, satisfied I belonged.

Tuck was thinner than last I'd seen him, the plain brown robe hanging loose around his middle for the first time I could remember. His hair was shaved in its usual tonsure, but the fringe over his ears was now silvery-grey and lines creased his ruddy face, evidence of worry and care. He looked worn and tired, although he made a valiant effort to hide it behind a broad smile.

'Well met, Marian, well met.' He stood up and took my hand, guiding me to sit next to him. 'Kate and Robbie are well and safe?'

I smiled for the strangers watching our meeting and murmured, 'They're warded as best I could. Beth is staying with them until I return.'

'That's news to cheer an old man's heart,' he said. 'There's little enough good news about friends and those I hold dear. Thank you for offering to help, Marian. I know how heartsick you must be over Will, but some things can't wait to be mended by prayer.'

Tuck had always been practical in all things, including his faith. His belief in God never interfered with him seeing what needed to be done, or the best way to go about it. He held to that at all times, even if the solution was magic. We'd always been friends as a result.

'Will wouldn't want me to do nothing but weep and leave others in danger. And we both know he'd be the first to offer help,' I said. 'Tell me what you've learned about how Alan and the others died. If I'm to have any chance of finding the person behind this spell, I need to know all I can. There must be something that ties all of them together.'

'You mean other than knowing Robin?'

He gave voice to the thought I'd not wanted to acknowledge.

Robin would work that out for himself too, if he hadn't done so already. His brother was dead, along with his best friend's son, and others who'd followed him wherever he led. For all his faults and arrogance, he wasn't a stupid man.

'Robin brought us together in Sherwood, but he hasn't left the monastery for close on twelve years,' I pointed out. 'His ties to anyone but his brother broke long ago.'

One of the serving girls set a fresh tankard of beer in front of Tuck. She turned to put a second down in front of me, but when I waved her away, she smiled and gestured at the innkeeper. 'It's only water. Malcolm said you'd be thirsty from walking and water'd be what you'd want. The well's deep and clear, so you won't be getting sick from it neither. That's a promise.'

'Give him my thanks.' I took the tankard from her, wrapping both hands around the dulled, dented metal. She'd spoken the truth: the water was clear and clean – but even so, I breathed a spell to banish illness before I drank.

Tuck passed the girl a penny, took a long drink of beer and wiped his mouth with the back of his hand. 'Most of the story you'll have had from Tim. I've little more to add. All of our friends were found just like Will, off alone somewhere with eyes open and staring. The only person I've talked to myself is Midge's wife, Meg. She found Midge kneeling next to the horse trough with not a mark on him. Meg said he looked surprised, as if he'd seen someone he hadn't expected.'

Midge hadn't expected to die in his own yard. I stared at the water in the tankard, thankful I'd never know if Will had recognised the face of death before it took him. 'What about the others?'

'I don't know anything more than what Tim told you,' Tuck said. 'Alan was in a tavern in York staring out of the window. Gilbert and Gamelyn were setting up their wares for the fayre in Sheffield.'

'There has to be something. Let me think.' I closed my eyes, hoping to recall everything I'd heard about these men since I'd seen them last. News did reach me from time to time. 'I thought Gilbert had stopped travelling? The last word I had was he'd found a girl he fancied and settled down – so what was Gamelyn peddling that would have tempted Gilbert back on the road?'

'Trinkets, mainly – hand-mirrors, ribbons, buttons, combs – the kinds of goods that attract merchants' wives and daughters.' He took another sip of beer and shook his head, as puzzled as me. 'Nothing they haven't peddled before. I can only guess at what might have sent Gilbert back on the road – could be the young woman he liked didn't want to be courted.'

There was one more death to ask about, one that tore my heart as badly as Will's had. Putting it off only made this harder. 'And what of Ethan? Tim told me he'd died, but he never said how.'

Tuck wrapped his fingers around the tankard, squeezing tight enough that the veins on the back of his hands stood out. 'I don't know how Ethan was taken from us. As soon as I heard, I went to the farm to offer a friend's comfort. Emma refused to talk about what happened and John flew into a rage when I offered to pray for Ethan's soul. He sent me away, and none too gently. I was told not to come back.'

Shared loss was still loss. It wouldn't lessen the pain for any of us. I'd helped bring Ethan into the world, and I felt sure John would tell me what I needed. John would want me to find the person who stole Ethan from all of us.

'One of them will talk to me,' I said. 'If not John, then Emma. I will go on to Midge's mill at Mansfield from John's farm and from there to Sheffield – someone will know more about how Gamelyn and Gilbert died. If I have to, I'll find the inn where Alan died as well. Can you get word to Beth for me? I don't want her to worry if I'm gone longer than a week or more.'

'Don't fret, Marian, I'll carry the message myself. It's been too long since I visited Kate and Robbie.' The Tuck of old wouldn't have patted my hand like a worried father. He'd changed, grown older and cautious. 'It pains me to think of you travelling that far, being apart from your children for so long. Do you have a place to stay the night? If not, I can find a room for you. I'd have done so already, but I didn't know what you had planned.'

I'd filled my basket with jars, packets of dried herbs and small vials, thinking to trade them at market. I had no great need for the wares peddled in Nottingham, but there was always news passed from stall to stall which I'd not hear otherwise and some little bit of gossip or farmwife's chatter might lead me to the person responsible for the curse. It was a faint hope, but I found it hard to let it go. 'I'm sure I can trade a potion or two for a room. I've some coin to use along the way and I'll barter for the rest. There's always call for love charms, if nothing else.'

Tuck paused with the tankard lifted halfway to his mouth. 'You told me love charms don't work.'

'They don't,' I said, 'but people want to believe that a scrap of cloth and ribbon left under a pillow or tucked in a pocket will bring the one they fancy to their side.'

I ran a fingertip through the water droplets clinging to the side of the tankard, weighing how much to say. In all the years I'd known Tuck, I'd never felt the need to explain everything. Strong spells did exist, many of them tied to simple charms, to trick a person into someone's bed or to compel them into pledging devotion. But compulsion was an ugly thing and I'd never use my craft for such. 'Belief oft-times makes people bold enough to speak. That's usually all it takes for things to work out on their own. You have my promise any charms I trade for bread are harmless.'

He patted my hand again. 'I never doubted you, Marian. Come along now, let me help you gather what you need for travel. And I've just the place for you to spend the night that won't make me worry. I'll feel better if I see you safely on your way come morning.'

I picked up my basket and followed him from the common room into the sunshine, both of us blinking against the bright- ness, sunblind after sitting so long in the dark tavern. Tuck took my arm to guide me to the market square, leading me down the narrow alleys, through side streets I'd never have found on my own. Nottingham was growing quickly these days as tradesmen and merchants arrived, all hoping to supply King John's castle when he was in residence. They brought their families or started new ones when they arrived. The sleepy hamlet I remembered was becoming a real city.

We turned a corner and the market spread before me, hand-carts wedged between farm wagons and the brightly coloured caravans of pedlars who travelled from one fayre or market to another. The scent of sweaty horses left standing in harness was strong, vying with the smells of cooking onions, animal shit and unwashed bodies. I'd been away from towns too long and the stench quickly unsettled my stomach.

One side of the square was set aside for the canopied stalls run by the shopkeepers who made their home in Nottingham. I could see a cordwainer selling stout boots, a baker piling his counter with meat pies and thick trenchers of bread and a draper doing brisk trade, judging by the goodwives clustered around her, selling lengths of cloth as well as clothing already made hanging from hooks in the back of her space. They'd most likely been ordered by someone in town who'd not then had the brass to pay for them. Trying to get what coin she could for her labours showed good sense.

Having Tuck at my side made bargaining easier; I suspected the traders were asking less for their goods than if I'd been alone and Tuck was content with the prices I paid as he pulled me from stall to stall. It didn't take long: I acquired a cloak from the draper that would double as a blanket and a pair of boots from the cordwainer better suited to walking than my own worn shoes. One farmer's wife was happy to trade a sturdy hessian bag with long straps for my faithful willow basket and a poultice to ease the ache in her crooked fingers. I repacked my jars and herbs in the bag and slung the strap over my head so it lay comfortably across my chest.

Tuck steered me towards a woodcarver's stall filled with intricately carved animals and birds, and creatures I thought were meant to be Fae – or at least the craftsman's idea of what the Fae looked like, for I'd never seen any creature who resembled the winged beasts and serpents that sprang from his imagination.

'I'd like to take a gift to Kate and Robbie,' Tuck said. 'What do you think they'd like?'

I smiled and shook my head. 'A kind gesture, Tuck, but you don't need to bring them trinkets. Kate and Robbie are always happy to see you.'

'Don't deny an old man his pleasures.' He tucked his thumbs in the rope belt tied loosely around his waist and set his feet. Many were the times I'd seen him stand just so while settling arguments between Robin's men, or when refusing the sheriff entrance to his church, so I knew there'd be no moving him. 'Choose something they'd like.'

When I studied the creatures, the choice was obvious; I wondered that I hadn't spotted the carvings right off. I picked up a frog for Robbie and a fox for Kate, both so finely worked I fully expected to see them breathe. He tucked the presents safely in his bag, patted the flap and smiled.

'Now for a room for the night,' he said 'There's a clean inn near the abbey where I sometimes pass a convivial evening with friends. The innkeeper is trustworthy, and he owes me a favour or two. His wife is an excellent cook as well: you won't find scorched stew on her hearth.'

'A decent supper before bed would be very nice.' I threaded my arm through his. 'You're a good friend, Tuck. Show me the way.'

We turned to go. The pretty Demisang, Maddie, stood behind us, arm in arm with a handsome yeoman dressed in a castle guard's tunic. In a simple gown of peacock blue, her loose hair hiding the Fae shape of her ears, Maddie looked like any other young maid out for market day. A fairing, a sheaf of colourful ribbons, had been tied around her arm in a lover's knot: a courting gift from the yeoman with dream-clouded eyes. He held the Demisang's hand, the market and the people milling around him unseen. Ribbons fell from his own sleeve as well, wrapped three times around and knotted tight, but these were bindings, not a lover's gift, designed to hold him close until she grew bored.

Anger and the need to sever his bonds churned inside, but a crowded market square wasn't the place to openly challenge Maddie and wrest away control. Nothing the Fae did was ever easy to predict and I couldn't take the risk that she might hurt the boy rather than surrender her prize.

Looking past me as if I wasn't there, Maddie gave Tuck a delighted smile. A game, no doubt, learned in her mother's court. 'Father Tuck! What a surprise to see you at market. I thought you'd still be shut up in the abbey saying mass for the earl's son.'

'The earl has Father Gil to say mass for him and lead prayers for his son's soul.' He felt me stiffen and squeezed my hand in sympathy. 'I haven't seen you at services in a long while, child. I hope you're planning to make confession next month with the rest of the parish.'

'My mother is ailing, Father Tuck. Carrying another child is hard at her age. I did what any good daughter would do and went home to offer all the help I could.' She lowered her eyes, demure and proper. 'My father is away and I don't know when he'll return. I may be called back to tend my mother again.'

Only half a lie, and well told at that. Tuck would believe every word. Knowing that Maddie wouldn't turn a hair over deceiving the kind-hearted priest, not any more than she'd hesitated to bind the yeoman, made me even more furious.

'You did the right thing. The Lord tells us to honour our father and our mother.' Tuck sketched the sign of the cross in the air. 'I will remember your mother in my prayers.'

Not a hint of magic showed when I looked at Tuck with other sight. Most likely he was acting as he always did, accepting the simple girl he thought Maddie to be, but it troubled me she was in Nottingham enough he'd chide her about missing mass. Why she went to Christian services at all disturbed me even more.

But a Demisang's life among the Fae was never easy, especially for one as pretty and bold as Maddie. Living away from her mother's court would help keep her alive – as long as she didn't push the Lady of the Fae too far. No refuge would save her then.

'We should go, Tuck.' I stepped between them, blocking his view of her. His eyes were clear when he met my gaze, guileless as always, and another worry fell away. What he saw in my eyes I couldn't say, but his gaze flicked over my shoulder to Maddie and back to me.

'Dear me – I promised you supper, didn't I?' He took my arm again and nodded to Maddie and the young yeoman. 'Blessings to you, Joan, and to you as well, Tom. Give your father my best.'

Names have power: a name can bind and unbind both. Tuck's use of the boy's was a gift. Pretending to stumble, I caught hold of Tom's sleeve to keep myself from falling. One whispered word wrapped in anger and will and the ribbons that bound him to Maddie came away in my hand.

Shock, then rage filled Maddie's face as her bindings crumbled. She glared at me, her pretty green eyes promising murder if she could manage it.

'My pardon,' I muttered and hurried away with Tuck, the ribbons bunched tight in my fist.

The dreams were already clearing from Tom's eyes as we left. He'd see the truth when he looked at Maddie now, notice the cruelty in her smile and her ire at losing her plaything.

He wouldn't be easy to fool or bind again. I'd take the one good thing to come from this day and be glad.

Chapter 5

Though I am young, and cannot tell
Either what Death, or Love is well,
Yet I have heard, they both beare darts,
And both doe ayme at humane hearts ...

BEN JONSON

The inn Tuck favoured was in sight of the abbey, close enough I could easily imagine him strolling over in the evening to spend time with friends. Big windows covered the building front, each one fitted with stout wooden shutters and framed with faded red clay bricks. The sign swinging on chains above the door had *The Sea Maiden* painted under a picture of a bare-breasted mermaid. I'd always thought it an odd name for a Nottingham tavern, landlocked and many leagues from the coast.

Supper was as good as Tuck had promised, and the place far cleaner than most I'd stayed in – I didn't even need the spell I'd readied to clear the mattress of fleas, lice and other crawling and biting things left behind by travellers. When dawn woke me, I felt well rested after a night of dreamless sleep. After dressing, I repacked my bag and went downstairs, where the innkeeper waved me towards a table in the common room. As I settled in to wait for Tuck, the wondrous smell of fresh-baked bread drifted from the kitchen, setting my stomach growling loud enough that I was sure everyone in the room could hear. Before I could ask after breaking my fast, the innkeeper's wife put a jug of fresh water in front of me, a thick chunk of that aromatic rye bread and a slice of boiled beef from last night's supper. I started digging in my purse for a penny, but she waved the coin away.

'Father Tuck asked for me and Kit to feed you well, soon as you showed your face this morning and I'm not 'bout to go disobeying our abbot. Put your money away and eat up now. If you be wanting anything else, you just ask.' Her good-natured, gap-toothed smile banished the weary look around her eyes. I didn't think she was much older than me, but a hard life had left its mark.

The food was as good as any I'd had, the warm bread free of grit and the meat tender and full of flavour – and no sooner had I swallowed the last bite than the innkeeper's wife was slipping another hunk of bread in its place. I was hard-put to finish, but conscious that I wouldn't eat this well again until I returned home, I managed to down every crumb.

I watched the door so I wouldn't miss Tuck coming in, keeping an eye on what was going on around me into the bargain. Other than the innkeeper's wife, I was the only woman in the common room. I studied two monks who bent their heads in prayer at a table near the window before starting on their food, wondering why they weren't taking their meal with the other brothers of Tuck's order, but in the end, I decided it was none of my business.

A richly dressed merchant came down the stairs and, pausing, looked around the room as if searching for someone he knew. His beard was shot through with grey but his hair was still a thick dark brown. The window shutters were thrown open and bright sunlight made the gold thread embroidered on his blue velvet sleeves sparkle and the white silk panels gleam. His keen blue eyes lit on me and the confident smile that followed spoke of trouble, but the innkeeper had seen his face too and after a quiet word in the man's ear, the merchant allowed himself to be led to a table across the room.

More travellers, all men, came down, some seeking tables, others settling their accounts and leaving straight away. Although the room was filling up, no one else sent more than a passing glance in my direction and I finished my meal, happy to be left in peace.

By the time Tuck arrived, the room had almost emptied again. He frowned at the two monks still lingering in their cosy spot by the window and they hurriedly got to their feet and murmuring blessings to the landlady, took their leave. I'd no doubt they'd shortly be finding themselves with extra duties of some sort to atone for their laziness.

He'd saved a smile for me. 'Marian! Good morrow to you. I hope you slept well.'

I stood and let him kiss my cheeks. 'Thanks to you I was well fed and well taken care of. I'm in your debt.'

'Nonsense! Friends do what they can to take care of each other. All ready to leave, I take it?'

'I'm ready,' I said, 'and I've got good weather for starting out.'

He shifted his weight nervously, his gaze drifting towards the door and back to me. On anyone else I'd have said his expression spoke of guilt, but I'd never known Tuck to feel guilty over anything.

I slung the bag across my shoulder, draped the heavy cloak over my arm and asked, 'What's wrong? Has there been more bad news?'

The door opened again, momentarily flooding the common room with the sound of a wagon rumbling past and a coster-monger shouting his wares on the street outside, and when it swung shut again, Robin was standing just inside the room. His hair and beard were more grey than brown now and new lines had been carved in his face. He wore a forester's tunic and breeches and a bow and quiver hung from one shoulder. A heavy travelling pack dangled from his free hand.

Tuck's crime was suddenly clear.

'No! I won't have him following at my heels.' I dropped my bag so it thunked against the floor, setting all the jars inside rattling.

Both men flinched and Tuck took a step back. The innkeeper's wife hurried her husband into the kitchen ahead of her, but she didn't hide her smile as she glanced over her shoulder at me.

'I've done well enough on my own for going on twelve years, Tuck. I don't need his help or his protection.'

Robin tossed the pack in his hand so it landed at my feet. 'I told you she'd be furious. These are the clothes you told me to bring for her, Abbot. With your leave, I'll go back to the mon-astery. She doesn't want my help and I don't want to fight over the fact she needs it.'

I opened my mouth to answer, even more furious than Robin could conceive at the thought that I needed a nursemaid, but Tuck grabbed my arm and spun me to face him, the unaccustomed scowl on his face warning me to hold my tongue.

'Sit somewhere and be quiet, Robin. I'd be most grateful if you wouldn't make things worse.' His bulk was blocking my view of Robin, who'd slouched over to a bench against the wall. It was hard to hold onto my anger with Tuck watching me; his expression was that of a worried and disappointed father. 'I'm not questioning your ability to take care of yourself, Marian, but it isn't wise for you to make this trip alone. Someone out there is killing people – friends we care about – and if they can't strike at you with magic, they will likely try a more direct attack. You can't guard against everything. Please, take Robin with you. Kate and Robbie need you to come home safe.'

I could admit to being wrong. For all swallowing my pride would leave a bitter taste, I'd done so many times before and never felt the worse for it. Tuck was right: once all this trouble had been sorted, I needed to come home safe to my children. Still, I made one last plea. 'There's no one else? No one you can spare from their duties?'

'The only person I'd trust is John, but I can't ask him to go with you, not now. Emma needs him.' He leaned closer and lowered his voice. 'Robin thinks overmuch of himself, but he's still the best man with a longbow in all of England. I wouldn't force him to go along if I didn't truly believe he'd keep you safe.'

I wanted to laugh. 'No one has ever forced Robin to do anything against his will.'

'I'm head of the order. Robin's sworn to obey me,' Tuck said. 'He won't be allowed to take his final vows until I say he's ready. I've let him hide inside the monastery for almost twelve years, hoping he'd find a way to face you and himself. I know now that was a mistake. This journey is penance for his sins.'

'A perfect reason to send him with me, when his sins are the

49

heart of everything between us.' Kind and giving, that was the Tuck I remembered, but there was iron inside him too, which was why he was abbot. Swallowing the taste of betrayal, I turned away.

'Marian, Robin used to put himself between you and danger and never gave it an instant's thought. He may hide it from you, but he's still the same man he ever was.' Gentle hands on my shoulders pulled me back to face him. 'Don't forget I married you, and I did so with joy and the hope you'd live a long and happy life together. Robin has many sins to atone for, but you're not one of them. You never were.'

He believed every word he said. I was having a harder time. At last I sighed, and nudged the pack at my feet. 'All right. I won't fight you. What clothes did you have him bring?'

'Clothes more suited for travelling and sleeping under the stars, nothing you haven't worn before. The breeches might be over-long and the tunics a little big, but the hat should fit well.' Tuck slung my own bag on his shoulder and held out Robin's. 'One of the sisters shortened two linen shifts to go under the tunics for you. While you change, I'll make arrangements with the innkeeper's wife to store your gown until you come back.'

Practical in all things, that was Tuck, and with a good memory of the past. He was right, of course: I wouldn't draw as much attention dressed in a baggy tunic and breeches, and we wouldn't be forced to stick to the king's highway between towns either. Cutting through woods and fields would shorten our journey and we'd move faster without my skirts catching on every hedge and bramble. If fate was kind, I'd bypass the spellcaster's attentions as well.

I hurried up the stairs to change. Tuck had done everything he could to ease my way and keep me safe. If there were a way for him to unravel the curse on his own, he'd go to work with a will and keep me well clear – not that I'd thank him for keeping me from a fight that was mine as well as his, or let him, if I knew. In any case, as things now stood, the bulk of righting past wrongs and stopping new ones fell to me, even if that meant Robin dogging my steps.

Chapter 6

Let other bards of angels sing ...
WORDSWORTH

Robin set a fast pace leaving Nottingham. His legs were longer, but I was used to roaming Sherwood and kept up easily. Morning passed into afternoon with very few words exchanged between us. He spoke only if he needed to ask a direction or to warn of some small hazard on the path. I wasn't eager to coax him into conversation – birdsong and the soughing of the wind through the leaves was all the company I needed. My thoughts were full of Will, my heart empty and missing him.

Twice that morning I saw Will's shade watching me from the trees and each time I looked away, words of warding and refusal on my lips. I'd asked him not to haunt me, but his phantom still continued to seek me out. The bond between us was strong and hard to sever, his ties to life stronger still. Forcing Will on his way was within my power, but I didn't have the heart to set the spell, not when in time Will would forget the world and those he'd left behind. He'd move on then, without a push from me.

John's farm was less than a league north of Hucknall. Farmers who couldn't cart their wares to Nottingham or who didn't have enough to make the trip worthwhile would sell or trade their goods at the weekly market there. Wagons and carts crowded the narrow track as we drew closer, most now holding nothing more than a few stray onions or empty crates that used to hold birds. The warm weather and sunshine had brought people out and the farmers didn't have any unsold goods to take back.

The men making their weary way home smiled and tipped their hats to us. A few gave Robin curious looks when he returned the greeting, as if thinking they should know him – and mayhap they did. Robin had risked his life for more families around Sherwood than even I knew. Nottingham's sheriff had collected taxes in the name of Prince John far beyond anything Richard had ever asked from his subjects, demanding full payment of all tithes from even the poorest farmers. Stealing back the money and livestock taken and returning it all to the farmers hadn't been an easy task, not when getting caught meant a death sentence, even for the Earl of Locksley's son.

But Robin, Will and John weren't about to let hard-working families starve, not to satisfy the greed of a man who'd never been hungry a day in his life. Stories about Robin spread, growing grander with every telling, until it was impossible to know what was real and what was little more than an ambitious bard's fancy. Still, we never lacked for shelter or a hot meal as a result, or a friend to point the sheriff's guards in the wrong direction.

Throughout the day I watched him walk ahead of me, looking relaxed and easy for the first time in years, and wondered if Tuck was right, if maybe the Robin we'd known was still inside him. For Kate and Robbie's sake, I hoped so.

As the midday heat eased, Robin left the rutted road, cutting over the fields to skirt the edge of town. Smoke curling from cottage chimneys in the distance was blown tattered on the wind and spread thin over the valley. We crossed a score of small streams all winding their way towards the River Leen.

Twice I heard children's high, thin voices, then saw them with long switches in hand, driving their family's sheep or cows from pastures back to fold and byre for the night. Some of the boys were smaller than Robbie, but they showed no fear of the lumbering beasts towering over them. The girls ran after lambs and ewes, swift and long-legged as a spring colt, driving them back to the flock.

Life is never as peaceful, never as tranquil or safe as it looks from a distance. Ethan had been one of those fearless small boys a month ago, herding his father's cows back to shelter. Like most children, he never gave a thought to not seeing the next day, or any of the days that followed. Death still carried him away.

Early evening was darkening the sky by the time we reached John and Emma's farm. The faint glow of lamplight shone between cracks in the tightly closed wooden shutters. John had built the house beside a small ash grove. The trees helped break the wind in winter storms and cast shade to help cool the house on the hottest summer days. Twin springs that gave rise to Whyburn Brook were close by, a ready source of fresh water. The wide stream burbled and sang in its banks within sight of the doorstep.

The anguished cries of an infant came from inside the cottage and Robin stopped at the edge of the yard, hesitant to go on. He glanced back at me.

'All's well, Robin. Babies cry.' He'd not been there when Kate and Robbie were infants, when the wailing of one invariably set off the other, or when lack of sleep and not being able to soothe them had set me to weeping as well. 'Their youngest is only a few months old. She probably has a touch of colic.'

He pulled off his hat and wiped his sweaty face on a sleeve. Robin was still strong, not even close to being an old man, but he probably hadn't walked for a whole day in years. 'How many children do John and Emma have now?'

'Now that Ethan's gone . . . ? There are two little girls.' I rummaged in my pack, looking for the herbs to ease the babe's colic, if that's what it was. 'Emma's had a harder time with each birth. Another might kill her. I don't know if there will be more babies.'

He stared at the cottage, his voice even and calm. 'If it's God's will, Emma will bear more children. Holy Writ says a wife should provide her husband with sons.'

With all the years we'd been apart and the differences between us, I was still shocked he'd say such a thing. Robin might have been commenting on the weather for all the feeling he showed. 'And the God you believe in would have Emma die in childbirth, trying to give John a son?'

Robin met my gaze and I knew he was considering how to answer. 'If that's His will, then yes: all women but Blessed Mary bear the punishment of Eve's sin.'

'Then I hope your God never turns his eyes Emma's way.' I managed to hold tight to my temper. If I started a brawl on his threshold John would ask why and I didn't want to tell him.

He clearly believed what he said and Tuck's faith in him suddenly struck me as misplaced. Robin saw nothing wrong with thinking sons were more important than the mothers who bore them. He'd changed from the man I'd once loved to the point where I wasn't sure I knew him at all.

The cottage door opened and the babe's hiccoughing wails grew louder. John sauntered out, swinging a bucket in one hand, with his tiny four-year-old daughter trotting at his heels. With a mass of fair curls framing her face, Rose was the very image of her mother. John doted on his daughter and spoiled her as much as Emma would allow. Seeing her play shadow to him didn't surprise me at all.

John noticed us standing at the edge of his yard right away, dropped the bucket and scooped Rose into the safety of his arms. 'Who are you?' he called. 'What do you want here?'

'It's Marian.' I tugged my hat off and shook out my hair. 'Forgive us, John. We meant to knock on the door, not startle you like this.'

'Mari?' His long legs crossed the yard in just a few strides and he gathered me up with his free arm as easily as he had Rose. Holding tight, he murmured, 'Em told me you'd come. She kept saying you'd come when you could and not to think you wouldn't. I'm so very glad you're here.'

I hugged him back just as fiercely, hoping to ease the ache for one of us. 'I'd have come sooner if I'd known, but word only reached me a few days ago. I'm so very, very sorry. How is Emma?'

'Em's stronger than me most days. She has the girls to look after and that mostly keeps her too busy to think.' John brushed soft curls back from Rose's face and planted a kiss on her forehead. 'At night, when they're sleeping and the house is quiet . . . that's when it's hardest. For both of us.'

Robin's men had named him Little John back in our outlaw days, a jest that made all who met him laugh, for he stands a full head taller than Robin or any other man in Sherwood – he positively towered over Emma. Some – a few – of the most powerful Fae Lords grew as tall, but no one was dim enough to ask John if one of those Lords had got his mother with child.

His hair was thinner then when I'd seen him last, a few months back, his beard shot through with new streaks of grey and white. John's shoulders were stooped from years of hard work, but there was nothing little about him, especially when it came to his heart. If anything, John grew kinder as he got older. The anger Tuck had talked of was unlike him, but grief often bled all the sense from a man.

'I know why *you're* here. For the life of me I can't fathom what he's doing with you.' John glanced at Robin and back to me. 'Where's Will got himself off to?'

Robin dropped his pack and quiver at his feet, the sting of knowing he was unwelcome plain in the set of his shoulders. 'Will died a fortnight ago. Tuck sent me to guard her on the road or I wouldn't be troubling you. I know you don't want me here, John, but there was no one else to watch over her.'

John pulled me against him, offering the comfort and understanding I wouldn't get from anyone else. 'Ah Mari, no! Not Will too? I'm so sorry. Losing Will and the boy both in the same season is too much.'

The boy. Seeing he couldn't even bring himself to say Ethan's name made me wonder if I'd said Will's to anyone but my children and to Marlow. I'd been right in thinking shared loss didn't dull the pain. The edge was sharper somehow.

'An angel came and took my brother away.' Rose's tiny hand reached out and petted my hair, her big blue eyes full of sadness. 'Did she take Will too?'

'Hush now, Rosie. No more of that.' John patted her back and set her on the ground. 'Run on inside and tell your mam we have company for supper. Maybe you could rock Annie's cradle while she finishes getting things ready? Get on, now. I'll bring them inside in a moment or two.'

She skipped into the cottage, humming a tune under her breath. John didn't take his arm off my shoulders but kept me tucked up tight, frowning until Rose was safe inside. He turned his frown on Robin. 'You're right, Robin, I don't want you here. But since Tuck saw fit to send you along, we'll make the best of it. You can earn your supper by fetching the water for Em while I have a word with Mari. You know where the spring is.'

I feared for an instant that Robin would balk at taking orders, but he snatched up the bucket and stomped off. Shadow and twilight swallowed him, leaving me alone with John.

'I'm sorry, Mari. Em and I have both told Rosie to stop going on about angels, but she's young yet.' He gave my shoulders a squeeze and stepped away, staring into the darkness. 'She don't mean any harm asking if an angel took Will.'

'I know that, John. She's not much more than a babe.' I touched his arm. The muscles were bunched tight, tense from holding himself in. 'Tuck said he came to see you and my guess is he told Rose stories about her brother being with the angels. Believing such things gives him comfort and he'd want to make it easier for her.'

He didn't answer. John had always needed to take his time to think things out. I'd never hurried him in the past; I wouldn't rush him now.

The wind picked up, bearing with it the smell of sun-warmed hay and water-soaked earth and rattling, sword-sharp reeds along the banks of the brook. A dog's warning bark sounded from somewhere; a sharp whistle called the hound back. Scents were always stronger and sounds carried further in summer darkness. Frog songs and the soft call of owls sounded close enough to touch, a trick of the falling night.

Scudding clouds fled across the face of the moon, shining bright and full as power rose, buzzing across my skin. I crossed my arms and breathed in deep, listening for what might hide where I couldn't see. The Fae would be abroad tonight, gathering to dance, seeking mortal partners where they could. They'd hunt in equal measure for innocence and for those weak enough to fall under their spell.

I didn't worry that any in John's house could be tempted out by weakness, but innocence and belief were another matter. Casting wards around the house wasn't a simple task and would tax my strength, but I'd rest easier knowing protections were in place.

Deep in thought, I jumped when John finally spoke.

'I sent Tuck away because thinking about what happened to the boy made me angry. And I just couldn't get the words out to tell him what happened, or put the anger aside long enough to hear what Tuck had to say. I wouldn't blame you for not wanting to talk either. But I hadn't heard about Will then, and I'm feeling that knowing might be important.' John lifted his hands and let them drop, helpless in the face of words he didn't know how to say. 'Will . . . how did he die?'

Talking about those we'd lost was why I'd come. Best to start – to say Will's name – to someone who had also called him friend.

'They found Will in his rooms at his father's manor. He was sitting in a chair with a scroll in his lap, as if he'd been reading and something had interrupted him. His . . . his eyes were open, staring.' Cold that had no place in a summer night crept up my spine, followed by grief I couldn't ward against, no matter how much power rode the moon. 'The earl's physician couldn't give a reason for why he died, just that he had.'

'All was well when he went into his room – no sign of anything troubling him.' He wasn't asking a question but making sure he understood.

'Will was joking with the stable hands before he went inside.' I closed my eyes, holding on to the thought of him laughing a little longer. 'There was no sign, John. No warning.'

He threw his head back and stared at the sky. John knew as well as I that wounds left covered fester and never heal. I waited for him to find a way to begin.

'Rosie was with the— with Ethan when he died. I made him take her along to fetch water. The baby was sleeping and I wanted some time with Em. With the young ones underfoot all the time . . . I latched the door so they'd not surprise us coming back.' He looked at me, unshed tears glittering in the moonlight, and I reached for his hand, holding on tight so he'd not be so alone in his remembering. 'We fell asleep until Annie began to fuss. Ethan and Rosie hadn't come back, so I went looking for them. I kept calling for Ethan, calling and calling, getting further from home without his answering. The moon was all the way up, like it is now, before I heard Rosie crying.'

'The moon?' I squeezed his hand, trying to recall when Tuck told me our friends died, counting days. 'Was the moon full that night?'

'Only a day or two past full, maybe three. There was lots of light to see where I was going – and to see—' He looked away, raking his fingers through his rumpled hair. 'Rosie was curled up next to her brother, crying and calling his name, speaking so soft I could barely hear her. Both of them were dripping wet, soaked to the skin, but Ethan was just ... lying all still. Not moving. I'd never seen him that quiet.'

Staring, eyes open.

John didn't need to say the words for me to recognise that common thread, but it wasn't one I could pull loose or follow to the weaver. Not yet.

'The angels – tell me why Rose keeps talking about them.'

'I will. Give me a minute to get my breath.' He closed his eyes, trembling at the memory. 'I couldn't do nothing for the boy. Rosie was shaking with cold and wouldn't stop crying, so I picked her up, thinking I'd take her to Em and ... and go back for Ethan, but she started kicking and screaming that we couldn't leave Ethan again – that she ... she left him and the angel took him away. She was so scared, Mari, so very scared. So I put the boy over my shoulder and I carried the two of them home together.'

'Oh stars, John.' I couldn't imagine that walk home, what part of him withered away with a dead child in one arm, his daughter terrified and sobbing in the other. 'And Rose thinks it's her fault.'

He nodded, tight-lipped and grim. 'Rosie told Em she saw an angel in a scarlet gown walking on the stream, following them. She tried to show Ethan, but the boy told her to stop lying and pick flowers for their mam while he got the water. Rosie keeps saying she turned round to find the angel smiling at her. That's the last she knew until she woke up next to her brother – she says she doesn't remember how they got to the place where I found them.'

Now I was shaking and couldn't stop, knowing how close John had come to losing Rose too. He and Emma couldn't bring themselves to believe her story – the idea of a messenger from God taking away their child was just too horrible to think about. Believing sickness or some taint had carried Ethan into death was easier.

But Rose's story had the ring of truth to me, the words of a child gifted with other sight who saw what her brother couldn't. She named the creature an angel because angels were what she knew and understood. Rose was young, far younger than most when their gift woke for the first time. There'd be lots of time to teach her control – and to accustom John and Emma to the idea. Now wasn't the time to say anything.

'Rosie follows me everywhere now, Mari. She always did, of course – but not like this. I woke up last night to find her standing at the side of the bed, watching me and Em sleep.' John breathed out, a long sigh, and rubbed a hand over his face. 'It's odd for a grown man to feel his baby daughter is guarding him from harm, but that's what she thinks she's doing, I'm sure of it.'

Robin cleared his throat behind us, warning that he'd come back from the spring. He looked from John to me. 'Did you tell him?'

I shook my head. 'Not yet. We'd other things to speak of first.'

John turned to me, ignoring Robin. I knew ill feeling had lingered between them since Robin put me aside, but not how deep it ran. 'What else is there to tell?'

'Nothing that brings me any pleasure to say. We've lost more friends, John.' I wasn't happy to be the bearer of such bad tidings, bringing more grief to a friend already awash in loss, but I couldn't stay silent. 'Alan, Midge, Gilbert and Gamelyn . . . they've all died since midwinter, and all went without warning or reason, just like Will. Tuck has set me the task of finding out why.'

'And just like the boy.' John stood silent, his head bowed. I'd expected sorrow, not the anger in his eyes when he met my gaze again. 'Robin, take the water to Em. She's been waiting long enough. Tell her Mari and me will be in for supper soon as we're done talking.'

'I don't mind doing favours if you ask nicely, but I'm not your servant.' Robin dropped the bucket at his feet, slopping water on his boots, but not upsetting it. 'Don't give me orders. It's not your place.'

'It's my place if I say it is.' John planted a hand in the centre of Robin's chest and pushed hard. 'If you plan on sitting at my table and eating my food you can damn well work for it. About time you had to work for something.'

Robin's breath came harsh and quick with fury, but I stepped between the two of them to keep them from coming to blows.

'Take the water inside, Robin. Please. This isn't worth fighting over and John has the right to say what he wants done in his house.' I shoved the packet of herbs for the babe into his hand. 'Give these to Emma for the little one. She'll know what to do with them.'

He snatched up the bucket and stormed off. I waited for the door to slam, but he closed it quietly.

John scowled, fists clenched at his side. 'How long has Tuck known?'

'A fortnight, no more. He saw how this fit together after Will died and sent for me. The news took a long time to find us.'

His shoulders relaxed, some of the anger gone, though not all.

'I did what I could to protect Kate and Robbie and came here. I'll do what I can to protect you and yours before I leave.'

'Then it is magic?' Both hands raked through his hair again.

'Of course it is. I'm a fool for asking. Tuck wouldn't come to you, or take you away from your young ones otherwise.'

'It's a curse, if I'm reading the signs right,' I said. 'I'll lift it if I can. But first I have to find the one who cast it.'

'There's nothing normal about any of this, Mari – not Rosie seeing angels, nor the way Will and the boy died. But I'd be twice damned as a fool if I didn't see this all leads to Robin one way or another. Our friends are dead and his brother too, yet Robin's still right as rain.' He took my hand, sounding weary and older than I knew him to be. 'Stinks to the stars, if you ask me, and there's something just not right about any part of it. You're welcome in my house tonight, but I won't have him under my roof once he eats. He can sleep in the barn or go. It's all the same to me.'

'John . . .'

He crossed his arms and set his shoulders. 'I've a family to think about, Mari, and I won't put them in more danger. It's decided. Now come inside and eat. Em will be itching to see you and cross I've kept you so long.'

The moon was higher, bathing the house and yard in power. There wouldn't be a better time to ward John and his family. Food could wait a few minutes longer.

'Tell Emma I'll be along in a moment or two. I promised to do what I could to protect all of you. The best time is while the moon is riding high.' I picked up my bag and cinched it tight. 'Would you take my things inside? I won't be long.'

After he'd kissed my forehead and left, I turned my mind to what needed to be done. Calling power on a full-moon night was akin to drinking too much wine, a giddy feeling that changed how you saw the world, making everything appear beautiful and luminous. One of the first lessons learned in true craft was to only take what magic you needed. Drunk was drunk, whether from power or grape, and both made it far too easy to believe you could do anything.

Sherwood had a magic of its own that dampened and dimmed the moon's changes. Other sight showed each blade of grass in John's yard studded with baubles, each leaf and twig rimmed with inner light. Beauty was everywhere I looked, some of it real, some glamour. The night was alive in a way even I rarely saw.

Why the Fae held their revels bathed in moonlight wasn't hard to understand, nor why they used the moon's magic to call mortal lovers to their side. For one night each month, these creatures with so little beauty of their own could steal from the moon and all who saw them would believe.

I gathered power and spun it into a web around the house: a spider casting strands of protective silk. Three times I walked around the house to keep out harm, cast threads three times around each window, the door and the chimney. Each crack, each hidden mousehole, was warded with memories and the love I held for all those who lived in this home.

Too many I'd loved were gone already. I wouldn't risk losing another.

The high-pitched yip of a vixen among the streamside reeds prickled the hairs on the back of my neck, making my heart beat faster. I was afraid Bridget had come to warn me of danger and fetch me home. But an instant later the deeper bark of the vixen's mate answered her from somewhere downstream. I sucked in a shaky breath and started inside to supper.

My hand was on the latch when the sound of laughter and music circled around my head, beckoning me to follow, but I was far from an innocent. I shut the door behind me and pretended not to hear.

The Fae needed to hunt elsewhere.

Rosie sang me awake in the morning. She was sitting on a low stool next to her baby sister's cradle, crooning lullabies in a high sweet voice that hushed little Annie's colicky cries. Emma bustled around the hearth, fixing porridge and slicing cheese for breakfast. She was too busy with getting all of us fed to pay attention to her older daughter but I took note, watching how the touch of Rose's hand stopped the baby's fussing. More than just a touch of other sight hid inside this snip of a girl. I'd have more to teach her than I'd thought.

Once we'd finished eating, John and I gathered cloaks and hats and went outside, followed by Rose, who was carefully carrying a wedge of bread and cheese Emma had asked her to give Robin. Annie started howling again as soon as her big sister went out the door, each cry more heartbroken than the last.

Robin was waiting in the yard, silent and pouting. He looked surprised when Rose held out the food, but he knelt to take it from her with a smile. 'Thank you, Rose. Give your mother my thanks too.'

I hadn't wanted to ask John to show me where he'd found Ethan, but knowing I'd need to see the place, he insisted on taking me there himself and nothing Emma or I said could shift him away from the idea. Walking into the room where Will had died would have been more than I could bear, but John had always been brave.

I still asked one more time, 'Are you sure you want to do this, John? We can find the field on our own.'

'I can't spend my days avoiding the place by walking around the long way or not taking cows to graze that pasture.' He shooed Rose inside to Emma and closed the door firmly behind her. 'Let's get going before Rosie gets it in her head to follow.'

Rain threatened and the sky hung low and pregnant with grey clouds. The dank wind ruffled my hair as I followed John, cool and moist and carrying the scent of wet fields. Robin trailed behind us, still sullen after his night alone in the barn.

Tiny brown wrens flitted in and out of the reeds along the brook, our passage flushing them from one patch of cover to another, but inquisitive sparrows and shyer dunnocks held their places, swaying on thin branches as the wind set them to bobbing. Bright eyes watched us pass and some called out, high trills warning their more timid brethren to take flight or hide while we travelled alongside the stream.

The brook narrowed to a fast-moving runnel as we reached its source, the spring-fed pond. John stopped walking, though I didn't need him to tell me this was where Ethan had died. The way he stood, shoulders sunk, head bowed, was enough.

A pall hung over the field, an air of loss and things gone wrong. More had happened here than Ethan's death, terrible as that was: being sure of that, and not being able to give what I sensed a name, was the worst part.

'Forgive me, Mari. I thought I could do it . . . but I can't. This is close as I can go.' John pointed to a spot a few paces from the pond's edge. 'It's just over there, near those rocks. Rosie and the boy were so wet, I thought at first they'd fallen in. That was before she told me about the angel.'

'Rose saw an angel?' Robin stepped up eagerly and looked around. 'She saw one here?'

The bright, hopeful look in his eye, his need for the angel to be real, made me nervous.

'Rose saw something, Robin, but not an angel,' I said. 'Not unless your God has taken to stealing away innocent children.'

The palms of my hands itched and rubbing them against the heavy weave of my cloak didn't ease the feeling away. I took a single step towards the pond and the itch grew, pulling me forward. 'There's something very wrong about this place. You stay here, both of you, while I try to puzzle this out.'

Other sight showed that the Fae had once built a faerie ring around this pond, but that was long ago. Less than a day after a full moon a ring still in use would glow silver-bright; mistaking it for anything else would be impossible. The signs here were faint to the point of vanishing. Generations had lived and died since the last time a Fae Lady's court danced in this ring.

And in any case, Fae magic was clean, pulled from the earth and sky and growing things. Death had no place in their rituals. It's true the High Lords and Ladies played games with mortals, did things no one outside the Folk would understand, but I'd never before known leftover magic from their weavings to fill me with loathing.

Without me needing to ask, John took my bag from my shoulder and I paced slowly forward, searching with other sight for whatever was making me want to claw the skin off my palms. The itch spreading up my arms as I drew nearer the pond and the tumble of rocks was becoming a true misery.

A broken circle of salt mixed with bone dust surrounded the rocks, its jagged edges glowing the same sickly yellow colour as the grass dying inside its boundaries. I couldn't say whether John undid the weaving when he came for his children, or if the spellcaster dispersed the magic. Fragments of the spell lingered yet, turning the ground inside the circle dead and barren, but most of the power had dissipated. I was more than grateful for that. Foulness spread all around me, its horrid taste filling the air until all I could think of was carrion rotting in the heat. The stench coated my tongue and try as I might, I couldn't swallow the taste of rot away. The thought of Rose and Ethan lying there amongst that filth made me feel sick to my stomach.

That powdered yellow bone and salt crystals were still visible in the grass after a month of rain, wind and sun, a full month of cows wandering the pasture, gave me pause and set me thinking about why magic would persist so long in this place. I walked the edge of the circle, searching for reasons, for why I wanted to claw the skin off my arms and why the salt forming the circle hadn't dissolved.

My answer was on the far side of the stones.

Dull shards of weathered bone, most of them split and broken, covered a flat rock which had been used as an altar, by the looks of it, just out of sight of the place where John had found his children. More shattered pieces of skeletons littered the ground, some in piles against the base of the rock, others scattered as if a foot had kicked them in passing. Dark stains marked the stone, wide streaks that ran down the side and darkened the ground.

Bones and tiny skulls belonging to fox kits and baby rabbits were piled off to the side. Their remains were mingled with what looked to be a farm dog's new-born pups and lambs so small they too must have been stolen just after birth. Whoever had drawn the circle had chosen only the very young to sacrifice, infants still unmarked by the world.

Ethan was older, but even by the strictest teachings of the

Church he was considered below the age of innocence. The bodies in the circle told me that innocence was the reason he died.

I could only guess why Rose was spared. Other sight let even the youngest child see the world as it truly was – the good and the bad, the beauty and the ugliness. Her ability to see the creature she'd named an angel might have saved Rose's life.

That creature was responsible for all the death here, I was sure of it, but what I couldn't understand was why, or what there was to gain. Marlow would know what power sprang to life with the death of the very young, but the dragon and his knowledge were leagues away. Guesses I had aplenty, but that wasn't the same.

None of the skulls I could see looked human, but I'd no desire to venture any closer to be certain. Death that comes too soon always dims the world a bit and I couldn't bring myself to face darkness that complete. Nor did I want to risk leaving young spirits trapped here, unable to start their journey again, so I'd do what I could to cleanse this place and if it disrupted the plans of the one who'd drawn the circle, well, so much the better.

I muttered charms and set wards against evil as I retraced my steps. John and Robin were standing several paces apart when I came around the rocks, each staring off in a different direction. Grief tugged at John's shoulders and left unfamiliar lines in his face, but Robin wasn't sparing him so much as a glance. Once they'd been the closest of friends. Now they were strangers.

John saw me first. 'Did you find what you were hunting for, Mari?'

'I did.' I took the bag he was holding out and hugged it to my chest. 'Now I need to try and fix things. I'll need some wood, John, wet or dry makes no difference.'

He nodded and pointed behind him. 'There's an old apple tree over there that fell last winter. Give me a few minutes.'

John had never questioned what I needed or asked why. My craft didn't frighten him and he'd helped me with spell-casting before this. He loped off across the pasture, his long legs covering more distance in one stride than I'd manage in three. I searched through my bag, hunting for dried rosemary and rue.

'What did you find behind the rocks?' Robin leaned on his bow, watching me with the wary look in his eyes I knew too well. He'd done his best in the years we lived together to distance himself from my craft, even when magic was the only thing keeping us out of the sheriff's hands or a step ahead of the prince's troops. Now Robin was faced with me working craft again and I could practically see him squirming at how near he was forced to stand. He'd like what I planned to do even less.

'Things you don't believe in. There's a salt circle to keep in power and the bones of new-born animals that were killed here. I'm going to cleanse the circle and put any spirits left behind at rest.' I found a half-used tallow candle in the bottom of the pack which would provide the spark I needed. 'I can't be certain all the bones belong to animals and it's too dangerous to try and sort them out. Ethan died here too, Robin. I won't trust to chance his spirit isn't tied to this place.'

'Ethan is safely buried in hallowed ground.' Robin reached for his cross, his fingers gripping the piece of carved wood so tight his knuckles shone white. 'The village priest judged him to be under the age of reason and he went to God free of sin. You needn't concern yourself with Ethan's spirit. God the Father has care of his soul.'

Even after all our years apart, Robin still knew the ways to make me spitting mad and start an argument – and I was determined not to let him. 'You've lectured me on the evil you see in the world more times than I can recall, Robin, but you don't recognise real evil, or the harm it does. I doubt you ever will, not until something you swear can't exist plants a knife in your chest.'

'You've damned yourself in God's eyes a hundred times over and you still insist on doing it again,' Robin said, his mouth pulling into a hard line. 'Would you damn Ethan with your witchcraft?'

My use of craft, an old quarrel between us, was the reason he'd ended our marriage. Biting back the anger he'd stirred to life, I added a small sack of salt to the pile at my feet. Letting him goad me would make the spell harder to weave and just the thought of fighting ancient battles anew made me weary. 'If you're right and Ethan's safe with God, nothing I do can harm him. But I won't take the chance of trusting that's true and doing nothing. Make no mistake, Robin: what happened here was dark and foul, whether you believe or not. I can't bring Ethan back, but I can untangle him and any other innocents from the spells woven here – so stay clear and let me get on with it.'

'It's not too late.' He tipped his head to one side, watching me the same way I'd seen a yeoman watch a mouse before tossing it to a pack of cats. 'I can help you make peace with God, Marian.'

When I stood up straight I was nearly eye to eye with Robin. He was always taller in my memories. 'I don't need your help. I do fine on my own.'

His face flushed crimson and I braced myself for an outburst, but he turned away abruptly and stalked off. I was thankful to let him go.

John returned at a run, breathing hard, his arms full of apple branches. 'Where do you want this, Mari?'

'Just at the edge of the dead grass – but don't step any closer to the rocks than that.' I gathered what I needed into my arms and followed him. 'I'd be grateful if you'd keep Robin well away until I finish. Things could go badly if he interferes.'

As he eyed Robin, nodding, I blessed him anew for trusting me.

I sprinkled dried rosemary and rue over the branches, still wet with morning dew, glad to see the herbs stick. A dusting would have done, but having more to hang the spell on eased my mind. I walked the edge of the circle, tossing the branches inside, then walked all the way around again, this time pouring salt to form a new boundary, leaving open a space the width of my foot. I picked up the candle. Calling flame to a wick was a simple bit of craft, one every hedgewitch could master. Keeping a candle burning in wind and damp took a bit more skill, but I'd mastered that trick out of necessity during our outlaw years. Sprinkling a bit of the rosemary and then rue on the flame caused it to flare. The candle burned green for an instant before settling into a steady yellow flame.

'Remember life, remember who you were, remember your purpose.' I fed more power to the flame, tossed the candle into the centre of the circle and closed the open space with the last of the salt. Flames began to feed on the wood, the faint pale-green flickers threatening to die in the damp wind until I wrapped my will around the memory of Ethan's smile and kept them burning.

I walked the circle again, adding rosemary and rue to the salt, coaxing the flames higher. Behind me I half-heard John quarrelling with Robin, but I didn't have any attention to spare for either man.

'Death is not meant to tie young souls to stone and earth, nor bind bright spirits to the place they died. I call on the power of fire and air to cleanse. I call on the might of water and earth to open the way. Seek your place and start anew. Remember life, remember your journey and find who you're meant to be.' I reached the place I'd started and sealed the herbs as I'd sealed the salt. Flames shot higher, spreading from wood to grass, lapping at the piles of bone.

A maelstrom rose, tangled my hair and whipped it into my face: the creature's magic sought to hold her victims tight. The wind keened and moaned, singing a song of despair to muffle my call to life and renewal. Death wrapped its claws around the fledging spirits trying to escape, sank its fangs into them and pulled them back towards darkness.

But life holds power of its own, born afresh with each child's birth-cry and the first buds of spring. We all cling to the days granted to us and fight to stay in the world, often long past the time when slipping away would cause less pain. I channelled that power through me, pulling it from the damp-beaded flowers scattered across the pasture, memories of what it was like to suckle my children and how it felt to lie in the arms of someone I loved.

I wrapped all my will and anger around the magic, feeding the flames. 'You are not bound here,' I cried. 'Go!'

The roar of flames drowned the cry of the wind and fire filled the circle, burning away blood and pain and fear. Flames ate through the remnants of the original circle, turning powdered bone and salt to ash. The spell shattered then, and the sound on the wind echoed the trapped spirits' death cries.

Slowly, the fire died away, dwindling to feeble flickers among the ash and embers. The first small ghostly shapes began twisting upwards, ill-defined phantoms barely outlined against the sky.

Too weak to stand, I fell to my knees. Now scores of young

spirits were rising from the ashes and vanishing into the flat grey clouds, far too many of them with a human shape. None of the bones I'd seen were large enough to belong to a child, but their souls were bound here nonetheless. I'd been right to cleanse this place.

Tear-blind and shaking, I watched until the last little shade had disappeared. I'd hoped for a glimpse of Ethan's face, to recognise him and know he was free, but that was a desperate wish, one I knew would never be granted. I watched anyway.

Chapter 7

. . . those days are gone away,
And their hours are old and grey,
And their minutes buried all
Under the down-trodden pall
Of the leaves of many years.

JOHN KEATS

I don't remember much about the walk back to John's cottage, other than stubbornly refusing to let him carry me home. John let me have my way, but without his arm around me, I'd have pitched straight onto my face.

Once, near the end of our outlaw days, I'd been forced to pour that much of myself into a spell. Travelling with Alan, Will and Robin in the far north of Sherwood, we'd been betrayed and the four of us found ourselves running for our lives, hounds and hunters both on our heels. Keeping them off us and hiding our passage took all the strength I had. Robin was the one tugging me along that time, whispering encouragement in my ear and making sure I kept my feet under me. Weeks later, Alan told me that Robin had been terrified I'd pushed myself to the edge of death and that he'd lose me.

Now Robin trailed far behind, wordless, the expression on his face not giving away a hint about his thoughts. I welcomed his silence, too weary to cope with his anger or to argue. Funny to think there was a time when I lived for a word from him, when the sound of his voice lifted my heart. Now my thoughts were all of Will and what I'd have given to hear him call my name, or to see him smile.

John did have to carry me those last paces. He called from the yard for Emma to open the cottage door and she was beside herself, insisting he tell her what happened and all the while preparing broth and feeding me sips until my hands grew steady enough to hold the cup myself. When I'd swallowed all I could, she helped me climb the ladder into the little loft under the eaves, where I slept half the day away, not waking until late afternoon.

Rose sat on the edge of the bed, solemnly watching over me. 'I don't hear Ethan crying or asking me to help him.' Her small hand wrapped around my fingers. 'He's safe now, isn't he?'

This bit of a girl was full of surprises. Rose was naturally stronger at craft than many a fully trained woman I'd known. Those stories about Fae blood in the family might be true.

I brushed soft curls back from her face and tried to smile. 'Yes, little one, he's safe. You don't need to worry about him.'

She nodded, more serious than a child of four had any right to be. Innocence died many ways and for some, far too soon. 'I wanted to help him, but I didn't know how. Will you teach me, Mari?'

I sat up and pulled Rose into my lap. Over her head I saw John at the top of the ladder, tears glittering in his eyes. He met my gaze and I knew he'd heard everything. We'd been friends far too many years for him not to know what it all meant. I waited, letting him decide before I spoke, for all that if he said no it would make little difference. She'd have to be taught, but I'd feel easier doing so with his consent.

He swallowed hard and nodded, putting his trust and his daughter into my hands.

I hugged Rose tight and kissed the top of her head. 'I'll teach you all I can, but we need to wait until you're a little older. There are other things you need to learn first to keep you safe. I have to go away for a while, but when I come back you can visit me and we'll get started.'

John cleared his throat, but Rose's expression made it plain she'd known he was there all along. 'Emma sent me to see if you were awake. She's of a mind to feed you before you leave.'

'Tell her I'll be right there.' I rested my cheek on Rose's hair. 'I need a moment first.'

He disappeared down the ladder and I turned Rose to face me.

'I need you to swear an oath to me, Rose. It's important, or I wouldn't ask you.'

She peered up at me with her big blue eyes and nodded solemnly.

'Promise me that if you see this angel again you'll run inside this house as quick as ever you can. She can't get inside here, I've made sure. Can you do that?'

She tugged on my hand, tears in her eyes and breathing too fast. 'Make Da promise to come with me – make him *promise*, Mari. He doesn't believe me when I talk about the angel. If she comes back she'll hurt him.'

I kissed her forehead. 'I will. I'll make both him and your mam promise. I don't want any of you to be hurt.'

Rose slid off the bed, fingers twisting in her skirts. 'She won't hurt me, only Da.'

I cocked my head to the side, watching her with other sight for any hint of a spell I'd missed before. 'You can't know that, Rose.'

She sighed, the weariness that had no place in one so young creeping back into her eyes. 'The angel said she could forgive me . . . because I saw her. But she couldn't forgive Da his sins, so she took my brother. Why did she do that? What did Ethan do wrong, Mari?'

'Nothing, Rose. He did nothing at all.' I gathered her into my arms again and rocked her, hoping with all my heart she'd believe me. 'Ethan didn't do anything wrong. She lied to you. I don't know why, but I promise I'll find out.'

I held her until John came up the ladder again to find us. She clung to me but never shed a tear, staring wide-eyed and silent into the corners of the loft, guarding against terrors no one else could see.

Robin and I left the farm in the misty half-light before dawn. The land surrounding the cottage was quiet and still. My wards were still shining bright, the spell-lines as strong as the night I wove them. I walked away and tried not to look back at John and Emma standing in the yard. I'd done all I could do. With luck, it would be enough to keep them safe.

Birds waited for the first rays of the sun before they began to sing in the day, ending the quiet and lightening my heart. Dark clouds and rain of the day before moved away, leaving bottomless blue skies behind. The grass looked greener, the flowers brighter. I didn't question why that might be, whether it was a bright sunny day or my need to hold to tight to something other than thoughts of death.

Neither Robin nor I talked. He had the brooding look on his face that meant I'd be better off if I left him alone. I used the peace and quiet to sort through all that happened the day before, go over all I'd learned. Being left with more riddles and fewer answers unsettled me.

Mansfield was two full days' walk from John's farm if we didn't have to wait out bad weather. Once we left the valley, the path ran through thick woodlands until we neared the River Maun. This was a part of Sherwood I hadn't travelled in many years, but I knew we needed to be on guard. Bands of highwaymen fleeing King John's justice roamed the forest pathways, watching for unwary travellers or merchants whose purses were heavy and guards few. These robbers showed little mercy to anyone who tried to win free with their supply of coin intact: they were truly outlaws, without a cause to fight for other than their own greed.

The gristmill where Midge had lived and died sat on a spot where the river curved and grew deeper. A swift, strong current turned the water-wheel, powering the huge grinding stones with ease. He'd prospered in his mill, living close enough to King John's market to sell flour to the castle bakers and the goodwives of the town, but far enough away from watchful eyes to do business with anyone who didn't want notice.

I'd heard from a woodcutter that Midge had married a year or so back. The man who'd carried the tale said Midge's wife was a smart, cheerful girl, with dark curls and eyes that lit up at the sight of him. I'd hoped the next I'd hear was that his house was full of children, something I knew he wanted; that his laughing-eyed young bride was so soon a widow was a very sad thing.

Robin set a good pace and we entered deep woodlands before noon. The day had grown warm as the sun climbed higher and I welcomed the cooler air and dappled shade. We hadn't gone far beyond the fringe when Robin called a halt.

'Sit and rest a while, Marian. Have a bite to eat if you're hungry.' He tossed me the bundle of food Emma had gifted us with. 'If I remember rightly there's a stream not far over that way. I'll refill the water-bags and maybe scare up a pigeon or two for supper later while I'm at it.'

'There's no need to stop on my account.' I pulled my hat off and fanned my face, hoping a cool breeze would dry my sweat-damp hair. 'Refill the water if you like and then we can go on.'

'Sit down and stop being so stubborn. We're in no hurry.' He slung the straps for both water-bags over his shoulder and grabbed his bow. 'You've been stumbling along for a good bit now – a few times I thought you'd trip over your own feet. I don't fancy carrying you all the way to Mansfield.'

It was true. I was wearier than I was comfortable with or willing to admit. Knowing that Robin made sense and I still argued against it was a measure of how bone-tired I was. 'All right, we'll stop and rest. I'll sit quietly while you fetch the water. But there's really no need to coddle me.'

He snorted. 'I don't plan to coddle you, just not let you run yourself into the ground. You came close yesterday and I'd be blind not to see that. The abbot will nail my hide to the chapel door if I don't look out for you – and you may believe I'm not a cruel man. Another day's rest at John's would have done you good, but I'd stretched his patience thin enough.'

I moved deeper into the shade, put my back against an oak and sank to the ground. The ache in my bones convinced me that shifting myself again might take more effort than I'd thought. 'You're both stubborn men. I don't know what the quarrel between you is, but you should find a way to mend it.'

'John or Will never told you?' Robin stood over me, emotions closed away so I couldn't read them. 'You really don't know?'

'The last time I saw the two of you together was more than twelve years ago, Robin.' I took hold of my patience, knowing he never said anything without going the long way around. 'John never spoke of you. I knew there was ill feeling between you, but not how deep it ran, or the cause.'

'We had much more than a quarrel between us and it's not something that can be mended.' Robin turned away, looking back the way we'd come. 'John came near to killing me when he found out I'd ... I'd put you aside and left. He kicked in the door to my room, yanked me out of bed and slammed me into a wall – but he was only getting started and he'd learned a thing or two in the sheriff's jail. It took Will and Tuck both to pull him off me. I hurt so bad after the beating he gave me, I almost wished he'd managed to kill me. I'm surprised Will never told you the story.'

'Carrying stories was never Will's way,' I said. 'He wouldn't have taken any pleasure from telling me how you'd been hurt.'

'No, I suppose not.' He hitched the straps over his shoulder. 'Eat something. I won't be gone long.'

A mouthful or two of food was all I wanted, enough to keep Robin from nagging. I dug a wedge of Emma's cheese out of the bundle and broke a piece off the end. Tired as I was, eating even that small amount was an effort.

I leaned my head back and closed my eyes, listening to the quiet rustle of leaves moving with the breeze. Up in the crown of the oak a male greenfinch sang, claiming the tree for him and his mate. Other males answered from other trees, each bird setting boundaries the others shouldn't cross. Squabbles broke out, high-pitched and frantic, but quickly over.

Squabbles and quarrels. Best if I didn't dwell on that.

I woke to the smell of pigeons roasting and the pop of fat dripping into flames. My bag was tucked under my head. I opened my eyes to late afternoon light, having slept half the day away again. The false twilight that settled early in heavy woodland would be on us soon. With the moon just past full, we might travel on for a while, but we wouldn't get far before the light failed and in any case, Robin would need to sleep sometime.

We'd lost the best part of a day, sacrificed to my need to recover after breaking the angel's spell. I didn't know whether to whimper or rage.

Robin sat next to the small fire, feeding sticks to the flames. Two pigeons hung on a spit, making my mouth water. He saw me stir and smiled. 'I hoped you'd wake on your own. Supper will be ready soon.'

I sat up and tried to rub my eyes free of grit. Foul barely described my mood. 'Why did you let me sleep so long? We were supposed to leave once you fetched water.'

'I did try, Marian. You swung at me and went back to sleeping like a stone.' He turned the birds so they'd brown on the other side. 'You left me little choice. I still don't fancy carrying you, so I let you be.'

No matter how much I wanted to, I couldn't argue with that.

He never said the fault was mine, but I knew it was. 'Your pardon, Robin. I won't let it happen again.'

'There's no need for forgiveness. I don't begrudge you the rest.' He glanced at me, a strange look in his eye, as if he couldn't tell jest from honest speech. 'Your magic isn't anything I approve of, but even I could see your spells took everything out of you.'

'Most charitable of you, Robin, not holding the need for rest against me. Almost as generous as allowing you saw I needed it.' His disapproval was nothing new, but I was too tired not to snap at him. 'How far is the stream you talked about? I'd like to wash my face before supper.'

'Not far. I can show you if you'd like.'

'Just point me in the right direction.' From anyone else the offer of help wouldn't have raised a ripple, but anger is never reasonable. 'I can find it on my own.'

'Do you see the trio of ash just to the right? Go past them and keep going until you see a split oak. The stream is two or three hundred paces further on from the oak.' He pulled the spitted pigeons back from the flames so they'd stay warm but not cook as fast. 'There's a pool there, knee-deep or more. The bottom is rock and sand, not mud. I'll hold supper until you get back.'

Robin might be forgetful at times but he'd remembered that I wouldn't return quickly if there was a pool for bathing. I set off to find the stream, vowing to myself that I'd be more reasonable when I got back.

I soon found his pool where the stream ran through a clearing, sun-warmed and still, and swiftly pulled off my boots and clothes. Soft sand billowed under my feet near the edge, changing to smooth pebbles as I waded in up to my waist. Sun-warmed the water might be, but still chill enough that the first touch made me shiver. Silver minnows swam around my ankles and tasted my flesh, each tiny nibble tickling until I couldn't help but smile. The fish swam away once they were satisfied my toes weren't a new kind of food.

Birds sang lustily in the trees, calls echoing from one stand of trees to the next, nesting birds calling to their mates or males warning away rivals. Flashes of colour darted between cover as one parent or another went to find food for hungry nestlings.

Splashing water on my face wasn't going to be enough to wash away old resentments and grief. I rinsed sweat and dust from my face and hair, then floated on my back, my eyes closed, letting my hair drift around me, until some of the ache left my muscles and calm filled the space left by pain and anger, letting me think.

I couldn't spend my whole life angry at Robin. He was what he was and that wouldn't change. I thought I'd accepted that long ago, but time blurred memories with everything else. And if I were honest, at least some of the anger I felt now was that Robin was still alive while Will was dead.

Grief would soften over time as well. The sharp thrusts each time I remembered Will would blunt to an ache, albeit one I'd never lose. Surviving until the memory of his smile didn't fill me with pain – that was a task I wasn't sure I had the strength for. Without Kate and Robbie depending on me, I might not have tried.

Shadows stretched long across the pool, making giants out of saplings. Warmth fled as the sun made way for Mother Moon. The evening breeze made me shiver and I opened my eyes to a sky barely holding on to day. Ripples broke around me, reformed and continued on, driven before the wind. I'd hidden away for as long as I could. I sank to the bottom of the pool one last time before getting out. Water dripped in my eyes as I stood, blinding me to anything but faint sparkles and glimmers in the shadows.

My first thought was that Water sprites or nymphs had left behind tiny pieces of magic that shone brighter in early twilight. I brushed the hair out of my eyes, thinking nothing more of the light until I noticed the shimmer swirling in the deepest part of the pool. Red-tinged water bubbled up from the bottom, darkening to deep crimson as it spread across the surface. Other sight showed flickering flashes of gold under the red. I took a step closer.

'Witchling, come away!'

A Fae Lord stood at the edge of the pool, the scars he'd earned gaining status gleaming against his dark brown skin. His black hair was pulled back and tied with a strip of leather, the tiny bits of grey over his ears the only hint of age I'd ever seen in one of the Fae. Cornflower-blue eyes looked to the centre of the pool and back to me. He offered his hand. 'Leave the water and go back to your fire. I'll deal with this.'

Waves caressed my ankles, warm and soft as the fall of night. The lap of water became a song, faint, as if coming from far off and calling me closer. My eyes grew heavy and I shut them to listen. I wanted to find the music and join my voice with the one singing, to lose myself and soar on the melody. Whispers wove through the tune, full of promises that Will waited to dance with me if I'd follow. The need for him pulled me towards the churning crimson.

'Marian!' The Fae Lord's voice cracked like a drover's whip, jolting me out of the waking dream. 'Look at me and come away.'

A gust of cold wind raised goosepimples, shivers reminding me that my clothes lay draped over a branch out of reach. I splashed back to the edge of the pool, but stopped short of taking the Fae Lord's hand.

His voice softened. 'You've nothing to fear from me. The Lady sent me to watch over you. You have my oath I'll do you no harm. Dress quickly, then go and warm yourself by the fire.'

I scrambled from the water, more than a little afraid at how quickly and completely I'd lost myself. My hands were clumsy with cold and pulling on my clothes difficult. 'Have the Lady's protections worn thin so soon? How safe are my children?'

'The Lady's guardians still watch over the cottage and keep your children safe. The old dragon wards them as well.' The Fae Lord stood over me, blocking my view of the stream. 'The Lady didn't know you'd be venturing so far from home when you called her to the circle. I'm pledged to protect you in her name.'

He glanced over his shoulder at the pool where the water was bubbling and boiling loud enough that I could hear it. I didn't try to look past him, partly from fear of falling prey to the spell again, but even more afraid of what I'd do if a shade wearing Will's face beckoned to me.

'Go now, eat your supper. Ward your camp well before moonrise. I'll weave my own wards once I'm finished here.' He smiled, perfect teeth shining in the twilight. 'You'll find the Archer by the fire, fast asleep and unaware of time passing. He'll wake when you return. Tell him as much or as little as you choose.'

I tugged on my boots, settling my feet into them with a hard stomp. 'I don't think I should tell him anything. He wouldn't believe a man of God could be spelled by the Fae and I'm not in the mood to try to make him see reason.'

'Oh, he believes. The Archer hides behind his God like a shield, but he believes in the Fae and their power.' The Fae Lord's smile grew wider. 'This isn't the first time one of the Fae have touched him. Ask him if you don't trust my word.'

Mischief shone in his eyes, but so did truth and left no room for me to doubt. I fled the grinning Fae Lord and the bespelled pool, running until my breath came short and painful and his laughter faded away. I ran until I couldn't run any more.

Robin was indeed dozing by the fire when I stumbled into camp, unaware I'd been gone much too long. The fire slept too, flames frozen and unmoving, spitted pigeons unburned. Everything woke – including Robin – as soon as I sat on my cloak.

The confusion in Robin's eyes as he saw how dark the sky was cleared almost at once and he handed me one of the pigeons without comment. We ate in silence, the final light of day fading into night. When the last of the bones had been fed to the fire, I rolled into my cloak and tried to sleep.

Nights were never quiet in Sherwood, but the calls of owls in the treetops and the screams of dying rabbits weren't what kept me awake. Memories of the Fae Lord's words and the glee in his eyes as he told me about Robin did a fine job of keeping me awake.

Robin had never told me of being charmed or beguiled by one of the Fae. That didn't mean it wasn't true.

Chapter 8

'Tis strange that death should sing.
I am the cygnet to this pale faint swan,
Who chants a doleful hymn to his own death,
And from the organ-pipe of frailty sings
His soul and body to their lasting rest.

WILLIAM SHAKESPEARE

Rain began not long after we left camp the next morning. Iron-black clouds had dimmed the dawn, prolonging night so that we hardly knew when the sun rose. Fat drops collected on the tips of branches, many of them finding their way down the back of my neck. The morning was dreary and cold and miserable, matching my mood. Simple questions from Robin earned answers sharper than he deserved until he lapsed into silence after I'd bitten his head off one too many times.

Constantly jumping at shadows was part of my foul mood. I used other sight to watch for the smallest glimmer of magic, hoping for some kind of warning before a spell overtook me. This part of Sherwood was filled with piskies, wood-goblins and sprites of all sorts, each one of the minor Fae leaving a touch of sparkle behind when they passed through. By midday my head was pounding, but I hadn't found anything that didn't belong.

The casting on the pond had been meant for me, a trap I had walked into blindly. Blaming weariness and anger at Robin for why I'd missed the signs was the easy answer, but the truth was I hadn't been paying attention. In cleansing the circle and releasing the trapped spirits, I'd made an enemy and put myself in danger. I hadn't given that a thought before. Now I couldn't forget.

We stopped in the shelter of a small beech copse to eat the last of Emma's provisions. Rain still drizzled, dripping from leaden clouds, looking determined to keep it up all day. The trees offered some little shelter so I claimed a stump for a chair and sat mulling over how Rose's angel knew to set her spell on that one pond and no other. How she'd found me was the question I'd been worrying over all morning.

The Fae Lord chose to show himself a moment later, appearing next to me as if conjured from raindrops and mist. Knowing he still dogged my steps was both a comfort and a worry. I wanted to ask him about the spell, if he'd broken the weaving or if he knew how the caster had found me, but he put a finger to his lips, hushing me before I spoke.

'Be still, little witch. The Archer is blind and deaf to my presence. He'll wonder why you speak to the air.' He pranced and pulled faces like a jackanapes, while Robin looked right at him. 'The Lady sends word your children are safe in her care and you need not worry how they fare. She bids you to find the person who built the circle, quick as you can. The Lady won't let the person twisting bright magic into something foul go unpunished.'

With those words the Fae Lord faded back into the shadows. I stared at the place where he'd vanished, wanting to call him back. Questions I had a-plenty, but answers were hard to come by. Why the Lady chose to involve herself was yet another riddle I couldn't unravel.

'What's wrong, Marian?' Robin watched me, his brow crinkled in puzzlement. He'd withdrawn from me and the world for more than twelve years, but he was no innocent when he left, or now. I'd never have believed a man his age could find the world so hard to understand. What the Fae Lord said about shields came back to me.

'Nothing to fret over. A Fae noble carrying a message to let me know Kate and Robbie are safe.' I brushed rain off my nose and pulled my hat down tighter. 'In the years we ranged across Sherwood, you saw me talking with one of the Fae many a time.'

Robin frowned, the corners of his mouth pinched and sour-looking. He offered the water-bag, but I shook my head. I waited while he drank deep, preparing for the sermon I knew he'd feel compelled to deliver.

He didn't disappoint me.

'I've seen demons and devils roaming the darkness, but no creature I'd call noble,' Robin said. 'Who you call the Fae are children of Lucifer, hiding evil behind a fair face. God warns of the danger to our mortal soul if we consort with demons. I want naught to do with them.'

'You've never faced a real demon if you'd hang that name on the Fae. They walk the world differently than you and I, but I'd never call them evil.' I pressed him, wanting to see where it led. Shields hid secrets more often than not. 'I find it strange you've never passed a word with one of the Lords or Ladies. Even Tuck sought the aid of Fae Lords when he needed their help.'

'Tuck can look to his soul and I'll look to mine.' He scowled and turned away. 'No need is great enough to seek their aid.'

'Not even Kate and Robbie's lives?' His head snapped around, the puzzlement and surprise on his face real this time. 'I needed to seek protection for them, Robin. The Lady of the Fae guards our children while I'm away. She sent the messenger to let me know all is well.'

Anger and fear warred inside him, each skirmish outlined in his shifting expression until fear won. I saw it in the way his fingers twitched towards his knife at small sounds, the way his eyes slid sideways to watch the shadows. Fear of me or fear of the Fae? I couldn't say which.

'Robbie and Kate are far from safe in Aelfgifu's keeping. She is the mother of lies and rules a nest of vipers. May God have mercy on their souls.' Robin stood and quickly gathered his things. He strode away into the rain and the gloom, leaving me to follow on my own.

I roused myself after a moment and trailed behind him, not really seeing anything beyond the angry set of Robin's shoulders as the Lady of the Fae's name rang in my head, wrapped in power that left me in no doubt this was her true name. The court had scores of High Lords and Ladies of varying degrees of power who held their names close, and out of them all he'd named the most powerful. Not even Marlow, ancient as the oldest tree and stone in Sherwood, knew the name Aelfgifu.

Mother of lies, Robin had called her, and all the while he lied with every pious condemnation, the words falling from his lips with an ease that left me wondering if any word he'd ever spoken to me was truth.

He shouldn't know her name, but now I had the answer to how she'd known mine.

Another day and a night passed before we neared the River Maun. I spoke as little as possible and Robin, still holding his secrets close, said even less. We circled one another like cats, wary and ready to hiss and spit at the smallest offence.

The Fae Lord showed himself often now, his manner grave and solemn and all traces of mockery gone. He peered from behind massy oaks or between poplars growing no more than a hand-span apart, oftentimes with lesser Fae clustered around his feet. I ventured to guess the brounys and sprites were scouts to range far afield, for he never spoke, nor gave me the chance to ask. An army was accompanying us through the forest and Robin saw not a one of them.

Oaks gave way to saplings, sweet chestnut and rowan, alder and birch. The paths grew more open as we drew closer to Mansfield. Flowers stretched towards the sun in places free of deep shade, bright splashes of colour that took me by surprise. Deer ran at our approach, leaving heathland for deeper cover in hidden thickets.

The outlaw bands in this part of the greenwood lived off the land, finding food where they could; King John's strict laws against poaching meant nothing to them. For the herds to be this shy of men, these men must be bolder and more numerous than I'd heard.

We came to a well-worn muddy track, full of deep ruts from farmers' carts and wagons: the road to the king's market at

Mansfield and the river beyond. Remnants of the old Roman road endured, plain to see, if not as easy to travel. The old stone mile markers still stood in places, although chipped and overgrown with creepers, and from time to time we passed smooth sections of paving stones running along the edge of the dirt road.

Reminders of the blood spilled in ancient times also endured. Other sight gave me visions of shades dressed in strange garb, bearing long iron-tipped pikes or swords quite unlike those carried by King John's guards, marching in neat rows on a flat paved road – a road that crumbled to mud once they'd passed.

Sadder ghosts trailed behind the Roman soldiers on that shattered paving, prisoners wearing little more than rags. Kin of my kin, they were bound to haunt the land they'd died for. Their eyes begged me for release, but there was nothing I could do to free them all.

One of the shades touched my hand, a woman with dull red hair and a baby riding in a sling on her back. Cold gripped me, crawling up my arm into my chest and taking root. I saw her last days, beaten and abused until she found a knife unguarded and the courage to free herself. The child was gone by then, abandoned because its crying was an annoyance to the Roman commander. They'd left her body at the side of the road for carrion crows and marched on.

Her touch left me no choice: if I did not unbind her, I would carry the haunt with me for the rest of my days. Cursing myself for a fool I moved off the road, away from pleading eyes and grasping hands. There was no time for a circle or a proper summoning of a guide to carry her to the next life, but her name rode the memory of how she died. I hoped a name would be enough.

'Forget this place, Eithne. Let go,' I whispered. My will cradled her need to be gone, nourished the desire to live again. 'Forget the passage of time. Forget pain and death and what was done to you. Your child has lived a hundred lives, died a hundred times and lived again. Seek your next life, Eithne.'

She wavered in and out of sight and I thought at first she'd gone – but she returned, standing apart from the other shades, holding out her infant son where I could see him. I couldn't answer her silent question. Some ghosts lingered because of fear, clinging to what they knew, but Eithne held to this place for fear of leaving her child trapped and alone.

A tall red-haired young man appeared next to her, rippling in and out of view, his spirit anchored elsewhere. The infant in her arms vanished. Eithne's son smiled and took her hand. She touched his face and the two of them came apart, clouds fraying on the wind. I blinked and they were gone.

I wiped my face on a sleeve and took a shaky breath, looking around for Robin. He hadn't gone far for he'd stopped in the middle of the road to talk to a farmer leading a donkey cart. Two young boys stood in the front amongst the cabbages, wide-eyed at whatever story Robin was telling. The stream of shades parted to go around the farmer and his sons, not a one going near them – but phantom after phantom reached out to Robin, touched his face, his hand, moved through the centre of him and walked on. He didn't flinch or give any sign he felt any echo of their suffering. His kin were truly dead to him. If I'd asked, I wasn't sure he'd admit they'd ever lived at all.

Robin believed in ghosts no more than he did in anything good that might arise from my craft. He'd told me once that a man secure in his faith knew what waited after death: reward for a good life or repentance for what the Church called his sins was all Robin believed in, all he'd ever allow existed. He lived his life shutting out anything that might call that belief into question.

On the other side of the old road, the Fae Lord watched, unsmiling and grim-faced. I took some small comfort that he stayed close and on guard. He'd told me the truth when he said Robin was blind and deaf.

And I was beginning to wonder what good Robin would do me against the one casting this curse, how he was meant to protect me. There was so much he couldn't – or wouldn't – see. Promise to Tuck or not, it might be long past time to leave him behind.

The wild rush of water was a sound I hadn't heard in far too many years, a roar loud enough to drown all other sounds long before the river came into view. The Maun was a child of the First Rivers, born when the land was new and still untamed. Most waterways were settled long ago and easily tolerated the workings of men, freely lending their strength to turn millstones, but the Maun demanded payment for her help. This river thought little of leaving her banks, washing away farms and homes and carrying tokens of the lives she took as offerings to the sea.

Sailors' tales spoke of hunger in the crash of waves on deck and of the way Mother Ocean's laugh rode tempest winds before she pulled men under the surface. I heard some of that laughter in the splash of rushing water against river rocks, heard hunger in the groan of timbers as the waterwheel caught and robbed the river of her strength.

The mill loomed on the riverbank, twice as tall and more massive than any house in Mansfield. Midge's cottage and a good-sized barn stood back from the water, sheltered from the wind by a stand of rowan trees. Two horses, a matched pair, stood in the fenced-in paddock next to the barn. Chickens roamed the yard, staying well back from the large black and white dog tied to a stake near the front door.

Even before we'd emerged from the trees the dog was stretching to the end of his rope and barking furiously, jerking on the tether, lunging again and again until the stake began to pull from the ground. No one appeared to call the dog off and Robin readied his bow.

I quickly searched my bag until my fingers closed on the charm I wanted. I'd made the talisman to calm anger in a man, but the spell should work just as well on the dog. 'Wait, Robin. Let me try. I'd rather not introduce myself to Midge's widow by killing her dog.'

'I don't want to kill the beast either, but if no one calls him off I may not have a choice.' He sighted down the arrow. 'I don't want my throat torn out by some scruffy cur. Be quick about it before he attacks.'

I warmed the charm with my breath, waking the spell. 'Good dog, brave dog, we don't mean your mistress any harm. She's lucky to have you guarding her so fiercely, but there's no need. That's right, go to sleep now. I'll let her know how brave you are.'

The hackles on his back went down and his tongue lolled out the side of his mouth. I'd no idea what breed he'd sprung from, but he'd seen hard use. One floppy ear had been half-torn away, judging by the crude stitching, and a virulent red scar covered one back haunch where the fur was gone and would be for the rest of his days. His sharp black eyes watched me keenly, ignoring Robin for now. He'd calmed down nicely. If I could get the charm around his neck, we'd have no more trouble.

'There, that's a good boy,' I coaxed. Another step closer and his tail began to wag. 'I knew you were a good dog.'

'Put your weapon down, bowman, or I'll shoot your friend where he stands. Do it now!' A man stepped half-round the corner of the barn, his bow aimed square at my chest. Robin glanced at me and tossed his bow away. 'Back away from the dog, boy. I'm in the mood to be generous if the two of you leave quietly.'

I took a few steps back. The stranger eased the rest of the way around the corner, a small, curly-haired woman clinging onto his tunic. I didn't know who he was, but the woman must be Midge's widow.

The dog began to growl again, but he didn't lunge towards me.

'Stand down, Julian, that's a good boy. I've got it now.' Julian lay down, but his growling increased, rolling up from his chest. The man kept his body between us and Midge's widow, shielding her completely. 'Get back to whatever gang of thieves you belong to and pass the word that any who try to bother my sister will deal with me.'

'We aren't here to cause your sister any trouble. Midge was a friend. I've come a long way to get here.' Moving slowly, I pulled my hat off so he'd see I spoke the truth. Travelling in a man's garb might be practical, but at times I forgot that meant not everyone immediately saw me as a woman. 'He'd likely have spoken of Robin and Marian in passing.'

Midge's widow peeked out from behind her brother. 'Marian? You sent us a marriage gift.'

Her brother lowered his bow, still eyeing us with distrust, but she stepped out from behind him, a tiny woman not more than a head taller than Kate. Men frequently married women half their age, but I was still surprised at just how young she was; she couldn't have been more than eighteen, nineteen at the most. She looked frazzled and worn thin, the lines in her face new and too deep for someone her age. The bright eyes I'd heard about were dull, all the sparkle gone. Grief might have started the change in her, but I was afraid there was more.

I smiled, hoping to smooth over a bad beginning. 'The crock of spices was meant for you both, but the shawl was for you.'

'Midge liked to see me wearing it. He'd wrap the shawl round me so I'd not take a chill after—' She put a hand to her stomach, tears glittering in her eyes. 'I know it was on the back of the chair when we went to bed, but now I can't find it anywhere. It's not like me to lose things.'

Her brother put an arm around her shoulders and kissed the top of her head. 'It'll all come right, Meg. We'll find your shawl, I promise. Let's get you back inside so you can lie down. I'll sort things out with Midge's friends once I get you settled.'

'I'm sorry, Marian.' Meg sighed and pushed dark curls off her forehead, leaning hard on her brother. 'I've felt poorly since before . . . Jack will take care of you. I'm sorry.'

'There's no harm done,' I said. 'Go, get some rest now and we'll talk later.'

She was too pale and too tired to blame solely on grief. I worried that Meg might be with child, and being so tiny and so young meant it would most likely go hard on her. Once she'd rested I'd speak to her.

Robin snatched up his bow and slammed the arrow back into the quiver, fuming silently until they were out of sight. 'A fine greeting to give visitors. Does that lout threaten to shoot everyone who walks into the yard?'

'He has a right to protect his sister and what's hers,' I said.

'This isn't your father's estate, Robin, and more times than not, strangers coming out of the greenwood are up to no good. I'd say she's lucky to have her brother here. There's not a hope of her running this place on her own.'

That he'd been manor-born never left Robin, not completely. He'd slept rough with all of us, dressed game and taken his turn with chores, but he was an Earl's son to the bone and raised to be his father's heir. Even after knowing him most of my life, the things he took for granted or just plain didn't know still surprised me.

Robin had always found it almost impossible to admit he might be wrong and I might be right and living in the monastery for more than twelve years hadn't changed him or made him more humble. Without a word, his back and shoulders stiff with anger, he left me standing there. Settling under a tree on the edge of the yard, his back to the trunk, he pulled his hat down over his eyes and sulked.

Julian's ears perked up as he watched me move around the yard but save for his tail thumping hopefully if I came close to his tree, he stayed quiet, so I paid him little attention. I wanted to see the spot where Midge had died, or any sign that Rose's angel had touched this place too.

The horses crowded the gate leading into the paddock, but they moved back with a quiet word, calmed with a scratch behind the ears. A half-barrel full of water sat against the barn wall. From the look of the wood, the barrel was newly placed, unweathered. Fresh straw filled a manger inside the barn and harness for the horses hung neatly on the walls above Midge's wagon. I saw nothing to say things had been any different the day Midge died. Tuck might have remembered wrong.

The horses stayed well back as I left the paddock and latched the gate. I nearly trod on Jack's toes when I turned around. He was clearly Meg's elder brother, the same curve of the chin, a tousle of dark curls around his face, though his were salted with grey and he looked nearly old enough to be her father. His eyes were river-blue where hers were peat-black and he was just shy of being as tall as John, but there was no question they were kin. They shared the same father, but I'd wager Meg's mam was a second wife.

'What are you doing?' He looked down at me, arms crossed over his chest and feet planted. 'Poking your nose in where it don't belong makes me question if you're really Midge's friend. I've no proof you're who you say.'

The way he looked at me set my teeth on edge and I wouldn't stand for being bullied.

'I don't venture away from home and my children lightly, but I made the journey to try and discover how Midge died. That's hard to do without poking my nose into things.' I planted my own feet, crossed my arms and matched him glare for glare. 'Tuck told me about a horse trough. You could save me some time and tell me where the trough is.'

'Father Tuck sent you to look around?' He unbent a bit at the mention of Tuck's name, but his stubborn streak clearly went deep. 'I don't know what good that will do. The trough's got nothing special about it – nothing that's going to bring Midge back anyway, or make things right for Meg.'

'Stars above, Jack! Why does it matter to you if I look at it or not?' I took hold of myself, reminded of what I'd said to Robin. Jack did have the right to protect his sister's property, for all I was wishing he wouldn't stand square in my way while doing so. 'There's more to my coming here than Midge dying. Tuck and I – we've lost other friends too. John and Emma lost a child. I'm doing what I can to find the one who killed them.'

'Father Tuck never made mention of anyone else dying.' He scratched his neck, still looking sceptical. 'And not a breath out of him about anyone being murdered the whole time he was here. Wonder why that is?'

'He didn't know. Word didn't reach Nottingham until after he'd seen Meg. It took time for all the news to find him and he didn't put it all together until Will—' Telling a stranger about Will was still far too hard. I looked away for an instant, fighting not to cry, sorely tempted to tell Jack he was being a damn fool. 'Tuck saw a pattern in how our friends died. Thinking it might be a curse, he asked me to find the person responsible. You can trot off to the abbey and ask him yourself, if you like. Or you can take my word that good men are dead, all friends to Midge.'

He eyed me, chewing on my words. 'Am I right in thinking Will Scarlet is one of the dead?'

'Will . . . Will was the last to die.' That mention of Will was enough to start my throat closing up. 'I won't rest until I find the one who took him.'

'Midge was right fond of Will Scarlet. He told me lots of stories about the trouble they got up to – he claimed that you were in the thick of it more times than not.' Jack hooked his thumbs in his belt and set his shoulders. 'The trough is gone. Meg cried so much each time she saw the bloody thing I took an axe to it. I burned the pieces on the riverbank where she couldn't see. There's nothing left for you to look at.'

'The magic will still be there.' I glanced at Robin, but he hadn't moved, nor shown any sign that he was listening. 'Show me where it stood.'

'Magic,' he repeated. 'Midge always claimed you had the sight.'

'I have that and the craft to make it useful.' I'd expected to be challenged; not having to prove myself was a blessing. I thanked Midge. 'Tuck wouldn't have asked me to come otherwise.'

Suddenly Julian began to bark, twisting and pulling at the rope as if frantic to break free, and that did get Robin's attention. He pushed his hat up and stood, waiting to see what the dog would do.

The abused stake pulled out of the ground and Julian charged towards the woods, baying like one of the king's own boarhounds on the scent, the rope and stake pulling behind him.

'Damn dog, always running after something. Catching him will take half the day.' Jack kicked at the turf, clenching his fists at his side. 'At times I think it might be easier just to let him go until he comes back on his own. You have the sight: tell me what he's chasing this time.'

I gave a quick look, ready to give him a piece of my mind if he was making sport of me, but a pair of wood-goblins were dancing in the distance, making faces at Julian, teasing him until he'd given chase. The dog was heading straight for them.

'A pair of wood-goblins. They're luring him into the trees, but they won't harm him.' I turned to Jack and saw him nod.

'I thought as much, but I've a hard time seeing them that far off. The goblins will tire of the game soon enough and let the dog come home. It's the trice-damned lobs and brounys who make him run till he's worn to a nub.' He ran a hand through his hair. 'I'd best go after him or I'll be gone till dark. The trough was back behind the barn. You'll know the spot. The grass is dead all round it.'

The mark of Rose's angel: a circle of dead vegetation and a world of grief left behind. The need to find the woman casting the curse grew, but all I had was the word of a young girl and her memory of a woman wearing a crimson gown looking down at her – that, and a trail of death. I still didn't have enough threads to lead me to her.

I held up a hand to stop Jack from haring off into the woods after the dog. 'Hold on. Let me try to call him back.' I wrapped my will and the need to obey around the dog's name and cried, 'Julian, come back!'

How hard Julian resisted surprised me: the dog did slow, but didn't stop, still loping after the wood-goblins.

I pulled back harder, putting more force behind the command. 'I said, *come back!*'

This time he turned and slunk out of the woods and lying on his belly in the shade cast by the rowan trees, he looked back into the forest and whined.

I called him a third time, pitying Jack for all the times I guessed he'd had to go after the dog on foot.

'The goblins will never let you catch them, stubborn dog,' I told him, but not unkindly. 'Get over here and maybe one of us will scratch your ears.'

The dog gave up the chase and trotted back, the stake bouncing behind him.

'I'm grateful, Marian,' Jack said, and this time he sounded it. 'The lesser Fae have pretty much left him in peace since we came to stay with Meg, so I was half-witted enough to think it was safe to give him space to walk about.' He scowled and took hold of the rope round Julian's neck, but he relented enough to give the dog the promised scratch behind the ears. 'I'll tie him to a tree from now on, with chain or a stouter rope; they'll be the only things that will hold him.'

Julian looked at me and whined, sorrowful as a child denied a sweetmeat. 'I'll not let you free either,' I said, trying not to laugh. 'You've no sense at all. As many times as Jack says you've chased after lobs and goblins, you'd have to know they're up to mischief. Go on with you, do what you're told.'

Robin stayed out of it, but his lips were pressed tight in the way that meant he'd plenty to say. He must be near to bursting over the dog chasing after wood-goblins like they were farm cats and Jack not turning a hair. I counted it a blessing that Robin had decided to stay quiet rather than start preaching about the wrongs and the harm done. Jack didn't strike me as the sort to take kindly to a lecture on dangers to his mortal soul.

While Jack tied the dog up, I went around to the back of the barn. The circle was impossible to mistake: grass the colour of old bone ran in stark lines and an odour sour as a pond turned green by summer heat filled the air. This circle was just big enough to trap a man and carry him to his death.

Jack came to stand with me, thumbs hooked in his belt again. He eyed the circle with the self-same dread and disgust I felt; it kept me from setting a foot inside. 'What does your sight show you now?'

'If you've seen small Fae luring Julian into their games, I'd say you've a touch of other sight as well. Tell me what it shows you. Between the two of us maybe we'll find some of the truth.'

'I've just enough sight to keep me out of trouble and stop a will-o'-the-wisp from leading me into a bog.' Jack rubbed his hands over his face and took a breath. 'But it's true enough that I don't like looking at that piece of ground. Someone paced a circle out deliberate. At times I think I see footprints all around the edge, one set lapping over another, but when next I look there's nothing to see but salted earth.'

A circle of salt and powered bone, death and poisoned earth. Other sight showed me the same small footsteps, three rings laid one over another, hate and revenge sealed with the touch of her hand. No shades haunted this circle: she'd meant to kill, not bind.

Robin had told me stories of angels barring the way with flaming swords, their faces too bright and beautiful to look upon. Entire towns had been destroyed by angels, to hear him tell the tale, the people living there deemed too evil in the sight of his God to spare a single one. Other tales had God sending his angels to kill the first-born sons of his enemies in their cradles. I'd never understood how Robin could see the deeds of angels as righteous and somehow glorious – to my mind that last particularly was an especially cruel, personal way to take vengeance.

Rose had named the creature she saw well, though she couldn't have known. Vengeance was at the heart of this and somehow, with each scrap of truth I learned, glimpsing the secrets he held so close, I was growing more convinced that so was Robin: that he was the common thread Marlow had set me to find.

What I couldn't say was if he knew the cause of all this death and misery, or if he was as mystified as me. We'd had our troubles, but he'd been a good man once, putting himself at risk to keep the poor from being crushed under the sheriff's greed and the prince's indifference. The man I'd known wouldn't hold tight to secrets that put our friends and our children in danger.

The thought that Robin might know the name of Rose's angel and not tell me, or lie if I asked him, made me feel ill.

I didn't want to think he'd changed that much.

Chapter 9

Ouphe and goblin! imp and sprite!
Elf of eve! and starry Fay!
Ye that love the moon's soft light,
Hither – hither wend your way . . .
JOSEPH RODMAN DRAKE

Meg was brighter when she woke, more life shining in her eyes and shy smile. Glimpses of the girl Midge was smitten with peeked through the veil of grief. I understood why he'd married her, young as she was, for fire and iron were the core of this woman. Once the rawness of loss eased, that strength would serve her well.

Jack fussed over her, something I sensed she'd never allow when fully herself. He cooked supper for the four of us, going about the task cheerfully. While we ate he joked and coaxed smiles from his sister, pulling her attention back to us whenever that faraway, lost expression fell over her face. Even Robin, determined as he was to stay apart, took note and tried to draw Meg into conversation.

The cottage was larger than mine by half. The room held a wide stone hearth, deep enough to keep the fire well back from the wooden floor. In the far corner a ladder led to a loft nearly as large as the great room below. The stout shutters stood open in the wall next to the door, letting in the warmth of the summer day. I recognised the touch of Midge's hand in the carvings on the cupboard, the chest at the foot of the big bed and the curved spindles of the chair backs. The sturdy table might be workaday, but the top had been oiled to a rich lustre and rubbed smooth, making it easy to keep clean. He'd always been a good carpenter and a better woodcarver, the care he'd taken with his work evident in every piece.

I'd told Jack what little I knew about how the others died and how I'd cleansed the circle to free Ethan's spirit. The thought of Meg being questioned about the morning Midge died didn't please him, but he understood why I needed to. He'd agreed it would be easier for Meg if I spoke to her alone while he saw to the evening chores.

'I could use some help, Locksley.' He scraped the supper scraps into a bucket. 'If you'd feed the chickens and lock them up, I'll deal with settling the horses for the night.'

'You've a thing or two to learn about how to treat a guest.' Robin rocked back in his chair, arms crossed in front of him. 'You can do the chores yourself.'

'Robin, he asked for help with one small thing.' I glanced at Meg, who was watching Robin and her brother with fearful eyes. 'You've tended to a flock of chickens in the past. Doing so again isn't asking too much.'

'I say it's too much.' Robin spoke to me but he never looked away from Jack. 'I admit it's been overlong since I've travelled the country, Marian, and what's considered good manners can change, but last I knew, feeding a man supper didn't make him your thrall or oblige him to do your chores. If he wants the chickens fed and put away, he can do it himself.'

'Thrall?' The bucket thudded on the floor. Jack held himself tight, but the set of his jaw warned me that Robin needed to tread carefully. 'You're awfully quick to take offence where none was meant, Locksley. I thought only to give Meg and Marian a few moments alone to talk. My sister has had no woman to talk to since Midge died.'

'Jack, don't. Please don't quarrel with him over this.' As quietly as she spoke, Meg still drew both men's attention. She looked from Robin to her brother, her bottom lip trembling, wide-eyed and frightened. 'I can feed the chickens – I don't mind.'

Robin stared at Jack, the arrogance in his eyes draining away; even he wasn't blind to how scared Meg was. He stood and bowed over Meg's hand, his rarely used court manners not all forgotten. 'Your pardon, madam. Truly, I didn't mean to upset you. That was thoughtless and I beg your forgiveness. I'll leave you in peace with Marian so the two of you can talk.'

As soon as her brother followed Robin outside, Meg left her chair next to the fire and started opening the cupboard to rummage inside, then began digging through the chest at the end of the bed, muttering to herself as she made her way around the room. Dullness filled her eyes again and she kept returning to search the same places again and again.

I took her by the shoulders and turned her around so that she was facing me. She stared, but I wasn't sure she saw me at all. 'Tell me what you're looking for, Meg. I'll help you find it if I can.'

'My marriage shawl ... it was a present ... and I can't find it . . . I don't know where it's gone.' Meg's strong hands gripped my arms tight. Her dark eyes were suddenly burning fever-bright, all dullness gone. 'Help me, Marian, please – she took the shawl when they went away – she told me to forget what they did to me, but I can't . . . I have to get my shawl from her. She said they'd come back, that he'd hurt me if I told anyone . . . and . . . and when my baby came they'd . . . changed her . . .'

The fire in her eyes flickered, her hands dropped away and she wandered back to the cupboard, muttering under her breath again as she searched all the shelves for a piece of wool and lace that wasn't there.

'Stars,' I whispered. 'Mother of us all, forgive me for being a twice-damned fool.'

I'd searched with other sight for signs of the angel's passage in the yard, the barn and the mill, but I'd never thought of Meg. Looking at her now, I wanted to weep. She was wrapped in bands of bindings and blood-red spells of forgetting, a writhing nest of serpents meant to control her and keep her silent. I couldn't imagine the strength it had taken for her to break free and speak, even for an instant.

'Meg, come, sit with me.' I put an arm around her shoulders and led her towards the bed. 'You don't have to search any more. I'm going to find the shawl for you.'

'You know where I left it?' She slumped against me, somehow looking even smaller as the fight went out of her. 'I don't think I can look much longer. I'm so tired.'

'I know, sweetling. I know.' I sat with her on the edge of the bed and hugged her. I had to think of the child she carried as well, find a way to untangle both of them. If I made the wrong choice here I'd do more harm, and she'd been hurt more than enough. Right then, pushing her into sleep was the only thing I felt easy doing. 'Lay back and rest now, Meg. You'll feel better in the morning.'

She sighed, grief leaving her face as her eyes fluttered shut. I pulled the cover over her and brushed curls back from her face, my anger growing with each slow breath she took. This creature grew more cruel with every innocent she touched.

I hadn't known for sure that Rose's angel was Fae until Meg spoke, and the spells this pair had left behind suggested a powerful Lord and Lady, which only added to the puzzle. High-ranking Fae played vicious games for power, but I'd never known their struggles to go outside the bounds of the Lady's court, or for one to set his or her hand against a man. Status amongst their own kind was all to them.

Robin's offence, his 'sins' as Tuck called them, must be great indeed, but try as I might, I couldn't imagine what he could have done.

Not a scrap of this made sense to me, and what had been done to Meg perplexed me most of all. Any reason this pair of Fae would come back to gather up any child Meg bore was too horrible to think on.

One thing was certain. Aelfgifu's protection was tainted, riddled with lies and half-truths. If she truly didn't know who in her court was behind all the death and twisted magic, her days as ruler of the Fae were surely at an end.

Jack came back inside, his arms full of firewood, but seeing Meg, still and pale against the blanket, he dropped the wood next to the door. 'What happened? Is she all right?'

I couldn't answer him, not yet, and not with Robin standing in the doorway behind him listening, while I was wanting nothing more than to shake the truth out of him. 'Meg is only sleeping. Do me the favour of bringing the dog in here, Jack. Tie Julian to the bed so he can watch over her.'

Jack struggled with my request for an instant, torn between hovering protectively over his sister and doing as I asked. He held my gaze as if searching for a reason to believe me, and he must have found one for he brushed past Robin to bring Julian in from the yard.

Robin put his own load of firewood in the box next to the hearth and went back to gather up the logs Jack had abandoned. He watched me from the corner of his eye, weighing, as he always did, whether to speak or not. I'd never been fond of this old habit and hadn't missed it: I wished he would just speak his mind and be done with it.

I smoothed Meg's curls once more and turned to face him. 'Just say what you're thinking, Robin. If you have questions for me, ask.'

'I'm thinking Midge's wife needs a priest to tend to her body and soul, not a demon-chasing dog. I'd have to be blind not to see there's more wrong with the girl than you're saying. And I'm thinking that if Jack trusts you she'll end up buried unblessed and sins unforgiven, just like Midge.' Robin stood, brushing bark and dirt off his hands. Anger and the righteousness he wore like armour twisted his smile. 'I think you'll go your own way and never pause to consider God's will or the state of her mortal soul. But both of us know you don't care what I think.'

'I might care more if you put a moment's thought into what you say.'

I covered my face and took a breath, weary of fighting, weary of how he made even tiny things a struggle. After years of living with Will, I'd forgotten what life had been like in Robin's company. In truth, I'd wanted to forget. 'For pity's sake, Robin. She's not dying. I wouldn't be standing here and doing nothing if she was.'

One hand wrapped around Julian's rope collar, Jack stood in the open door, listening. The scent of wood smoke and crushed grass clung to the dog's fur, growing stronger with each wag of his tail.

'What is wrong with my sister?' he asked. 'Don't lie to me, Marian. I'd know.'

'I don't lie well and in any case, there's nothing to gain by trying. You do need to know the truth if we're to help her. Bring Julian over and I'll show you what I can.'

Jack tied the dog to the foot of the bed. The rope was long enough to allow Julian to jump up next to Meg, where he settled down between her and the wall, whimpering a bit as he licked her hand.

I pulled the cover back to Meg's waist. 'Look at her, Jack. Push your bit of sight as far as you can. I'll help if need be.'

The dog saw the bindings right off and set to licking Meg's face and nudging her shoulder with his nose.

Jack took a little longer. 'Mother of God . . . What is that?' He reached a hand towards his sister, but stopped short of touching the red coils twisted around her from neck to ankles. I wouldn't want the rage on his face turned towards me. 'Who did this to her?'

Meg sighed and began to mumble nonsense, as if she'd heard Jack and was trying to answer. I laid a hand on her cheek, sending her deeper into sleep. 'Save your strength, Meg. Trust us to take care of you.'

Gesturing for Jack to follow, I started for the door. Robin stepped in front of me. 'You're leaving her?'

'Of course not. But it's better if I speak to Jack outside, where she can't hear.' I glanced back. Julian's head was resting on Meg's shoulder, his eyes closed but ears twitching at every sound. 'Stay with her, if you would, and keep the fire going. It's best that she stays warm. Call if you need me.'

Robin bowed, deep and mocking. 'Keep the fire going. I'm good for that at least. Any other orders, milady?'

'If it's orders you're looking for, I've got one, Locksley. You're supposed to be a man of God.' Jack's hand shook as he took my arm to guide me past Robin. 'Do us all a service and act like one. Pray.'

The muted roar of water greeted us as we stepped outside. Yesterday's rains had swelled the river, filling it from bank to bank. Mist hung in swirling clouds where water splashed against the rocks, drifting to glisten on leaves and the stone walls of the mill. Sister rivers and brother streams flowed into the River Maun, all of them laughing in a race towards the sea. There was joy in the sound, and a gladness that lightened my heart, for all this night held little enough joy and all too much sorrow.

I stayed quiet while Jack paced. It was best for him to burn off some of his anger before I gave him fuel for more. Listening to the night sounds calmed me as well, giving me time to think. Frogs sang in the shallows, their deeper voices carrying over the rush of water. Nightjars called from behind the cottage and others answered from downstream.

An owl glided in front of me and across the yard on silent wings, dipped to the ground and rose again, a mouse hanging from its talons, outlined for an instant against the stars. One life ended and allowed another life to go on. We didn't always get to choose, but I thought it better to be the hunter.

'I don't understand what I saw.' Jack stopped a few feet away and looked to the sky, not at me. 'What's got hold of Meg?'

'Spells to make her forget what happened the day Midge died. Another spell binds her to the person who wove them, making the need to forget stronger.' I folded my arms, shivering despite the warm night. What I'd seen was hard. Telling Jack would be harder still. 'A token, something Meg cares about, keeps the bond strong: the shawl she keeps looking for . . . They took her wedding shawl with them that morning.'

'They?' Jack looked at me now, his face not much more than a shadow in the darkness. 'How do you know there was more than one person here the day Midge died?'

'Meg broke free long enough to tell me some of what happened. She's strong, Jack, stronger than many people I've known, but fighting the binding is taking all the strength she's got.' I hadn't told him the hardest things yet, the things that would wound him deepest. 'Unless I'm reading the spells all wrong, the pair who bound her are high-ranking Fae, a Lord and Lady. I can't tell you why, but at a guess, they want Meg and Midge's child. They told her they'd be back when the baby was born and they threatened to hurt her if she told anyone what happened.'

'Oh sweet Jesus.' He turned away and facing the river and the darkness, began to pace again, each turn a little faster. 'Bloody sweet Jesus. Killing Midge wasn't enough to muck up her life? Now the damned Fae want to steal her child too? What use is a miller's child to the high and mighty Fae?'

'I don't know. I wish I did.'

Memories of the circle I'd cleansed haunted me, but they

wouldn't need to bind Meg and enforce her silence just to kill another child. They wanted something more. I caught Jack's arm, forcing him to stillness. 'I'll do what I can for Meg, you have my promise on that, but this isn't a simple thing to mend. The Lord and Lady made her forget almost everything that happened and I can't be sure that I see all the spells tied to her. I could end up hurting her worse if I don't take care.'

'I can't leave her this way.' He ran a hand through his hair. 'There must be something we can do.'

'I've no intention of leaving Meg at their mercy, but I will need your help. Keep Robin here and don't let him follow me.' The moon was well past full, waning a little more each night, but enough power still rode the air to put out a calling and I suspected the one I needed wasn't far away. 'Julian will warn you if any of the Fae are nearby. Trust the dog more than your own sight.'

'Where will you be?' he asked.

Fire sprites sparkled under the trees, a sign the Fae Lord had already heard my call and waited somewhere out of Jack's sight. 'Looking for help. Pray I find it.'

My Fae guardian didn't try to hide or play games. Sprites festooned the trees along the path I should take, forming a corridor of light to point the way.

The greenwood grew dense and wild as I moved away from the cottage and the river, the only clear space the narrow track laid out for me. Old leaves crunched underfoot, smelling of mould and time past. The roar of the river faded into the distance. I thought for a moment the Fae Lord was leading me along one of the faerie roads, taking me a distance longer than time seemed to allow for, but the faint laughter of water was still bubbling behind me when I caught sight of him holding court, so I set the thought aside.

Back before men claimed the land round about for farms, before the mill stood on the riverbank and the king took a fancy to building his market in Mansfield, an oak larger than the one sheltering my cottage had stood in this clearing. All that remained of that great tree was the stump the Fae Lord now used as a throne. He sat atop it shirtless, the grub-white scars on his arms and chest flexing as he juggled. Lobs and goblins crowded the ground at his feet while a flock of lesser Fae perched in the trees behind him, Fire sprites jewel-bright among the brounys and hobs.

'You called me, fair witch?' He gave me a smile, quick and sly, his attention fixed on the objects he passed from hand to hand. One caught the light, flashing in the glow of Fire sprites and moonbeams, and moved around the circle again. A knife.

'I came to ask for your counsel and your help.' Truth would work nicely as well, though I'd little hope he'd tell me everything. He was a Fae Lord and if they spoke at all, it was in riddles. 'The man who died here was a friend and his young wife is in need of help I can't give. She's wrapped in Fae spells I've no craft to remove without hurting her badly. A Lord and Lady of the court bound this girl and afterward bespelled her to forget how they'd used her.'

The juggling stopped. An apple, the knife and a lady's fan hung in the air, framing his face. He tipped his head to one side, glamour painting the blank face of a harlequin over his own. 'What use would a Fae Lord and Lady have for a miller's wife?'

'As a brood-mare. They want the child she carries.' I didn't have his leave but I sat anyway, heedless of rocks and twigs on the path. If he took offence, so be it. 'The Lady who bound the miller's wife said they'd be back to take the child when the babe was born. She was supposed to forget, but the miller's wife broke free of the bindings and told me some of what was said. The Lord and Lady underestimated her strength and will and that puts the miller's wife in more danger.'

He frowned, the glamour slipping away. Though his hands rested on his knees, the apple, knife and fan began to circle again, slowly at first, but moving faster as his frown deepened to a scowl, until all I saw was a blur. The hobs and brounys clustered at his feet faded back into the shadows.

'What knowledge and counsel do you seek, witchling?'

'How to free the miller's wife without causing greater harm. Ways to keep the Lord and Lady from binding her again.' I straightened my back and met his gaze squarely. 'Who better to teach me how to deal with Fae treachery than you, my Lord?'

He snatched the knife from the whirling circle and for an instant, I was afraid I'd pushed too far. It wasn't until he smiled and grabbed the apple from mid-air that I knew I'd played him right. The Fae Lord cut the apple into quarters and offered me a piece from his own hand.

The apple was crisp and sweet juice filled my mouth. He watched me closely as I chewed, sending a thrill of fear into my belly. But we were not Underhill and if he sought to bind me to Sherwood for the rest of my days, it was wasted trickery. I was already bound.

'You were right to come to me, clever witch. Few know the treachery of the fair folk as I do.' He smiled again, but this time the glee was gone from his eyes. 'I have a question for you before we begin. Glamour lets treacherous Fae wear other faces if they choose and this Lord may have visited the mill before. If I discover the child she carries wasn't fathered by the miller, what would you do?'

'I've the means to purge her of the child if that's the only way to free her.' I licked juice from my fingers, not looking away from his face. The flicker of distress was brief, but real enough. 'I wouldn't do so lightly, or if another choice were open to me. Give me that choice.'

The fan floated like swan's down and came to rest in his lap. He cut thin slivers of apple, putting one in his mouth and tossing the next over his shoulder to the small ones in the trees. Fire sprites caught each slice and carried them to the other lesser Fae. The apple lasted until each had had a bite. The Fae Lord popped the last piece into his mouth.

A gust of wind whipped hair around my face and into my eyes, blinding me, and in that instant, the small ones vanished, leaving me alone with the Fae Lord. He held the fan open in front of his face, peering at me over the top. Moonlight shimmered over gold and crimson designs painted on silk, the patterns shifting and writhing so that I couldn't make sense of them. I kept tight rein on my temper, unsure if he was meaning to taunt me.

'This isn't an easy thing you ask of me. Not easy at all.' The fan snapped shut. He tapped the edge against his fingers and now I knew where I'd seen the fan before: in the Lady's hand. 'To know what must be done and whose child she carries, I'll need to touch the miller's wife. I can move without the Archer seeing, but the Warrior will know something is amiss. He won't take kindly to another of the Fae visiting his kin.'

'He knows I went to find help for his sister.' I stood, needing to ease the cramp in my neck from looking up at his tree-stump throne. 'I don't think he'll question how I came by it.'

'Brothers will do many things for a sister, Marian.' Graceful as a high-born woman, he opened the fan, hiding his face. Aelfgifu looked back at me when he lowered it again. 'Take me to the miller's wife. I'd see what my kind has done to her, and if I can mend it.'

The glamour rippled, shifting faster than my eye could follow. An old woman stood before me now, her hair thin and white with age. She leaned heavily on the walking stick clutched in one wrinkled hand. The other held a basket much like the one I used when visiting Marlow, filled with jars and vials, packets of herbs tied in scraps of linen tucked between them. Her gown was well used and worn, but tears in the skirt were neatly mended and covered by an apron stained with nut-juice.

He hobbled like an old woman too, the mask around him complete in every way. I slowed my steps to keep pace. 'Tell me one thing, if you can. Once the miller's wife bore her child, what use would a pair of Fae have for the babe? For all I can't bring myself to think they'd sacrifice a new-born for power, I've a harder time believing they'd go to all this trouble to steal her child without a purpose.'

'There is a purpose in all of this – if I knew the whole of what it is we'd not be here.' The Fae Lord paused his hobbling and leaned on the walking stick. 'The young spirits you freed served a different need than any child the miller's wife will bear. They won't sacrifice this baby for power.'

He knew more, or at least guessed at the reasons, I'd little doubt of that, and I was just as sure he expected me to pry his tongue loose. 'But this Lord and Lady have a need for a new-born child.'

'Or a changeling child to fill an empty cradle, perhaps one with a touch of Demisang blood to add to the illusion. If the babe sickened and died, there are those at court who would challenge the mother's power and right to rule.' A wrinkled finger traced the curve of my chin, making me shiver. 'A child of the Fae abandoned in a farmer's cottage would die as well, or so we've always been taught. The Fae seldom consider the love that mortals show their children, or the power it holds. They'd do well to show more of what they feel to their own child.'

Unsure how to answer, or if I should say anything at all, I stared into his eyes. I thought of him as a trickster and the mischief shining through the glamour was expected, but not that hint of regret. I didn't want to know what a Fae Lord might find to regret.

He smiled and hunched back over the walking stick. 'Come, witchling. The miller's wife awaits and I'd like to have an answer to part of this puzzle before dawn. We'll not catch this pair of renegades unless we find a way to track them.'

'We?' I took the basket from him. Glamour made him look aged, so for Robin's sake, I should treat the Fae Lord as if he really were feeble and bent. 'I thought your charge was to extend the Lady's protections, not to help me in the hunt.'

'What I'm charged to do and how I choose to act are not often the same.' His laugh was the sound of an old crone cackling, delighted at her own cleverness. 'And now I choose to join in this game of seeking.'

We came to the edge of the trees to see candle-glow filling the windows of the cottage, softly golden. The door stood open and I saw Jack sitting on the threshold, blocking the entrance and guarding his sister. I caught at the sleeve of the old woman's gown.

'The Archer and the Warrior will both want a name from me.

Something to call you.' Explaining why the old woman had come to tend Meg would be easy. Why she was to travel with us would lead to endless questions. 'What should I tell them?'

'I'd forgotten the mortal need for names.' His voice fit the face now, cracking with the weight of years. 'Pick a name for me, one that fits this form. If it's one you choose, I can't be bound with it.'

A name came to me easily. 'My mother had a friend named Nora. She was always kind to me. It's a good name and one I'll remember.'

'It will do for now. Be thinking of another, one that will fit when I look like myself. This body will help ease the Warrior's fears while I tend to his sister but I've no intention of hobbling from one end of the greenwood to another.' His sly, knowing smile looked odd on an old woman's face. 'I'll have need of names for the Archer and the Warrior. They'll know something's amiss otherwise.'

We were steps away from the cottage. Jack stood as we got closer, wary and watchful. 'Then I need a pledge from you, trickster: promise you won't bind them once you know their names. Not the Archer, nor the Warrior, nor the miller's wife. Promise me now, before we go inside.'

Julian began to bark, sharp and frantic, until the Fae Lord's fingers moved, the motion small, hard to see in the dark, and the barking stopped. 'You have your promise, sweet Marian. I'll include you in the pledge as well, even if you didn't ask. Come, tell me their names. Your Warrior grows impatient.'

'Jack. His name is Jack.' I lowered my voice. 'His sister's name is Meg.'

'So it is.' He tilted his head to one side, peering at me the way a heron watches a minnow before making a meal of it. 'And what do I call the Archer?'

I trusted him with my name more than I felt safe giving Robin's. The feeling twisted in my gut, though I'd nothing to pin my uneasiness on. Jack moved towards us and I had to speak. 'Robin. Call him Robin.'

'I thought him the Archer I knew, but mortals change from one time I might glimpse them to the next. Days flow differently Underhill.' He patted my hand. 'To work now, Marian. We've much to do.'

The bent old woman – Nora – brushed past Jack with no more than a nod and a wink, hobbling over the threshold and into the cottage.

He stepped back, staring until she disappeared inside.

Jack turned to me. 'Who is that, Marian?'

'The help I went to find.' I took Jack's arm to go inside. 'Call her Nora. She'll do her best by Meg.'

Chapter 10

Weep with me, all you that read
This little story;
And know, for whom a tear you shed . . .

BEN JONSON

Robin watched everything Nora did from his place next to the hearth. The old woman fussed and clucked around Meg, turning the cover back and smoothing the young woman's dark curls off her face. The mask of hedgewitch was complete, her actions absolutely in keeping with who she was supposed to be. Robin believed and so disapproved of Nora on sight. In his eyes a hedge-witch was but a step or two behind me on the road to damnation, as in league with the devil by using simple herbs as I was using true craft. I could only hope he wouldn't decide to say so.

Bringing Nora into the cottage earned me an equal share of judgement, measured out in scowls and frowns, but Robin didn't give voice to those accusations either. He avoided looking at Jack entirely and I guessed they'd had words. Cowing Robin into silence was a rare thing.

Meg, still sleeping, was somehow tinier with the room so full of people. Shadows played over her face, darkening the circles under her eyes, and I was struck again by how fragile she looked, how young and innocent. I could remember being that young once, but never that innocent.

Julian cowered at the end of the bed, his tail beating out a rhythm on the footboard and whimpering softly in his throat, until Nora held a hand out to him, palm up. 'Senseless dog. Get a good sniff so you'll remember friend from foe.'

He snuffled her hand, even venturing to lick her fingers when he had the scent.

Nora scratched behind the dog's ears and glanced over her shoulder. 'Your name is Robin, is it not?'

He stood up straighter, taking a step away from the wall he was leaning against. Robin glanced at me, seeking my permission or something else I couldn't guess at. 'That's my name. What can I do for you, Grandmother?'

'Take the hound out and tie him to a stout tree. Sit with him once he's there so he'll not bark at every piskie that wanders by. The two of you are over-large to share such a small room with the rest of us.' Robin opened his mouth to answer, but Nora's fingers twitched again. Surprise lit his eyes for an instant, easing away as the memory of wanting to speak left him. 'Take the dog out, Robin. When you see me again, call me Nora. I'm no kin to you and don't fancy being called grandmother.'

Jack stepped aside to let Robin lead the dog out, then moved back to fill the doorway. 'I'm staying. I'll stand in the door out of the way, but I'm not leaving my sister.'

Nora grinned, winking at me so Jack couldn't see. 'I wouldn't ask you to leave her. No, stand by the door just the way you are.

Keep Sir Robin from losing his way and wandering in. That's a good man.'

Spells still writhed around Meg, crimson flowing into tarnished gold and out again. Nora stood back, watching for a moment, muttering words under her breath I couldn't quite make sense of. No matter how I reached for understanding, their meaning danced just out of reach.

'You had the right of things, Marian: the ones who bound her wanted her to forget all she saw and heard.' Nora shook her head, breath hissing between her teeth as she touched Meg's cheek. 'My guess about young Meg was right as well. More than a drop or two of Fae blood flows in her own veins, enough that the Fae who bound her may hope to pass the miller's child off as one of their own.'

'Her mother was Demisang.' Jack unfolded his arms and hooked his thumbs in his belt. It was a warrior's stance, keeping his hands ready near a scabbarded sword or a dagger tucked into the belt. Many of the men who'd returned from King Richard's Crusades stood just that way, the habit ground deep into them. I'd missed it before, but I hadn't been looking.

I exchanged looks with Nora. 'You're sure?'

'I'm sure. My mother died of fever when I was fourteen. Meg's mother sat with mine day and night for more than a week, doing all she could with the lore and craft she knew. I'm not sure what you'd have termed Sara, herbwife or hedgewitch, maybe, but folks in the village and nearby farms knew to call her when there was sickness. It wasn't a secret to anyone Sara was Demisang, and her mother before that.' Jack gazed at his sister and his voice softened. 'My father married Sara a year later. Meg came along two years after that. Most families around us had Fae blood on one side or the other, so no one saw any shame in it. There's supposed to be a touch on both sides of my father's family as well.'

'And that explains why the Lord and Lady who killed the miller didn't just move on afterwards. Any Fae strong enough to weave these spells would hear the call of kin in Meg's blood.' Nora frowned. 'Now to puzzle out what to do about it.'

'I've only one question.' Jack hovered on the threshold, obeying the command to stay out of the way, but too anxious to stand where he couldn't see. 'It's all that matters to me, and all that would matter to Meg if she could speak. Can you release her and keep her free?'

'With Marian's help I can, but I warn you, it won't be easy. Now I've a question for you as well.' Nora stroked the hair back from Meg's face, touching her with such tenderness I had a hard time remembering a Fae Lord dwelt under the glamour. 'Would you have her remember what was done to her by the Lord and Lady?'

Jack left the doorway at her question, coming to stand next to Nora. I started to send him back to his place, expecting one of the ranking Fae to be angry over being disobeyed, but Nora was shaking her head, approval gleaming in her eyes.

'I'd have Meg be herself.' Jack looked me in the eye. 'I know my sister. She won't thank any of us for shielding her from the truth.'

Nora rummaged through the basket of vials and packets of herbs, picked out a few small bottles and scraps of linen and handed them to me. 'The best way to heal is facing what you fear, but I needed to ask before we began.'

Julian began to bark again, the sound rising from yips and yelps to baying, loud as a whole pack of hounds with the scent of wild boar in their nose. From the din I felt sure the goblins were back to teasing the poor dog. I could just make out Robin in the background, yelling about the noise, for all his shouting was doing little or nothing to quiet Julian.

'Be a good lad, Jack, and see if you can get your noisy dog to hush.' Nora pulled the stopper from a jar of oil and began to dab it on Meg's forehead and chin. The sweetness of mint filled the room, covering the fainter scents of groundsel and mallow. 'While you're at it, do what you can to distract Robin. You have my pledge no harm will come to your sister.'

She didn't weave a spell to compel him; I'd have sensed that. Jack's gaze flicked between Nora's face and Meg's and the lines of worry and doubt smoothed out the longer he looked. I'd no way to know what he saw, but he nodded and went to do as she bid.

'Come and stand by her head, Marian. Take care she can breathe, but clamp your hand tight over her mouth.' Nora dabbed more of the oil on Meg's hands, pulled her gown up and rubbed it on her legs, ankles and feet. 'Your Warrior will know I lied if he hears her scream.'

I did as I was told, tears burning my eyes. 'Isn't there a way to do this without causing her pain?'

'None I know the working of. I'd spare her if I could.' Nora poured the last of the oil into her hand, warming the liquid with her breath. I saw the colour change from ice-clear to glowing still water blue. She turned her hand palm down over Meg's belly. Oil dripping onto the gown spread in dark spots. 'Life is pain, sweet witch, and better a moment's suffering now than a lifetime bound. This will be quick and over as soon as I can manage.'

Each dab and drop of oil began to glow, spreading until the shimmer of blue surrounded Meg, swallowed my hands and crept halfway up my arm. Nora began to sing softly, her strange words and the tune blending until I couldn't tell one from the other. Any meaning to the language she used was still out of my reach, but there was no missing the power that grew to fill the room.

The first scream caught me by surprise, a small cry of agony escaping before I clamped my hand more tightly over her mouth. Nora wrapped strong fingers around barbed tendrils of the red bindings and ripped them from Meg's flesh. Blood welled up in a dark trail of ruby drops that glistened in the candlelight, disappearing again as the wounds sealed.

Meg bucked and twisted, struggling hard to escape my hold, and I fought just as hard to keep her still. I knew Nora had spoken the truth: there was no easy way to work the spell free. Each strand she sang loose tried to twine around Meg again and set down roots, but working as fast as she could, Nora flung each red spell thread into the hearth as she worked them loose.

Flames reached eagerly for each offering, sizzling and popping as if fed raw flesh. I turned away, unable to stomach the sight of red barbs curling, charring and turning to ash. Watching Meg's face was easier.

The tune changed, all the red streaks gone from the golden spell threads twisted around her, and Meg quieted a little. Forgetfulness was easier to banish, but returning her memories was no less painful: she was sobbing under my hands as the spell melted, the golden threads becoming thick honey oozing from a sun-warmed comb until they disappeared, vanquished by the Fae Lord's song.

Nora stopped singing, the blue glow surrounding Meg spread thin as smoke on the wind and vanished.

'You can let go, Marian.' Nora rubbed her eyes, looking shrunken somehow and more tired than I'd thought possible for one of the Fae. 'She'll wake soon. We don't want to give her more to fear.'

I pulled the cover up to Meg's waist. Tears were seeping from under her closed lids, pooling in the corners of her eyes and running down her cheeks. I wiped my own face on a sleeve, half-ashamed over crying for her, not understanding why. 'Will she remember all that happened?'

'She'll remember, but she'll have the peace of knowing she carries her husband's child. Thinking the Lord fathered the child was a lie they planted with the binding spell.'

Nora packed the unused vials and herbs, part of her mask to fool Jack and Robin into believing, back into the basket. 'And she will heal in time, as the young almost always do. We'll leave this place very soon, Marian. I'll summon a strong guardian to care for Meg while her brother is gone.'

The noise of Julian's barking and Jack arguing with Robin faded away. There was so much I wanted to ask, but I had little time. 'I can't see Jack leaving Meg on her own. Not unless he didn't have a choice.'

'The Warrior's path lies with us.' The trickster watched me through Nora's eyes. 'Someone must protect you from Robin's folly. I try, Marian, but even one of the Fae is limited in what he can do. Your Warrior moves openly in the world of men and possesses skills I lack.'

'I don't need Jack's protection, I've guardians aplenty. Tuck forced Robin on me, and you're here at the Lady's bidding.'

Meg whimpered softly, still lost in nightmares and trying to find her way free. I smoothed her hair, wishing I could take the dreams from her. It was the same wish I often had for Robbie; I wondered how he was sleeping with me gone.

'Far better for Jack to stay with his sister and help her heal,' I said. 'He's her warrior if anyone's. I've no claim to him.'

Some of his mask dissolved, the Fae Lord's laughing tone replacing Nora's aged croak. 'Ah, you didn't tell me you'd abandoned sleep, or sprouted a second set of eyes in the back of your head. To never need help is a feat few manage, or at least not for long.'

He was mocking me openly, but showing anger would only gain me more of the same. I held my tongue and didn't rise to the jibe, waiting for him to laugh at his own jest. Instead, his mood turned as quick as a minnow darting into a reed's shadow.

More glamour flaked away, the wrinkles in his face gradually filling in and easing the impression of age. Nora's back straightened and she stood taller. 'This isn't a matter of who has claim. It's a matter of what must be, and how this game plays out to the end. You have one sort of sight, Marian, letting you see the truth in things. I've another kind that comes and goes on a whim, giving me visions of what's to come, but never all I need to know, and never all that will happen. But what my fickle sight does show usually runs true. I've learned to follow the path set before me.'

No taint of a lie clung to his words. Regret was a heavy thing, necessity heavier still. I stepped away from Meg, betraying her just by asking the question. 'And this sight tells you Jack must come with us?'

'That it does, curious witch.' The hand that brushed Meg's cheek was smooth, the fingers long and graceful. His slow change puzzled me. 'Things will go badly for all of us if the Warrior stays behind.'

The scrape of a boot on the threshold was the only warning I had that Jack had come back. He braced his hands on the door-frame, staring at his sister. 'Mother of God . . . you freed her. I didn't think it was possible.'

'She is free for now. We have other work to do if she's to stay free.' The old herbwife faded from view little by little until all that was left was her wispy white hair and a gown that came nowhere near to reaching her ankles. A Fae Lord in a dress much too short for him stood there now.

Jack looked from me to the Fae Lord, his mouth set in a hard line. He stepped into the room and bowed. 'What do I owe for my sister's life?'

The Fae trickster grinned, eyes alight with mischief. 'Service for sweet Marian. An easy task for a strapping man like you, and best performed with a will. You're bound to her until I decide to release you.'

If the aim was to make me blush, I disappointed him. I'd spent too many years travelling with Robin, hearing crude talk in tavern common rooms or among bands of highwaymen and brigands in Sherwood. But Jack gave the Fae Lord everything he wished for and more, flushing scarlet to the roots of his hair and unable to speak. The trickster spun on one foot and laughed, delighted with the result of his joke.

'Explain to him what you mean by service!' My anger did little to dim the trickster's glee. My clenched fists and scowls set him to prancing in a circle, laughing harder. 'It's not what you're thinking, Jack.'

'I will leave explaining to you, witchling. He's bound to you, after all, and what service he gives is your decision.' The last of the glamour clinging to the Fae Lord fell away, the features of his face shifting as I watched. Scars gleamed on his bare chest and arms again, paler by candlelight against his dark skin. 'I'll return tomorrow with someone we can trust to care for the miller's wife. Keep the Archer well away from her when she wakes.'

Jack edged around the Fae Lord to sit on the floor next to the bed. Meg sighed, but didn't wake as her small hand disappeared into his. 'Locksley is over-fond of himself as most nobles are, but I've a hard time thinking he'd harm Meg. He's been nothing but kind to her so far.'

'Trust that I have a reason, Jack, and do as I ask. I've taken great care with young Meg. I'd rather not see my work undone.' He turned to me, smiling brightly. His smiles made me wary now, for good reason. 'I charged you to find a name for me to use among mortals that won't cause a fuss. Have you chosen yet?'

I hadn't given names a thought, for worry over Meg had pushed everything else out of my head. He knew that, but he'd toy with me and play at innocence while pushing for an answer. I said the first name that came to mind.

'Bert.' He tipped his head to the side, a bright-eyed magpie looking to add something shiny to its horde. 'It's common enough no one will think it strange or have reason to remember for long after you've gone. My uncle – my mother's brother – was named Bert.'

The Fae Lord's laugh filled the room, loud and booming. 'Clever Marian, you've lit on the perfect name. I shall be your Uncle Bert.'

I blinked and he was gone.

Jack stared at the spot where the Lord had stood for an instant and turned to me. If I'd any doubts about how he felt, the growl in his voice put them to rest. 'I can't believe you brought that creature here – calling one of the Fae to free Meg was a witless, careless thing to do! What were you thinking?'

'I was thinking I needed to do my best by your sister and I thought you felt the same. Witless I might be in your eyes, but I was never careless with Meg's life.' I knotted my fingers in the edge of my tunic, took a breath and fought down the temptation to fling something at him. 'We both wanted to see her free and breaking those spells was beyond my skill. I found what help I could.'

'And a fine bargain you made in the process, Marian: free the sister, bind the brother!' Jack stood, looming over me, his voice gone quiet with rage. 'Find someone else to give you service, witch. I'm sure Locksley will be willing to fill your bed again now that his brother's gone.'

'You pig-selfish bastard! You bound yourself by asking what you owed for Meg's life. I made no bargains and he set no price! You offered a Fae Lord payment when he'd asked for nothing. I won't take the blame for you being dumb as a turnip.' Tears blinded me, but I swung at Jack anyway, aiming to take his head off for what he'd said. I told myself this need to beat on him until my fists bled and wail until my voice broke wasn't grief. I'd no time for grief and mourning Will, only for revenge on those who took him.

He caught my fist in his big hand, the strength in his arm holding me tight. I wove fury around will to wrench my hand free of his grip and cursed being weak, but anger and weariness had goaded me into crying; now I couldn't stop.

We stared at each other: me fighting back choking sobs, Jack clenching his fists and breathing hard. Rage comes on suddenly, but drains away slowly in most people; only once anger leaves and gives them the space do they start to think again. I watched his expression change.

Jack covered his face with his hands and I heard him sigh. 'Christ's blood, I am an idiot. Marian . . .'

Meg screamed and sat straight up, her eyes wide. She tried to scrabble off the bed, blind with panic. 'No! Get away, get away! Don't touch me! Midge, make them stop— Help me! *Help me!*'

Jack caught her shoulders and eased her back onto the bed. 'Shush, Meggie, shush. No one's going to hurt you. Jack's here now. Jack's here.'

She stopped fighting him, sense coming back into her eyes. 'Jack?'

'I'm here, Meg.' He kissed her on the forehead. 'No one's going to hurt you while I'm here.'

Jack pulled her into his lap when she started to weep, rocking her in his arms. She didn't look much bigger than Rose that way. Neither of us said anything more about the Fae Lord or Jack's being bound to me. Not then.

It was all we could do to convince Meg that the monsters were gone.

The night was more than half over before Meg settled enough that I felt easy leaving her side. Cool air full of the scent of damp earth and rain falling upriver greeted me as I stepped outside. A few thin clouds ran before the wind, already spent and headed for the sea. The moon was nearly set and the stars cast little light, mere pinpricks of silver in a sea of pitch.

Julian trotted at my heels, a shaggy black and white shadow following me around the yard. Goblins still moved under the trees, but they weren't trying to lure the dog into chasing them and he was content to ignore them for now. I sensed the Fae Lord's hand in all of this, help of a sort, and one less worry.

Robin willingly agreed to sleep in the barn – Meg's sobbing scared him, although he'd never admit to being afraid. Not having to make excuses to keep him out of the house made following the Fae Lord's orders easier.

Truth be told, the way she was crying frightened me too, but I couldn't let fear turn me away from her. Some things Meg couldn't say to a brother, some of her questions Jack couldn't answer, so I did my best, wishing with all my heart that my words would be enough. The Fae Lord said she'd heal, but I doubted he understood human pain and sorrow, or the way it left a person so hollow and empty.

I wove the wards around the house with extra care; having little moonlight and the power it brought made the task more difficult. There was power aplenty in the river, wild and raw, but I didn't have the time to win the Maun's consent or wrestle away what I could steal, so instead I pulled threads of power from starlight, reeds swaying on the riverbank and the nearest trees, braiding them around each other until the strands shone. My will and what moonlight I could gather made the weaving stronger.

Wrapping wards around Meg's cottage took longer than with John and Emma's. The house resisted, its closeness to the river or some magic in the stone and timbers making it aware of what I did. Soothing the house's fears and convincing it that what I did was making Meg safer took far too long.

By the time I'd finished, weariness had nearly driven me to my knees. I wrapped my heavy cloak around my shoulders and tucked it under my drawn-up knees before I settled on the step, the wall at my back. Julian curled up at my side, company and guardian both. Sleeping under the sky suited me just fine. I doubted Jack wanted me back inside unless Meg needed me.

Julian's tail thumped in greeting as Jack knelt to scratch his ears. I watched from half-closed eyes as he nuzzled the dog, burying his face in Julian's soft neck and holding on tight. This was hard on him too. I needed to remember that.

'Come inside, Marian.' Jack wiped a hand over his eyes. His own weariness dragged at the corners of his mouth and his shoulders drooped. 'I'm an idiot, plain and simple. You tried to help Meg and the thanks you got was me acting like a spoiled lordling – I'm sorry for it. I'll make it up to you if I can.'

'There's no need for making anything up to me.' My head was muzzy with the need for sleep and dawn would arrive too soon. 'I've been known to speak without thinking a time or two. Ask Robin how many times my temper's got the best of me. We start fresh from here.'

'Come inside at least. Take my pallet for the night. You'll be much warmer and more comfortable in the loft than staying out here.' He sank down on the other side of Julian, long legs stretched out in front of him. 'I'll sleep on the hearth when I'm ready. I don't want to wander too far from Meg.'

'Is she sleeping?'

'For now anyway.' He rubbed his eyes again and stifled his own yawns. 'I keep thinking she'll come to the end of grief and crying, that's she's got to be worn to a shadow, but she gets quiet for a while, then starts in again. There's no end to the tears.'

'There is an end. Meg just hasn't found it yet.' I pushed back, bracing against the wall to sit up straight. 'Put Julian in next to her. She'll feel less alone.'

'A good notion. I don't think Julian will take a night on a straw tick too hard.' He ruffled the dog's ears. 'Just don't get the notion that you're too good to sleep on the floor from here on in. The royal kennels aren't in your future, lad.'

Julian laid his head on outstretched paws, watching me. He reminded me of Marlow, sunning himself in the meadow and pretending not to know everything that went on around him. For an instant I fretted about the dragon's wing and how his wounds were healing, but there was nothing more I could do for him until this business was finished.

'How'd you come to have Julian? He's not a farm dog, not big as he is and with those scars. Come to think of it, no farmer's going to name his hound Julian.'

'The old forester who gave him to me said that King Richard himself named Julian after the patron Saint of Hunters. I'm not sure I believe him, but it makes a good story.' Jack's hand brushed over the scars on the dog's flanks. 'Not sure how he came by these. I've seen scars on horses and dogs wounded by boars or gored by a stag; none of the scars looked like these.'

I touched the edge of the scar with one finger, half-suspecting what I'd sense. Julian's skin was seared smooth, not rough or puckered. 'I'd say a firedrake did this to him. A small one, newly hatched, or not far from it. Julian wouldn't have lived to chase goblins if the firedrake had been bigger than that.'

'Hare-brained dog,' Jack said. 'You don't learn, do you?'

Julian whimpered and thumped his tail, as if he knew what was said. I'd not wager against it, truth be told.

'If I can't stay here with Meg there are things I need to know. I'd be grateful if you'd tell me what you can. Where will we go when the Fae Lord comes back?' Jack stole a quick look at me, as if gauging how much he could say. 'I've no clue why he tricked me that way, or what good I'd be to you. I'm no use against the

Fae you're hunting and my skill with a bow is no match for Locksley's.'

A swarm of Fire sprites swept across the yard, looping in bright flashes so I wouldn't miss seeing them. Julian's ears perked up and he watched eagerly, but my hand on the top of his head kept him from barking. If the Fae Lord meant to stop me from speaking, I was going to disappoint him. Truth would serve Jack better.

'The Fae Lord – Bert – claims to see things before they happen. He says it's a kind of sight, different from what you or I have. But he doesn't see everything, only pieces, or there wouldn't be a need for any of this. He says your path lies with mine, and that I need you to protect me from Robin's folly. And he claims you can go places he can't, though I've a hard time believing the Fae can't go where they choose.' I was glad that darkness and shadow kept me from seeing more than the pull of Jack's mouth into a frown. 'Gilbert and Gamelyn were in Sheffield for the fayre when they died so I'm going there next. A fayre that size draws pedlars and tradesmen from all over Lincolnshire, even as far away as the Ridings, and people travel from every village and town for miles around to buy their goods. Someone saw something.'

Jack stood and walked a few paces, where he stood staring at the river. I pulled my knees up and rested my head on the wall at my back, too exhausted to watch him wrestle with what he'd learned.

He touched my shoulder and I came awake with a start, confused for an instant. He put a hand under my arm and hauled me to my feet. 'If we're going to chase this pair of Fae from one end of Sherwood to the other, you should get some sleep. I thought we'd agreed the loft was a better bed than the step.'

'So we did.' I scrubbed my hands over my face, fighting off the sick feeling of waking suddenly and too soon. 'Now it's my turn to beg your pardon. The day took more from me than I'd thought.'

'No apologies needed. This day took a bite out of all of us.' He ran his fingers through his hair. 'A last question, Marian, and then I won't trouble you again tonight.'

'Ask your question,' I said, the words muffled around a yawn. 'I'll do my best to answer.'

Jack grabbed the dog's rope collar and shooed him in the door ahead of us. Julian ran straight up to the bed, looked back at me, then hopped up next to Meg and stretched out with his back against her, his head resting near her shoulder and his tail draped over her legs. She settled against him, her face relaxing as she sank deeper into sleep.

'I don't like leaving Meg and I like it even less that one of the Fae thinks a stranger will be the best one to keep her safe, especially given that a pair of them killed Midge and hurt her to start with.' Candle-glow lit one side of his face, glinting on the silver strands in his beard. The shadows covering the rest of his features put me in mind of the Fae Lord's harlequin mask. 'I don't know how he – how Bert – came to be here with you. If not for Meg, I wouldn't think it any of my business, but as things stand, I need to know if we can trust him to play us fair.'

I thought hard before answering. 'The Lady of the Fae herself picked him to be my guardian. He's done his best to help Meg and he saved me from a trap Rose's angel left in my path. We can trust him as much as you can trust any of the Fae. I don't think it's in his interest to betray us.'

He thought on my words for a bit, then said, 'I'll take your word, Marian. You know more about the Fae and their ways.' He cocked his head. 'One last *last* question, if you will. What do you mean by "Rose's angel"?'

Not remembering that I hadn't yet told him this was another sign of how exhausted I was.

'An angel is what John's young daughter called the Fae Lady who murdered her brother.' I softened my voice, not wanting to wake Meg or her fears. 'Rose called her a beautiful angel in a scarlet dress, but she's four years old and angels are all she knows. She looked at the angel's face and couldn't remember anything after.'

'You should ask Locksley about that. There's something in Holy Writ about angels with faces too bright to look upon dealing out punishment in God's name.' He smiled wryly. 'Hear my gram tell it, I never paid any attention to Father Thomas' sermons, but I do recall that one – scared me witless when I was a boy.'

'Robin told me those tales years ago.' I shivered as the wind suddenly blew colder and pulled the cloak around me. 'Robin was with me at John's farm. He heard what Rose told me and he didn't say a word. I'll ask him about those verses, but I doubt he'll be eager to answer.'

'Then we'll find someone who will.' Jack grimaced and waved me the rest of the way inside. 'Odds are we can find us a priest in Sheffield who isn't a hypocrite.'

Another icy-cold gust of wind swirled through the yard, keening under the eaves of the mill. Laughter rode the wind, off-key and wild and full of magic: a calling, but unlike any I'd heard before. The sound lifted the hairs on the back of my neck.

I stepped back to the doorway and turned to peer into the darkness, still bleary-eyed as I woke my sight. Old haunts walked the night, faded to a whisper with age, but I couldn't see anything to explain the dread at the very core of me.

'Did you hear that, Jack?' I whispered.

He put a protective hand on my arm and stood beside me in the open doorway, on guard and listening. 'I hear the river running high and the wind trying to take the roof off the barn again, but nothing else. What am I listening for?'

'I'm not sure. A calling of some sort.' The sound raced down-river, growing fainter until it faded away altogether. I looked around at the peacefully sleeping dog and my galloping heart began to slow. 'Whatever I heard, it's gone now, and wasn't meant for us.'

'You're sure all's well?'

'As sure as I can be.' I rubbed my eyes. 'Julian will raise the alarm if we need to worry.'

Jack took a long look around the yard again before he shut and barred the door. He made sure I was safely in the loft before laying his blanket out across the threshold. Anyone trying to get in would tread on Jack first.

Between the dog and the warrior, Meg and I were well guarded. I shut my eyes and let the river's song lull me to sleep.

Chapter 11

Thou shalt not suffer a witch to live.
EXODUS 22:18

The sweet sound of panpipes woke me just after dawn. Each time the piper paused, a host of songbirds filled the silence with their voices. Note piled on note, musician and feathered singers taking turn by turn to weave a soaring melody rippling with joy. I lay still, listening as my Fae guardian piped in the morning, reluctant to face whatever trials the day would bring. His song was a welcome gift and I forgave him much for the giving of it.

Julian began to bark, running loops around the yard from the sound of it. Voices carried to the loft, the muffled words difficult to make out, but Robin's angry growl was a familiar herald of trouble.

I rubbed sleep from my eyes and tugged on my boots.

Meg was still asleep, a miracle given the racket coming from the dog and the yard – or maybe not: the faint glimmer of a spell over the bed tipped the Fae Lord's hand. I couldn't fault him for keeping her clear of the ruckus. I granted I might have done the same.

There was a pedlar's wagon in the middle of the yard, as bright and gaudy as any I'd ever seen at the Nottingham market. Two strong draught horses stood patiently in the shafts, colourful silk ribbons braided into their manes and tails. One gelding shook his head, setting the tails of yellow and blue ribbons to dancing and the tiny brass bells tied to the ends ringing. Poles set in each corner of the wagon bed held up a silk canopy, striped in the same strong blue and shiny yellow.

Round-topped wooden chests filled the wagon. Most of them were painted the colour of grass but the occasional red-topped one shone bright as overripe berries among the green. Brass braziers, tin pots, buckets and iron kettles dangled from ropes tied to the corner poles, clanging against one another when stirred by the breeze. The racket such a set-up would make bouncing along the road would be near to deafening; everyone within half a league would know where to find us. There was no way we'd be quietly sneaking into Sheffield with this rig.

Of course, real pedlars didn't go creeping into fayres or markets. They went out of their way to draw attention to themselves and their wares, anything to entice folk close. The Fae Lord knew what he was about, smarter about how people acted than I'd guessed. Give a market crowd noise and clatter and piping to make them tap their toes and they'd all see another group of hucksters eager to hawk their wares.

Now I thought on it, I saw another reason for announcing our presence to the entire county. Anyone who knew who we truly were wouldn't have any trouble finding us, friend and foe alike. Any hunter on our trail would likely think we were unaware of danger and thus unprepared. If Bert meant to lure the spellcaster out of hiding, this rig might do the trick.

The Fae Lord sat cross-legged on the wagon's wooden seat, beaming at Robin in the kindly way you might look at a befuddled child. His pipes rested in one hand, made of deer bones, dull and yellowed with age. He wore scuffed brown boots to the knee, dull tan breeches and a faded green tunic. His hair was clubbed and mostly hidden under a battered felt hat and his scars were hidden under his tunic. No glamour clung to him, or at least none I could see: the face he showed the world belonged to him.

Robin fell silent as soon as he saw me. He turned away from Bert, fuming for reasons I couldn't begin to guess at, but from the way he was glaring at me, I was clearly in for a share of his wrath too.

Jack leaned against the side of the wagon, ignoring the dog as he ran noisy circles around the yard. Thin strips of wood curled on the ground at his feet, shaved from a block in his hand. He caught sight of me and pointed with the knife.

'Our friend Bert tells me the vixen belongs to you and that chasing her will wear Julian to a nub. And I'm not to fret, because he won't catch her until she wants to be caught.' The corners of his mouth twitched, stopping just short of a smile. 'There was a moment when I wasn't sure Bert was talking about the dog. But we sorted that out.'

'Bridget!' I put enough command into calling her name that she couldn't ignore the summons. As long as I didn't look at Bert I could hold my temper, but finding Bridget here frightened and angered me both. I'd left her to help guard Kate and Robbie, her sharp fox ears and eyes more likely to spot trouble before Beth. 'Stop teasing the poor dog and get over here!'

She came straight for me, Julian running flat-out on her heels, and as she leapt into my arms, Jack grabbed the dog's rope collar to keep him from doing the same. Bridget watched Julian, bright-eyed, tongue lolling out of the side of her mouth, laughing at him. From the way the dog whined, I'd little doubt he knew that.

I held Bridget up so that she'd have no choice but to look me in the eye. 'What do you think you're about? I left you home with Kate and Robbie for a reason.'

'Don't scold her like that, Marian. Put the blame on old Uncle Bert that she wandered so far.' His wheezy wheedling voice was perfect for a favourite uncle trying to get by with something, but the trickster shone in his eyes. He was good at changing his voice to fit who he pretended to be: another kind of mask to hide behind. 'We'll have need of her soon enough and there's no harm done.'

'No harm?' I tucked Bridget under my arm, picturing the harm done so far and wishing with all my heart that there was a charm to undo it all. 'My children are at risk: who are you to decide calling away one of their guardians does no harm?'

'The vixen is not the only creature in Sherwood with eyes that see everything and sharp ears able to hear a bee's wing passing.' The glee in Bert's eyes faded and the teasing left his voice, which once again belonged to the much-scarred Fae Lord. 'An army of guardians watches your cottage, little witch, and not a sound goes unheard. The dragon sends his greetings and says you're not to worry. His wing heals nicely, helped along by visits from an old friend. I promise, your young ones are safe.'

'Dragon?' Jack stepped forward, his face alight with the eager-ness of wanting to believe but not willing to look like a fool. 'You've seen the dragon of Sherwood? He's real?'

Robin shoved between us, scowling and sour-faced.

Bridget growled and bared her teeth, all playfulness gone. I rubbed her throat, murmuring, 'Hush, Bridget, there's no call for that. He won't bite.'

'How many more demons will you call to your side, Marian?' Robin's lip curled, his eyes roaming from my face to my feet and back. 'You've given body and soul into the keeping of devils – you need not deny your sin, for I followed you into the woods last night and I saw what you did. Send them away now and beg God to forgive you.'

'I've called no one, Robin, and certainly no demons.' Bridget growled again, her heart racing. I held her tight, afraid of what she'd do and added, 'I stayed in the loft all night.'

'Just what are you talking about, Locksley? You dozed by the fireplace until Marian came back with – with Nora.' Jack shifted his grip on Julian's collar and glanced at Bert, who smiled, but never took his bird-bright eyes off Robin. 'She hasn't gone further than the yard since she came back.'

'This was much later, an hour or two before dawn. Voices woke me.' Robin's jaw set in those stubborn lines I remembered all too well. There'd be no shifting him now, whether he was right or wrong. 'I heard Marian laugh and when I walked to the barn door I was in time to see her run to the edge of the trees, to one of the Fae. He was half-naked – I'm not likely to miss those scars, even in the dark. Could be this one, for all I know. He kissed her and the pair of them went off into the forest.'

'You're daft, Locksley,' Jack broke in, 'or seeing things. Once Marian went up to the loft I barred the door and slept in front of it.' A frown creased his face. 'I'll grant I was tired, but she'd have had to stand on top of me to lift the bar – and anyroad, the door swings inwards. She couldn't get it open, not with me sleeping against it.'

Robin poked two fingers in Jack's chest and pushed. Julian and Bridget both growled, the vixen's a note above the hound, but Bert waved a hand and they quieted.

'I *saw* her. I followed the two of them and – and I watched what she did.' He swallowed and made the sign of the cross over his chest. 'I saw her rut with that demon like an animal until she cried out . . .'

'You *watched*?' Jack dropped the dog's collar and shoved Robin, making him stumble back a step. Jack took a pace forward and shoved him again, his face burning red with rage. 'Does watching make you feel more holy and free of sin than the couple you spied on?'

'Don't hit him, Jack. He can't help his nature any more than a viper can help striking. Beating him will change nothing.' Bert jumped down from the wagon seat. 'Archer, I believe you did see someone, but you're very wrong to think it was Marian. Once the wards were set and the door closed, no one left this house. The woman you followed didn't come from inside.'

'Who?' Jack's eyes opened wider and he turned to me. 'Christ's blood. She came back . . .'

'Yes, Warrior, the pair of them returned, and much sooner than I'd expected. They grow bolder, thinking the game is won. That will be their downfall.' Bert slipped the pipes up his sleeve and they promptly vanished. 'This changes things, but not too much. We will leave once young Meg's guardians arrive.'

'No, I'm not leaving her.' Jack planted his feet, arms crossed over his chest. Only the tremor in his voice betrayed any fear of what defying one of the Fae might cost. He understood what being bound meant, but he loved his sister more. 'I can't go now. If the two of them are willing to come back with all of us here, what's to stop them if Meg's alone?'

'You will go, Jack – don't think you have a choice. The bond can't be broken. Our enemies' actions don't change that a whit.' Bert reached up his left sleeve, pulled out four wooden balls and tossed them into the air. Once he'd set them in motion, each pass from hand to hand twisted faster until he was juggling more than a simple circle, though quickly as it moved, I'd be hard-pressed to say exactly how it differed.

'I'd never leave your sister unguarded, just as I won't leave Marian's children without eyes to watch for trouble. Have a little faith, Jack.'

Without breaking the pattern he tossed one of the balls. Jack snatched the ball from air and looked at the design on the side, the scowl on his face deepening.

'You had faith once, did you not? Why else leave your wife and son to follow Richard?'

The ball slipped from Jack's fingers, rolling to land at my feet. 'If you know I followed Richard, you know how well my faith was repaid.'

'I won't fail you, Warrior.' Bert looked Jack in the eye while the balls continued to fly from hand to hand unheeded. 'No one will harm your sister. You have my word.'

Jack held the Fae Lord's gaze. I had no way of knowing what he saw, but the wounded look in his eyes eased. After a breath or two more, he whistled Julian to his side and went inside the house.

I stooped and picked up the wooden ball, running a finger over the flaking paint in the etched royal crest before tossing it back.

Bert caught the ball without breaking his rhythm.

Robin's silences never lasted and this one was due to break. Instead, he stalked back to the barn, appeared again with a bucket in hand and walked to the river, disappearing around a curve on the other side of the mill.

Judging by the pleased smile on the Fae Lord's face, he'd pushed Robin into the actions.

I scratched Bridget's ears as I watched Robin stride away, feeling more than a little pity. Robin of Locksley believed himself a true man of faith, protected by his God from the wiles and magic of foul creatures like me, but the truth was, Robin was afraid of himself as much or more than me and that fear left him more open, which was just tempting Bert to toy with him. Scolding one of the Fae for acting according to his nature wouldn't change anything. Bert would do as he chose.

'Where is he going?' I asked.

'Not far. He'll be gone just long enough to be useful, no more.' The balls vanished up Bert's sleeve. He bowed to Bridget with a flourish. 'Little sister, a favour if you would. Find the Knight and his Lady on their way here and ask them to make haste. The game moves faster and so must we.'

She yipped and wiggled: now that he'd set her a task, there would be no holding her. I put her down and she raced across the yard, her bright red coat quickly vanishing into the shadows between the trees.

I turned to discover Bert gone – then I spotted him stretched out in the shade of the canopy, his feet dangling from the back of the wagon.

'You should rest while you may, kind witch. You got little enough sleep last night.' He raised his head a bit and peered at me through one half-open eye. 'We must go the long way round to Sheffield, travelling slower with the wagon. Keeping the Archer and the Warrior from each other's throats until we arrive will tax both of us.'

'I was thinking of sending Robin back to Nottingham. I know Tuck meant him to protect me, but Jack will do a better job.' I sat on the end of the wagon, swinging my legs as if I were no older than Kate. The shadows my boots made on the ground gave me something to watch and let me avoid looking Bert in the eye. 'Once I thought we knew each other, but I've begun to realise the truth, that we've always been strangers. Now he believes me a whore as well as evil: breathing the same air taints his very soul. I'm sure he'd be glad to be rid of us.'

'It's tempting, I'll grant you that.' Bert sat up and scooted over to sit next to me, swinging his long legs in time with mine. 'But he still has a part to play in this game, and many things to set aright. I can't send him away, not even to spare you.'

'I made my peace with how Robin sees me long ago.' I shrugged. 'I don't need to be protected.'

'You and Jack are much alike that way. He'd say the same.' Bert looked into my eyes and I knew with him I had no masks, no secrets. 'We all have a need to be spared from time to time.'

I took a breath and nodded, wanting nothing more than to let things alone for now. Bert began playing with a coin that had appeared from nowhere, rolling it from finger to finger, making it vanish, then reappearing it again. He looked content to be quiet, so I lay back and closed my eyes, drowsing in the sun the way Marlow slept in his meadow.

Seeing Will stride out of the greenwood, his eyes alight with mischief, was merely a dream, for even in sleep, grief threatened to blind me to anything else. But I couldn't put his memory to rest and I needed to remember more than just the pain of losing him, however sharp that was, more than a need for revenge on those who took him away. Our years together had been full of happy days and contentment. I feared forgetting that more than facing life without him.

So I held tight to the dream, to watching him walk towards me but never drawing closer, never being quite within reach. Memory could not ever be enough, but memory was all I had.

Bert's hand on my shoulder woke me. 'Meg's guardians have arrived. Time to wake and be about our business.'

I rubbed my eyes, not at all surprised to find my face damp. The Fae didn't cry, not that I'd ever heard tell, but Bert didn't say a word. I sat up and combed my fingers through my hair, longing for water to wash the dust and sweat away before we left, but already the day was moving on. 'I have clean clothes in my pack – let me change and I'll be ready.'

'We have a bit more time than that.' His smile was bright and wide and put me on my guard. 'The Knight's Lady bears a gift for you. She's bringing clothes more suited for a gentlewoman visiting the fayre in Sheffield. You'll have to give up your cast-off tunics and hose.'

'Why?' I slid off the wagon, tugging down my tunic and trying to brush it free of dirt. 'I haven't needed to worry about suitable clothes before now.'

'You're a player in this game, Marian.' The pipe appeared in his hands, conjured again from air, he trilled a few liquid notes and I heard Bridget's answering bark. 'And a player must always dress the part to be believed. People see what they expect to see and the proper clothes go a long way towards making that true. Come now and meet Meg's protectors. I promise you'll be well guarded while you bathe and dress.'

I saw them now; the people Bert had called the Knight and his Lady. The man dressed as one would expect of a miller, wearing a tan workaday tunic and breeches, black boots rising to mid-calf and a brown felt hat hiding his hair. He rode a grey stallion. The horse stood patiently as he spoke to Jack.

The woman next to him was dressed just as plainly, her dull burgundy gown of wool, her apron linen, russet hair coiled in braids atop her head. Her chestnut mare set to dancing impatiently until she quieted the horse with a touch. Bridget rode at the front of the Lady's saddle, her mouth stretched open, tongue lolling, in a fox's grin. Julian milled round the mare's feet, his whimpering at not being able to reach the vixen carrying across the yard.

Other sight showed me the truth of why the horses weren't bolting, or shying away from the dog's antics.

The Knight's chainmail shirt had sparks and oak leaf shadows playing through the closely woven links. Darker greaves covering his legs and arms shimmered with the leathery green of ferns in moonlight. Sapphires on the hilt of his sword twinkled like evening stars while river-blue jewels I'd no name for trailed the length of his black scabbard. At first I mistook the stag's antlers for decoration on the helm, until he turned and looked at me with calm brown eyes that stole my breath and I knew him for an ancient tale come true.

Where the Knight was forest-glade dark, the Lady at his side was meadow-bright. A garland of daisies crowned flaxen hair that rippled down her back. Her winter-sky blue gown matched her dancing eyes. She smiled, and kindness filled her face.

Meg was standing in her brother's shadow, shy in the face of the strangers, but showing no more fear of the Knight than of a neighbour who had stopped by for a visit. She blushed at something the Lady said, looking for a moment as young and carefree as she had every right to be. My fears of leaving her had already eased.

Bert clapped Jack on the back, staggering him. 'I told you Uncle Bert would find some good folk to stay with Meggie. How about you introduce Marian while I find where Robin's wandered off to.'

'He never came back?' I glanced up at the sun, measuring how long I'd slept.

'Now don't you go fretting over him.' Bert pulled a hat from air and settled it on his head. 'Most like the boy sat under a tree to sulk and fell asleep. You'll have your soak and get dressed in the time it takes me to hunt him up.'

He winked at me and was gone.

Jack's arm snaked around his sister's shoulders, holding on while he could. 'Marian, this is Ben and Cassie. They've kindly agreed to stay with Meg and help her run the mill while we go to Sheffield.'

Cassie slid off the mare, the scent of summer roses trailing behind her. She took the brown hemp bag Ben handed her, slipped the strap over her head and settled it across her chest.

'Your uncle asked me to bring a new gown for you – I did tell him it was silly for him to fuss so, but men are like that.' She gave me a conspiratorial smile as she lifted Bridget down and handed her to Meg. 'Will you keep this one out of trouble while I help Marian? For such a little thing she needs a deal of minding.'

'I'd love to take care of her.'

Bridget snuggled up under Meg's chin, her tongue sneaking out to lick the fingers stroking her fur.

'I've never even touched a fox before, let alone stroked one. She's so soft – and just as tame as Julian.'

'Don't let her fool you. She finds mischief in places you'd never think to look.' I took hold of Bridget's muzzle so she'd be forced to look me in the eye. 'Behave. Trust that I'll hear about it if you don't.'

Bridget nestled deeper into Meg's shoulder and closed her eyes, content for the moment to let someone fuss over her. I knew she'd be all right, at least for as long as she could resist teasing the poor dog.

Cassie led me behind the mill and down a path wide enough for two to walk comfortably abreast running alongside a gentle bend in the river. We passed through flower-dotted grass and by rustling reeds until the river broadened where a shallow pool had formed next to the bank, a little apart from the fast-flowing current.

Cassie knelt down and produced a gown from her bag, deep blue and full-skirted, sewn from fine-spun wool, softer than any I'd owned in years. She laid a linen shift that draped like silk on the grass next to it. 'Take your time, Marian. Sheffield and all the troubles there will still be waiting. Bert's hurrying you won't change a thing, more's the pity.'

A hard-packed path sloping down the bank to the pool eased my way into the pleasantly warm knee-deep water at the edge and I waded out a few paces, just until it was up to my thighs, and bent and rinsed my body and hair in the clear water. Pebbles slid under my feet, reminding me not to take the river for granted; the current a little further out was strong enough to carry me off if I didn't take care. I thought the rush of the water quickened in glee at the thought of having me at her mercy, and just as quickly, glee turned to disappointment as the power of the guardian warned the river away.

I hurried in any case, not eager to test Cassie's will against the might of the River Maun, feeling the water sucking at my ankles, trying to pull me back as I splashed to shore. I dried myself on my old tunic, then once I'd slipped the luxurious new gown over my head, took the bone comb Cassie handed me and worked the tangles out of my hair.

Cassie sat beside me, humming a tune, her voice chasing the melody as if trying to remember something from long ago. She plucked daisies from the grass and started making chains the way I'd done when I was a little girl. I watched her from under my lashes, trying to puzzle out who she might be.

'Ask your questions, Marian. They buzz in your thoughts like bees hunting nectar.' She dropped a necklace of daisies over my head and smiled. The tiny white and yellow blossoms shone against the blue gown. 'I can't promise to answer all of them, but I'll tell you what I can.'

Much as I wanted to ask her name, I knew better than that. 'The three of you have more craft and power between you than any of the folk I've ever heard tales about. If this is all a game, as Bert keeps saying, why not simply put an end to it?'

'That's Bert's way, to see life as a game and all around him as players. This time there's some truth in that.' Cassie wove more flowers into a circlet, plaiting chain after chain together until the crown was thick with white petals, yellow centres set like jewels. She placed the wreath atop my head as if crowning me lady of the flowers. 'All power comes with limits. The Knight's power is to guard and protect and in that he has no equal; mine is to heal and nurture. We'd be of little use in stopping the pair at the root of your troubles.'

'But perfect for keeping Meg from getting hurt again and helping her recover from her ordeals.' I stood and shook out the gown's full skirt, feeling a little silly bedecked in daisies. 'I know Bert's not any way near as dim-witted as he pretends. More's the pity he can't see everything that has to happen, or how it all ends.'

'Knowing the future is more a curse than a blessing.' Cassie stuffed the soiled tunic and breeches I'd dropped on the grass into her bag, started swinging it by the rope handle, faster and faster until the brown hemp was nothing but a blur, then let go. The bag arched out over the river and landed where the current was swift and the water deep. She greeted my questioning look with a smile and threaded her arm through mine for the walk back.

'Most in the Lady's court do see Bert as a fool, at least until they run afoul of him. Playing the fool is the part he's chosen in this game, but you must believe he wouldn't hold the Lady's trust long if he were nothing more than a trickster.' Cassie patted my hand. 'He's thrown his lot in with you, Marian, and that's a rare thing. Mind what he tells you and this will all come out right.'

I smiled. 'He'll leave me little choice about listening to him.'

'Indeed, Bert will do his best to herd you and that's his way too.' Cassie stopped just in sight of the mill and took hold of me by the shoulders. Her face was serious and solemn. Glamour gave her youth, but the eyes looking back at me spoke of age and time passing. 'You always have a choice, Marian. Don't let him push you into thinking you don't.'

We walked the rest of the way in silence. I tried not to think too much about the ways of the Fae and how they'd entangled themselves in my life.

Best I didn't think about that at all.

Chapter 12

I have heard talk of bold Robin Hood,
And of brave Little John,
Of Friar Tuck, and Will Scarlett,
Locksley, and Maid Marion.
But such a tale as this before
I think there was never none ...

17TH CENTURY BALLAD

The din and clamour made by the wagon bouncing its way to Sheffield was worse than I could ever have imagined. Pots and pans swung on their hooks and clanged together with each dip and rut in the road. The incessant crashing set my head to pounding within an hour of saying goodbye to Meg until I was convinced it would shatter.

The horses plodded along, keeping a steady pace and not wandering off the road, although Bert never bothered to touch the reins unless we met other travellers on the road, instead leaving them draped over his knee or resting on the wooden board between us. He played finger-tricks with coins or trilled tunes on his pipes, adding to the noise.

He must have been guiding the horses somehow, either with his tunes or some other hidden piece of craft, for at crossroads or junctions where the road split, he would sing a different sort of melody, something more akin to the soft hiss of rain on a thatch roof, the song's words in a tongue I'd never before heard, and each time the horses unerringly chose the way to Sheffield.

While I shared the narrow driver's seat, Robin walked, keeping pace with the wagon on Bert's side. Whenever I looked over at him, I could see his shoulders were tight with anger, but panic sat in his eyes each time he glanced towards the wagon seat. Bert answered each furtive look with a bright smile or a lively tune, as if he hadn't caught Robin on the road to Nottingham and forced him to return. Robin would never admit to running out on us, but that's what he'd done.

When Robin and I had started out on this quest, things had gone well enough. We might never have been easy in each other's company after he'd joined the monastery, but we hadn't been constantly at war. Now he saw me as the source of all his troubles, for I was forcing him to choose between his vow to Tuck and travelling with one of the Fae. His anger at having to endure my company grew three-fold as the day wore on, the clanging of pots and Bert's pipes adding to his foul mood, just as they added to my headache.

Jack was walking on my side, and he was definitely bearing the deafening racket with more grace. I considered it a blessing that the wagon was keeping the men apart and could even find it in myself to be grateful the clamour was keeping the pair of them quiet. Jack had already decided that Robin was somehow the source of all our problems and grief and they'd come near to blows before leaving the mill. Getting through the rest of the day with no more shouting between them would suit me just fine.

Fox and hound ranged far afield scouting for trouble, coming back every once in a while to make sure they hadn't lost us. Doing the Fae Lord's bidding both suited their natures and kept them out of mischief. Forcing Bridget and Julian to behave was no small accomplishment, I thought.

Julian didn't give chase to any of the small Fae, for all there were plenty around to tempt him. Small goblins, lobs and other minor Fae on either side of the road were keeping pace with us, small faces and big eyes glimpsed now and then between thicket and shadow. I saw fewer as the day wore on, but I trusted Bert had reasons to send them away.

We stopped to water the horses just after midday at a spring Bert found in the centre of a sunny meadow bordered by birch trees. Water bubbled up into a stone basin with a low spot on one side letting it overflow and tumble down into a lower pool. The long meadow grasses swayed in the light breeze while the leaves of silver birch rattled and sang summer songs.

The dog and vixen drank first, then raced off into the trees, Julian in the lead for once. Jack and Bert took the time to unharness the horses so they could graze freely and drink their fill at the spring. The Fae Lord and the Warrior put their heads together, speaking quietly, then disappeared into the trees at the far side of the meadow. Jack glanced back for a moment, as if making sure I'd seen them, but at a word from Bert he quickened his pace.

Robin seated himself on a rounded stone near the spring. Pulling arrows from his quiver, he checked the fletching on each, one by one, making sure the feathers hadn't worked loose and that the arrows were still straight and true. Watching him made me remember how patiently he'd explained to me, long ago, that a bent or crooked arrow was useless if you needed to hit your target; I'd laughed until my sides ached as he'd demonstrated what might happen. I'd seen him go through his arrows a thousand times, a normal thing for an archer who depended on his bow to eat and stay alive, but somehow, Robin doing something normal felt odd, out of place. Still, I left him to it. It would keep him quiet, I hoped, at least until he finished, or Jack came back.

Picking through the meadow, looking for herbs and digging for roots, kept me busy. We weren't so far from home that there were new and strange plants, but some were rare near my cottage, while others didn't grow at all in my part of the forest. I collected as many seeds as I could, wrapping them up in scraps of linen, taking note of where they grew, in shade or sun, and how near the water. If I couldn't coax them to grow, Beth would manage.

I'd worked my way back to the spring when the forest went still, birds fell into silence and the wind playing through the leaves quieted to a whisper before fading away completely. The horses stopped grazing and moved together, their heads shifting restlessly, their eyes wild. Bad storms were sometimes preceded by calm, but the sky was clear and cloudless – and I'd never known the quiet before a storm to make me want to go to ground like a fawn hiding from wolves.

Once, only once, Midge, Will and I had stumbled into a griffin's territory. Foul-tempered beasts, griffins were rare in Sherwood even then, all but the oldest having decided they wanted nothing to do with men and their settlements. The sheriff's guard wasn't far behind us that day: ill luck for them, as it turned out.

The forest had gone still and quiet, just as it was now, an instant before the griffin and her brood arrived. Six well-fed guardsmen and their horses were more of a temptation than three hungry outlaws; it was on them the griffin cast her spell. We'd crept away while the guardsmen calmly sat there, blind to death approaching.

Marlow told me later that not only were griffins contemptible in the way they hunted, they were lazy. Inflicting a waking dream on their prey meant they never had to chase a meal down.

A glance showed Robin with his head bent over an arrow, lost in his work but free of any spell. I stepped closer, turning in a slow circle, trying to look everywhere at once. 'Robin . . .'

'What is it, Marian?'

The irritation vanished from his face as soon as he noticed the motionless trees, too good a woodsman not to sense something was wrong in the sudden quiet, and he knew our griffin story.

He didn't waste time asking questions but slung his half-full quiver over a shoulder and grabbed his bow. Nocking an arrow, he nodded towards the wagon. 'Under the wagon, quick now. It's not much shelter, but better than being out in the open. Any idea where Jack and the bloody Fae ran off to?'

'They didn't tell me.' I wrapped will around need and sent out a call, but all I heard was a distant echo of my distress, not an answer, nor anything that could tell me Bert had heard. I tried again, and again, and each time it took more effort to remember why I needed him, or how to craft the calling.

The griffin was hunting me: this much I knew was true, a truth I clung to, using it as a prod to keep from falling completely into the spell.

Bridget and Julian slunk out of the forest, growling deep in their chests, moving quickly despite their bellies being pressed to the ground. Dog and fox began herding me towards the wagon,

Bridget going so far as to nip at my heels to make me move faster, while Julian grabbed my skirts in his teeth and tugged me forward, step by step.

The strange quiet was shattered by a griffin's roar. Both horses reared and bolted into the trees.

'Marian!' Hound and vixen dashed under the wagon as Robin slammed into me, carrying me to the ground. A rush of air passed over us and he was on his feet again, sighting down an arrow and letting it fly. I counted it a miracle he'd kept hold of his bow, for all I'd seen Robin roll off a swiftly moving wagon and come up shooting. The griffin roared again, this time with pain and anger, and the spell holding me snapped.

I'd always known Tuck was right: Robin was still the best man with a longbow in all of England. Two arrows sank into the griffin's feathered breast and a third found an eye. The beast threw its head back in agony and a fourth arrow took it in the throat. Robin readied another, but held his fire.

Every bowman in the country knew how iron reacted with magic and I'd yet to meet one who didn't tip his arrows with iron. The poison moved more quickly in smaller creatures, but the result was the same. Wisps of smoke rose from the griffin's body and I knew it was dead.

Robin helped me stand and pulled me into a hug, surprising me. His hands were shaking, but so were mine. 'Are you all right, Marian?'

'I . . . I think so.' I'd forgotten what his arms felt like, how tightly he could hold me, and how safe I felt. Missing Will with all my heart didn't keep me from remembering.

The calm shattered as the wind came rushing back, bending the birch trees almost double and breaking apart the smouldering remains of the griffin. Bones and embers were all that was left, but the wind pushed and rolled them across the meadow. A trail of scorched grass showed the path of the flaming skull and sparks rose up from the smaller bones as they were stolen by the wind and dropped into the spring.

An icy gust whirled around me and Robin, pelting us with stones, leaves and ash. He pulled my face into his shoulder and the wind blew harder. I knew I wasn't imagining the wind's angry scream, or the way Robin stiffened when he heard.

'It's all right, I'm here,' he whispered. 'I won't let them hurt you.'

All thought of being safe with him fled. I pushed against his chest, trying to get free. 'Robin . . . who—'

'Shhh . . . I'll protect you.' The wind tried to knock me off my feet, but he held me tighter. 'Don't be afraid, Marian. God is watching over both of us.'

The wind died as suddenly as it had begun, and echoes of the scream with it. Robin let go of me slowly, then started backing away, refusing to look at me. He retrieved his bow and the rest of his arrows, gathering them up fast as he could, and when he finally turned to face me, he was a stranger again.

'I'm going to look for the horses. Jack and . . . and Bert should be back soon.' He glanced over his shoulder. 'You'll be safe enough until then. The dog and the vixen can watch over you as well as me.'

I held myself tight, wondering who Robin would be when I saw him next. 'I owe you my life,' I said, keeping my voice together. 'I'm grateful for that.'

'Robbie and Kate need a mother. And I couldn't let you die with your sins uncleansed. The Lord will forgive you, Marian, as

I know he'll forgive me. It's not too late.' With that he turned and loped towards the trees.

I waited until he disappeared, then curled up on my side under the wagon, shaking head to foot and uncertain if the griffin or the stranger wearing Robin's face frightened me more. Glimpses of the man I'd once loved made it all worse. Julian greeted me with a thumping tail, a tongue licking my hand, and stretched out against my back. Bridget nestled against my chest, her sharp eyes watching for trouble.

Neither the slight vixen nor the over-large dog cared that I cried myself empty, more alone and afraid than I'd been since Robin first left me. No matter what Tuck believed, the Robin Hood I used to know was gone and what was left – the man I had to cope with – was a guilty stranger, a man who comforted then frightened me, turn by turn.

Robin knew Rose's angel wouldn't harm him. He knew who she was, that she'd sent the griffin after me – and that she wouldn't harm me if she had to go through him. I couldn't begin to guess all the secrets he was labouring so hard to hide, and that was the thing that frightened me most of all.

His sins were still at the heart of everything between us, as was his guilt. Robin's God might be able to forgive him, but he'd never forgive himself for the harm he'd done – and neither could I.

It was the sound of Julian barking and Jack yelling at the dog to quiet down that finally woke me. Bert was lying on his stomach, peering under the wagon to watch me, bright-eyed and far too cheerful. Bridget sat next to him, smiling the way only a fox can, looking well pleased with herself.

'Are you ready to come out, gentle witch?' Bert asked. 'I admit, it's a clever place to hide from griffins, but the Archer appears to have put an end to this one.'

'Who's to say there isn't another in hiding, waiting for its chance to take my head off?' I wiped a hand over my face. 'And if you want me to come out, you'll need to move, sly one. I'm not crawling over you.'

'I say, Marian, and I've reason to know this is the only one.' He moved out of the way, offering his hand to help me stand gracefully. 'The griffin sent to hunt you was old and dying, the last such beast in this part of Lincolnshire. Such a creature is easily bound by the pair running from me, but the Archer put an end to its suffering. You don't need to fear another will drop from the sky.'

'I need only fear they'll try to kill me again,' I said.

'They seek to warn me away by attacking you. Instead, they've made me more determined to end their folly.' Bert looked into my eyes, all trace of the trickster gone. 'My sight has failed me, and in turn, I've failed you. I regret putting you in more danger, Marian.'

Anger at the Lord and Lady we were chasing churned inside me, but I merely nodded and looked away. Bert held more power than anyone I'd ever known, and still this pair evaded all his traps, which made a part of me fear that no matter what the Fae Lord believed, we weren't really chasing them, but being led. My doubts and fears were human, mortal. One of the drawbacks to having so much power was that Bert would never think that way.

Jack moved around the meadow, the dog at his heels, gathering the griffin's bones into a pile. He wore heavy gloves I hadn't seen before; the thick leather protected him from embers and left-over magic both. Julian raced from the pile Jack built to uncollected bones smouldering in the grass, pointing them out with a bark and a wagging tail but never touching them, showing more sense in staying well back than I'd given him credit for.

Bert saw me watching. 'Iron took the griffin's life, but not the magic in its bones. Almost any of the High Fae and many Demisang have craft enough to fashion compulsion charms from a griffin's bones. Those with more power can turn the magic to . . . other things. Traps and lures spring to mind.'

'You plan to lay more traps for the Lord and Lady we're hunting,' I said. 'I grant you're clever, High Lord, but this pair are clever in their own way. I hope your schemes are enough to snare them.'

'Magic in a sliver of griffin bone will tempt the pair of them in and tangle them in my net. I admit destroying all the bits of bone would be wiser, but then, I'm seldom wise.' The gleam in his eye didn't match his serious words. 'I give my word we'll catch them when the time is right, witchling. They underestimate me at their peril.'

I eyed him. 'And when will the time be right?'

Bert laughed, startling birds out of the trees. 'Now that would be telling and spoil the surprise. Patience, young one.'

Holding up a small sack Jack called from the far side of the meadow, 'I've found all the pieces I can, Bert. The ones you wanted saved are in here.'

'Come and stand with us, Warrior. You shouldn't be too close.'

Jack grabbed hold of Julian's collar, trotted across the meadow and tied the dog to the wagon before coming to stand with me. Bridget ran over to sit with Julian, which stopped the dog from whining.

'What's Bert going to do?' Jack asked.

'Destroy the griffin's bones.' I smiled at the question in Jack's eyes. 'If you want to know how, you'll have to ask him.'

'A simple cleansing spell, Marian, helped along with a bit more power and craft.' Bert beamed at us, pulling his pipes from a sleeve and playing a string of notes, the run climbing higher and higher, then falling again until they faded away. Small flames began to lick the pile of bones, quickly growing larger and spreading to engulf the griffin's entire remains. He began to sing in a language I didn't recognise, coaxing the flames even higher.

The fire didn't burn long. Wind picked up the ashes, scattering them across the sky.

Bert took the small sack from Jack and slipped it inside his tunic. 'Time to summon the Archer and the horses back. We've a ways to travel before nightfall and I'd see you settled before I leave.'

Jack glanced at me, worry in his eyes. 'Where are you going?'

The trickster laughed and spun on his toes. 'Hunting the shadows for a pair of cowards and mayhap setting another trap or two. This game is well begun, but they grow bolder and more troublesome and my patience wears thin. I'd just as soon end this now.'

His pipes trilled another song, this one bright and lively. I could feel the summons in the tune and barely a moment passed before the horses ran out of the trees and across the meadow.

Robin trailed behind, each step reluctantly taken, resentment heavy on his face.

The day drew to a close and the sun dipped behind the trees. Shadows scored the road, a shifting patchwork of dark and light. Bert hummed a few notes, just loud enough that I heard the tune over the bang of kettles and pots and the rattle of harness. The horses angled off the road, plodding down a barely seen path I hadn't noticed.

Ruts in the narrow track rattled my teeth and the bounce from the wheels passing over the deepest dips came close to knocking me off the seat. Clouds of dust stirred by the horses' hooves hung like fog, the fine grains settling onto my hair as we rode through. I was glad when the dirt path gave way to a grassy-green clearing, the open ground surrounded by rowan and poplar. Small clusters of heartsease bloomed in the shelter of the rowan trees; the tiny yellow and purple flowers were easy to see even in twilight. An often-used firepit sat near a small stream on the far side.

Water raced down the stream, leaping from stone to stone, eager to join one of Sheffield's five rivers. The Rivers Don, Loxley, Porter and Sheaf were tamed when the first men came to England, a gift from the Gods that brought men here to share the land with the Fae. These four rivers shared their waters willingly and gristmills sprouted on their banks every few miles. A great forge overlooked the River Sheaf.

The fifth river, Rivelin, closest to where we made our camp, was still wild and jealous of its freedom, providing a home to water nymphs and a playground for mer who swam inland from the sea. Even in Bert's company, I'd avoid crossing the Rivelin.

Jack whistled Julian to his side. The hound loped into the clearing, Bridget running next to him. He scratched behind the dog's ears, earning himself a good face-washing as he asked, 'Can you keep these two with you, Marian? I'd thought to scare up a hare or two for supper. I'd rather not worry about hitting one of them by mistake.'

Bert smiled and made a small motion with his fingers, something I'd have missed if I hadn't been looking at him straight-on. The animals both yawned, curled up under the wagon and fell asleep almost instantly. 'Do your hunting in peace, Warrior. These absurd creatures will sleep until you return.'

'Useful skill, that. Many's the time being able to charm him into sleeping would have been a blessing.' Jack laid all his gear except his bow and quiver near the wagon. 'Is there anything you'd have me find for you, Marian? I might be able to find some herbs to season the pot.'

I rubbed my temples, trying to stop the drumming behind my eyes. 'Do we have a stewpot? To cook in, not to peddle at the fayre.'

Bert leapt into the wagon-bed and flipped open a red-topped chest. He pulled out a worn kettle and an iron tripod with a flourish. 'Just ask, fair Marian, and I will provide. We've herbs aplenty, onions and turnips as well. Once the Warrior slays his hares we will feast like noble monks and warrior-kings.'

'I've not heard tell of a king with a taste for roast hare and boiled turnips.' Jack nocked an arrow to his bowstring and started into the trees, winking at me on his way past. 'And if I recollect right, King John issued a proclamation banning anyone with noble blood from eating onions. Best leave those out of Locksley's share.'

I could see Robin on his knees at the edge of the stream, eyes closed as he splashed water over his head. He was quiet for now, but I'd little hope for silence lasting, especially if he'd heard. But Jack vanished into the trees and Robin didn't so much as look up to watch him go.

The silence didn't help my headache as much as I'd hoped.

Leaning against the wagon and shutting my eyes gave me some relief; pressing the heels of my hand against my temples eased the pain a little more.

'What troubles you, young witch?' Bert perched on the side of the wagon, bright-eyed as an owl atop a chimney. I'd be surprised if he ever missed anything.

'If we started down that road, we'd still be going come morning.' I sighed. 'But if you're in a mood to provide anything I ask for, you could start by doing something about the pounding in my head.'

He dropped to the ground next to me. 'There's many an ill that can't be mended easily or that lies outside my skill, but this I can do for you. Close your eyes again.'

I did as he asked. He hadn't played me false so far; he'd earned a touch of trust.

He cupped my face in his cool hands. His fingers were oddly callused for someone I'd imagined never doing a lick of work, but hours of playing pipes might leave such marks. 'You should have spoken earlier, Marian. There's no call for you to suffer from something so easily mended.'

Pain drained away quick as water flowing from a clenched fist. I opened my eyes to see Bert smile, warm and as close to human as I'd ever seen from him. Returning the smile was natural, done without thought.

'That's better now. Time to goad the Archer into gathering wood. If he steps quick I won't make him dance for his supper.' Mischief sparked in his eyes, the pipe appeared and he played a run of notes, brisk and meant to make toes tap.

Robin was still kneeling next to the stream, his head bent and shoulders hunched. He gripped the edge of his tunic so tightly, his fingers were white, bloodless. I'd never seen him afraid, not in all our years of running from the sheriff's men, but he was quivering now, obviously terrified.

Pity was an unaccustomed feeling when it came to Robin, but I couldn't deny I pitied him now. I was puzzled too, not knowing why Bert's jest had so unsettled him: yet another secret. 'I'll ask him to go for wood. You could ready the stewpot, if you would.'

The pipe whirled in his fingers and was gone as Bert grinned, full of trickster mirth. He leapt into the back of the wagon. 'As you wish. Stay well back when you ask him. He's become an ill-tempered hound and I fear he'll snap at you.'

Robin was on his feet, wiping his face on his sleeve when I came up behind him. When I put a hand on his arm, he jerked away, his breath coming harsh and sharp, hissing between his teeth. I stumbled backwards, belatedly heeding Bert's warning.

'Don't touch me, witch,' he said. 'For the love of God, don't touch me. Tell that evil creature to put his devil pipes away. I'll fetch your wood and build your fire, but nothing more. God in his mercy forgave me my sin once. I won't be tempted a second time.'

'Fetching wood is all I wanted from you.' I stared, stunned at his reaction. In my bones I now knew that Robin and Bert weren't strangers, but of their relationship I could guess nothing. 'I've no idea what you're raving about, Robin, none at all.'

Some of the wildness left his eyes. He turned away, running a hand through his greying hair. 'Ask him – he knows. There's even a chance he'd tell you the truth.'

My belief that I needed to know his secrets and hidden things grew stronger.

'No!' I cried, 'you've got a tongue, so use it. I won't ask Bert, or anyone else. I want the truth from you, Robin. Either come out and say what needs to be said, or keep quiet.'

I felt Bert behind me. He rested his hands on my shoulders, peering over the top of my head. Robin's anger-flushed face became ashen. 'Methinks he lacks the wit to tell you the truth, Marian, but it's well known that secrets fester and addle the brain. I know he lacks the will to speak, or he'd have done so years ago.'

He sidled to one side and now he was juggling again: his bone pipes, Aelfgifu's fan, a ring and a poppet not unlike Kate's made the circuit from hand to hand, but slowly, deliberately, this time, each hovering in air for an instant, impossible to mistake. Robin backed away, his eyes wide. His foot slipped on the muddy bank and he fell, landing hard in the water.

'So easily panicked, Archer? A few notes of a dance tune and a child's toy surely shouldn't unbalance a man of your reputation.' Laughter and faint drifts of melody swirled in the air, echoes of some long-ago Fae revel. Everything vanished but the ring, which Bert held out towards Robin, balanced on his palm. 'Or is it the trinket you offered in troth? It's a bad habit you have, Robin, making pledges and breaking them.'

Robin scrambled across the stream, sliding on the wet stones and stumbling to his knees before reaching the other side where he stood dripping and shaking and chanting prayers, making the sign of the cross over his chest, again and again.

Bert took a step closer and Robin jumped. His hand was trembling so hard I didn't know how he managed to pull his wooden cross from his tunic.

'Stay back! No one needs to remind me of how I sinned. I've spent twelve years doing penance, asking God's forgiveness for my weakness.' Robin gathered himself together, trying to find a bit of courage and dignity. 'If I had been steadfast in my faith she'd never have bewitched me, but I allowed her to bind me with pleasures of the flesh. I beseech God every single day to cleanse that stain from my soul.'

'You think I brought you to my bed with a *spell*?' After all our years apart I'd thought myself far beyond hurt, long past the tears burning my eyes. 'By the moon and stars, Robin, I *loved* you. I'd *never* bind you. I wouldn't bind anyone. Tuck married us because *you* asked him to, not from any need of mine.'

Bert wrapped an arm around my shoulders, his voice as gentle as my father had always been when soothing me. 'Hush, Marian, hush. The Archer speaks of following the Lady Underhill when she asked. He knows you never beguiled him.'

'Do I? One witch acts much like another.' Disdain filled his eyes, his fear forgotten, or maybe hidden behind a mask. Robin dumped water from his boot and stomped it back on. 'I'll fetch your wood. Jack can gut the hares.'

I watched the shadows swallow him up, barely marking his skill at blending into the greenwood, which was so much a part of him.

When at last I looked for him, Bert sat next to the firepit, the stewpot filled with water and swinging from the tripod's hook over yellow flame. I sat opposite him, pulled my knees up and wrapping my arms around them, and asked, 'How . . . how long was Robin Underhill?'

I didn't ask *when*. That I knew; I could name the winter day he'd vanished. He came back to me in summer, changed in ways I hadn't understood, into a man I didn't know. Robin never told me where he'd gone or why he'd sent no word, letting me believe him dead for all those months. Winter came again and saw him on the road to the monastery, by which time I was wondering if I had ever known him at all.

'Five years passed in the Lady's court before Robin grew restless. Two more years were gone before she sent him home. She hadn't compelled him to come and she wouldn't hold him when he asked to go. Time moves differently Underhill and I can't say if he was gone from Sherwood a year or a day.' Bert pulled five silver balls out of his sleeve, tossing them up one by one until all of them danced in the air. Two wooden balls joined them. 'The Lady bore him twins, a rare blessing among the Fae: one a daughter, touched by winter frost from the day she was born, the other a son summer-warm and loving. Their summer child was dead a season, no more, when the Archer left her. The Lady mourned both her son and lover. Their loss . . . distracted her.'

What he meant was their loss weakened her with the court, but he'd never say so outright.

'How did the boy die?' I'd never thought to pity the Lady for anything, but now my stomach twisted in sympathy, imagining all too easily the grief I'd feel if I lost Robbie or Kate.

A twist of his hand and the poppet joined the silver balls. The impassive harlequin mask now hid his face, splitting it between light and shadow. 'The story told to the Lady was of a fall from a high place: an accident, with no one to blame but bad fortune. Fondness for the one bearing the bad tidings let her believe the story was true. Not all believed the teller of the tale.'

'Their daughter – the winter child. She killed her brother.'

Bert, like all the Fae, couched everything he said in riddles, never speaking plain, but he didn't need to tell me her name, for she had her mother's eyes and Robin's hair. 'Did Robin know?'

His juggling ceased, the mask flaked into dust to float away on the breeze and Bert sat before me again, hands resting on his knees. He looked weary, older, as if spending time among men made him prey to all mortal ills. 'At least one at court thought Robin knew the truth of what happened, but the Archer kept his own counsel before leaving and the Lady – the Lady shut herself away and spoke to no one.'

The more time I spent in Bert's company, the more I wondered if tales of Fae heartlessness held any truth at all. The Lady had cared for Robin as I had; coupled with the loss of a child, the Lady must have faced bitter days when he left her, worse than I suffered when Robin turned his back on me. My children grew and thrived, bringing me joy, while she grieved alone.

And I'd had Will, although not for long enough. Not nearly long enough.

'Robin's known who we're hunting all along. Mother of us all, that lying bastard *knows*!' The poppet appeared in my lap, plaything of a cold-hearted winter child, as worn and well-loved as Kate's. I flung the rag doll away. The cruelty in Maddie's smile belonged to her alone.

His silence that summer was a lie worse than anything he might have said to explain where he'd been. He'd returned to my bed with a fervour and a hunger that had unnerved me at times. All the hurt and puzzlement I'd felt when Robin suddenly put me aside, even with my belly beginning to swell with the children I thought he'd wanted, was nothing in the face of learning he'd spent *years* in the Lady's arms.

With all the harshness that had passed between us, I hadn't hated him – not until now. He'd walked away and left Aelfgifu alone to grieve, and abandoned his troubled daughter in all her twisted pain; then he'd walked away from our children, leaving them all but fatherless. And he'd walked away from me, leaving me to find my own way. His friends had fared no better: a word from Robin might have spared Alan, Midge and Gilbert and Gamelyn; a word might have given Ethan the long life he deserved.

And I'd lost Will to his silence and might yet lose Kate and Robbie. He could have saved his brother and protected our children. Instead, he'd kept silent, choosing his guilt and twisted faith over the truth. I hated Robin for that most of all.

I laid my head on my knees and turned my face away, hiding from the sorrow in Bert's eyes, unable to stomach watching sorrow changing to pity.

The wool under my cheek smelled of sun-warmed grass and meadow flowers on a summer's eve, scents that eased my heart: a gift from the weaver, one I hadn't known of, or needed until now. I breathed a thank-you and knew she'd hear.

'Marian?'

Jack dropped four gutted bark-brown rabbits near the fire before he knelt next to me. He frowned and reached to brush a tear off my cheek. 'Will Bridget take one of these or does she need to go for her own supper?'

'She'll be happiest chasing down her own.' I wiped my face with a sleeve, liking him more for holding his tongue. 'She fancies herself a hunter and I've never told her otherwise.'

'That's wise of you. You don't want her turning into a lazy glutton like Julian – he'd starve if I didn't put a meal under his nose every night.' Jack rocked back on his heels, his eyes steady on mine. 'I'll get the biggest skinned and in the pot. Where have Bert and Robin gone off to?'

The dog and the vixen were stretched out near the fire, awake and watching the woods, no doubt guarding me while I was lost in woolgathering. 'Robin went for wood. Bert didn't say, but my guess is he went to do his hunting.'

'They'll be back soon enough.' He whistled, the dog trotted over and he dropped a carcass at Julian's paws. 'Under the wagon with you now. Keep your mess where I won't be stepping in it. And you, Miss Bridget, away you go. I left a few scrawny bucks running loose for your supper.'

She yipped and ran off. Jack busied himself skinning and jointing the rabbits, tossing the offal to the dog. He whistled tunefully, letting me be, other than looking over every little while and smiling, as if to let me know I wasn't forgotten.

I liked him the better for that too.

Chapter 13

Oberon, Oberon, rake away the gold
Rake away the red leaves, roll away the mould,
Rake away the gold leaves, roll away the red,
And wake Will Scarlett from his leafy forest bed.

ALFRED NOYES

Morning dawned clear and bright, birdsong rising with the sun to greet the day. After we broke our fast with the bread and sweet cheese Bert conjured up, we set off on our way to Sheffield. His sight said the Demisang and her Lord were near, though how close that was, he couldn't say, and none of his traps had been sprung. I'd never thought to see a Fae Lord frustrated and irritable, but Bert was both.

Robin went out of his way to avoid me, a more difficult task when travelling at such close quarters. He trailed behind the wagon, out of my sight, if never out of my mind, doing everything he could to keep distance between us. I was glad: speaking to him was more than I could force myself to do, more than I thought I could stand.

Keeping silent was for the best. I was afraid of what I might do if I didn't hold my anger tight inside.

Jack ranged just ahead of the wagon, allowing Julian and Bridget room to romp, calling them back when they roamed too far. He gave me space too.

As always, Bert left the horses to find their own way, the occasional trill or whistle all he needed to keep them on the right track. While birds sang the sun into a violet sky and the west wind blew clouds to the sea, he played his pipes, not dance tunes or toe-tappers to pull us from our seats and sending us laughing and whirling across the ground, but softer melodies, songs that made me remember other times, other places. Whether he played for me or himself, I couldn't say.

A full day's travel on rutted roads saw us into the edge of Ladies Spring Wood. Older than most of Sherwood, full of rowan and ancient oak trees, the wood ran to the River Sheaf on the west, overlooking the borders of Sheffield. The trees were brim-full of green woodpeckers, their scarlet topknots visible through the leaves as they drummed on the knotted tree trunks. Blue-grey nuthatches hunted for insects in the cracks the woodpeckers left in weathered bark and sang from the tallest oaks.

In older times Ladies Spring Wood had been home to large herds of firedrakes, but as Sheffield grew and men built roads and pathways, larger creatures of magic grew scarce. Stories were still told around the hearth by those who claimed to have spotted a firedrake feasting on a farmer's sheep, but they were rare now. There were lesser Fae aplenty roaming the wood, but Marlow's kin were almost gone.

The land rose as we got closer to Sheffield, gentle hills giving way to the occasional tall cliff which seemed to sprout from nowhere. Trees marched right up the slopes until they reached bare rock they couldn't sink their roots into, although flowers found purchase even there, bright reds, pinks and soft yellows springing up in the cracks of grey stone.

Twice we passed water falling in sheets from the tops of cliffs into pools below, sending rainbow-streaked mist rising up to sparkle in the sun. Birds bathed at the edges of the pool, water beading on slick feathers.

We stopped for the night under the shelter of a stone over-hang – the rain in the air smelled distant, but Bert thought the storm close enough that we'd likely catch it before morning, so a stone roof overhead would shield us from the worst of the downpour. Water bubbled up from a tumble of rock at the cliff base, spreading out into a deep basin. A small meadow began on the far side of the spring, stretching a few dozen paces before the trees thickened again. The lush grass was dotted with daisies and meadowsweet.

Even before the wagon had stopped rolling, Robin was stalking away towards the trees.

Bert helped me climb down from the seat. 'Start supper if you would, witchling. I need to stretch my legs, set my wards and bait my traps. You needn't worry about the Archer getting it into his head to wander off on his own. I put an end to that.'

He winked at me and was gone.

Jack unhitched the horses and let them wander off to where the grass grew thickest. The pot was swinging over my just-smoul-dering fire by the time he'd finished and he gave me a hand back up into the back of the wagon.

'Should be easy enough to make Sheffield before dark tomorrow, Marian, even slow as we're moving. If memory serves, we'll pass the abbey before mid-afternoon. The town's not much further on from there.'

He took the onions, turnips and herbs I handed down. The red-topped chest had turned out to be a bottomless supply, although I never knew what I might find each time I lifted the lid. Most mornings brought smooth, sweet cheese, sometimes even fresh-baked bread to break our fast. Jack hadn't turned a hair over the unexpected bounty and I guessed Robin hadn't noticed – I doubt he'd have eaten a bite if he had.

'The sooner we're there, the sooner we can go back,' I said. 'I've left Kate and Robbie with Beth too long as it is.'

'I won't be sorry to get on with what needs to be done either. I don't want to be away from Meg any longer than needs must.' He stood so I could put a hand on his shoulder and jump down. 'Now might be a good time to tell me what you and Bert have planned once we get there.'

Guilt came sudden and sharp. I'd almost forgotten that Jack had followed the two of us blindly, completely unaware of what he was walking into. He was trusting me to warn him of danger, so not sharing everything that I knew was unfair.

I cut up the onions and added them to the boiling water, using watering eyes as a good excuse not to speak for a moment, letting me weigh how much he should know. At last I said, 'He hasn't told me everything – Bert says people will talk freer to pedlars and not think much of it and he's right about that. We've little doubt that we're looking for a Demisang girl, even word of where she's been. Tracking her and the Fae Lord helping her will be the trick. His sight shows the two of them are near, but not where they are.'

'A Demisang?' He looked up from feeding sticks to the fire,

suddenly all sharp attention. 'I thought you said we hunted for a Lord and Lady.'

'And so we all thought when we started. But Bert and I talked things over and we have worked it out differently.'

I thought Bert might have suspected Maddie all along, but he'd waited to suggest that she was behind all our troubles until he was sure and I was ready to find the truth. I looked Jack in the eye, although I wasn't yet certain if telling him any of this was wise. 'We're searching for a Demisang girl who's part of the High Fae court. I saw the girl when I asked the Lady to protect my children, and again at market in Nottingham – Tuck knew her well enough to ask her why she'd missed Mass. She'd bound a young yeoman with love charms and thought nothing of taunting me with what she'd done. I made an enemy by setting him free. She's cruel enough to bind Meg without regret and to be Rose's murdering angel.'

He chewed his lip, thinking on what I'd said, then asked, 'Are you sure? I didn't think a Demisang could have the power or the craft for all she's done.'

'Sure as I can be. Craft can be learned – and I saw for myself the bindings she used on that boy; they took a great deal of skill. There are ways of harvesting power too, although not clean ways . . .' I told him about the circle where Ethan had died and the power stored there, all drawn from the death of innocents. 'I have been told some Demisang are born with almost as much natural power as a full-blood Lord or Lady, and those raised Underhill can learn as much craft as any of the High Fae.'

'And if she's part of the Lady's court, I'm guessing she grew up Underhill.' Jack rubbed his hands over his face, looking as sad and weary as I felt. 'But why kill Midge and the others? Or pull Meg into things? This Demisang can't have known them, can she? Or had reason? Why spread this curse beyond Locksley?'

I hadn't noticed that I'd stopped thinking of my friends dying as a curse, although just when that changed was hard to say. Curses were usually simple things, easily traced and undone. Nothing about Maddie was simple.

'I haven't worked out why, not yet,' I said. 'Maybe she thinks to hurt Robin more by hurting his friends?'

'Sweet Jesus. If that's what she's after, then she's missed by a pretty pace.' He snapped the stick in his hand and his bitter words left me in no doubt about how he felt. 'From the look of him and the way he acts, Locksley couldn't care less.'

His words were interrupted by a hound's baying. Bridget raced out of the trees and across the meadow, Julian a stride or two behind. A small leveret hung from the vixen's jaws, ears flopping with every bound. Bridget dived behind the rock tumble, but the dog wasn't slim enough to fit in the tight spaces between the rocks. He watched the spot where she'd disappeared and whined deep in his throat, as if begging her to share.

Robin returned an instant later, a brace of pheasants in one hand and two fat rabbits tied to his belt. He dropped them next to Jack. 'I caught them, you can clean them,' he muttered.

'I never said I wouldn't, now, did I?' Jack smiled, his jaw tight, prickly anger hidden in his jolly tone. 'We'd not want you to get your hands dirty, milord. Great lords hunt and leave the messy parts to the rest of us: that's always the way, Locksley. I'd more than my share of cleaning up messes while following King Richard to Jerusalem.'

The Robin I'd known of old had been as quick to laugh at

himself as to anger; this Robin did neither. His only response to being mocked was a flat stare and a closed-off expression.

'I'm going back out for firewood. Don't wait for me to eat.'

Without another word, Jack carried the birds and rabbits over to a flat rock and whistled for Julian. He threw one of the rabbits to the dog and shooed him under the wagon before setting to work. Bridget crawled out from behind her rock to beg for tidbits, her snout already blood-flecked.

'Tell me the truth, Marian. Are all the bards' tales of Robin Hood true?' He pointed at the man walking away and frowned. 'It's hard to believe Locksley is that man.'

'Robin and our friends saved men who couldn't pay their taxes from being hanged. They kept entire hamlets from starving. He was a good, brave man in those days. The tales are like all bards' tales, mostly true, but meant to entertain a crowd. Alan wrote the lion's share of those ballads, so the stories are true, right enough, but he sometimes forgot Robin was a man like any other.' I dropped the last turnip in the water and sat back to wait for Jack to finish dressing the birds. 'But Robin's not the same person I knew, not by half.'

He turned to me, more than curious.

I didn't make him ask what I meant, but told him another tale of Robin Hood, a story of spending seven years Underhill in the Lady's arms while I thought him dead, of a frost-touched daughter and the son who died at his sister's hand. Quarrels and bitterness, harsh words and me not knowing the man who'd come back to me were all part of the tale. That was the hardest tale to tell, now I'd learned the truth. When I'd finished, I told Jack what he didn't already know about Robin leaving me that winter morning to enter the monastery.

The pheasants were roasting on spits at the edge of the fire and the pot was bubbling briskly by the time Robin returned with enough wood to see us through the night. The look Jack gave him wasn't kind, but he kept his promise, holding his tongue for Kate and Robbie's sake, and for mine.

Bridget had begged for scraps until she knew there'd be no more, then slipped away to prowl the night. Bert hadn't returned by the time the food was ready, but he seldom ate with us. The pop and crackle of wood in the fire were the only sounds to break the silence as each of us brooded over our own hurts and troubles.

I worried most about how we'd go about finding a Demisang girl and a Fae Lord who didn't want to be found, and what I'd do once I caught them was another worry, one that was eating at me. Vowing revenge had been easy enough when I hadn't known the person I hunted was half-sister to Kate and Robbie. I did still long for vengeance, but now that thought gave me pause.

By the time Jack helped me clean up and put things to rights, Robin was wrapped in his cloak, his back to the fire, and deep asleep. He hadn't offered to help and I think Jack was just as glad as I was.

After a while, Bridget slunk back into camp to curl up under the wagon with Julian. Stars came out of hiding one by one, tiny points of light that did nothing to ease the darkness. The moon peeked over the top of rowan and ash and reflections rippled on the sky-black pond, twin of the waxing crescent above, cold silver against the dark. The moon edged a handspan closer to full each night, power riding the air growing stronger as well.

The thought brought me no joy. I was a long time hunting sleep.

*

'Marian!'

I sat up and rubbed grit from my eyes, not at all sure what I'd heard. Bridget and the dog were still curled tight in sleep, Jack and Robin still lying undisturbed. The familiar voice called again, faint, and sounding so far away that I almost didn't hear. 'Marian, help me!'

'Will . . . *Will!*' I threw off my cloak and ran.

Dew-beaded grass was cold and slick under my bare feet, growing treacherously slippery the further I went. I skidded, but kept running until I slipped again, this time landing on my hands and knees. The hem of my gown tangled my ankles when I got up, almost tripping me again.

'Marian! Where are you?'

His voice trembled. I knew Will was afraid – he needed me. He wouldn't call this way otherwise.

Wet wool weighed me down, the sodden hem slapping around my ankles threatening to trip me with each stride. Lifting my skirts freed my legs, but stole the strength I needed to run. I stopped long enough to strip off the gown, hesitating for an instant, then tossing it aside and going on. A thought tickled at the back of my mind, telling me something was wrong, but Will called again, his voice weaker and far away, and I forgot everything but finding him.

The path narrowed, winding between close-grown blackthorns that caught my shift and tore my skin until it burned with scratches, sweat and blood. Low branches snagged in my hair, yanking me half-off my feet. Something moved in the shadows, looming large at my side, fingers tipped with curved claws reached for me, but I gathered power and shoved the beast away with a word. 'No! Stay back!'

Finally, I glimpsed Will ahead and ran even faster, each breath burning my throat, heedless of anything but reaching him. He moved away, fading out of view behind the trees, disappearing for so long I thought my heart would stop. 'Will, wait for me! *Wait!*'

He reappeared from behind a massive oak and turned to face me, the glad smile on his face the one I knew well. A roar filled my ears, growing louder, drowning the sound of my heart hammering. Doubt returned for an instant and whispered for me to *think*, that there was something I should remember—

—and Will spread his arms wide and beckoned to me, sending what little sense I had fleeing.

'I knew you'd come, love. I knew you'd save me.'

A monster slammed into me from the side, knocking me clear off my feet. Arms trapped me, gnarled and thorny, oozing something foul-smelling from half-healed gashes and gaping wounds. The weight of the creature pinned me to the ground, keeping me from drawing a breath to force it away.

I panicked, frantically clawing at soil and dead leaves, fighting hard to win free, somehow more afraid of what this denizen of the wood would do to Will than of what would become of me. Deep growls rumbled in its throat, growing louder as I struggled harder. Sobbing in anguish, I waited for those talons to rake my back, for sharp teeth to tear out my throat, as the roar in my ears grew louder, presaging my death knells, and Will's as well.

Cool hands cupped my face, long fingers gently caressing my cheek. 'Marian, listen to me. It's your Uncle Bert and Jack. We've got you safe now. Can you hear me, sweet child?'

Twigs and small jagged stones pressed against my stomach, the odour of wet leaves, damp earth and salty sweat chasing away the memory of foulness. Pale blue witch-light blossomed and suddenly I could see. The arms holding me lost their thorns and gashes and became the arms of a man – Jack's arms – and I realised he was the weight pinning me down.

Will's shade was gone, the trees and solid path I'd seen behind him no more. I was lying at the top of a steep, muddy slope ending in powerfully churning water. Foam swirled at the base of boulders, crashing over the rocks and racing away with the current. Oddly, the roar in my ears was even louder, as if being able to see the rush of water pounding into the river from a waterfall far above it made everything real.

Two of the mer bobbed to the surface, the witch-light reflecting off water-beaded aubergine hair and dusky blue skin. Finger bones were tangled in their hair and necklaces of bone and shell hung around their necks. Amber eyes glinted in Bert's witch-light, angry at being denied easy prey.

The larger of the pair hissed and rose higher out of the water, row after row of needle-sharp teeth filling its maw, until Bert flung a shower of sparks towards them, fragments of fire and glow that rained down on the smaller mer's head. The larger mer hissed again, then pulled the smaller one under the surface.

Another spell; another trap, and using bait Maddie knew I couldn't resist. I began to shake, hurting all over, each breath burning my lungs and I started sobbing, which hurt worse, but I couldn't seem to stop.

Jack's weight shifted off my back, but he didn't let go, instead easing me up so that I was leaning against him. He kept one arm looped around my shoulders and rested his chin on the top of my head.

Relief filled Bert's voice. 'Aww, don't cry now. It's all right, little one, we've got you and you're safe with Uncle Bert. All will be well just as soon as we get you back to the wagon and tend to your wounds.'

Julian slunk up, belly to the ground, nudging my arm with his nose, begging to have his ears scratched. Jack patted the hound. Still breathless from running after me, he said, 'You're a good dog, Julian. I'd never have been able to follow her without you showing the way.'

'Time enough for that later, Jack. Let's get her back to the wagon.' Bert got a hand under my arm and with Jack, pulled me to my feet.

Lack of breath was all that kept me from screaming with blinding pain. One foot was badly cut across the heel and the muscles in my legs hurt nearly as bad. Only Jack's strong arms stopped me from falling when my knees buckled, but it was a near thing.

'Bloody sweet Jesus, I'm a right damn fool at times. Your foot is bleeding.' Jack picked me up, lifting me as easily as if I were no bigger than Kate. 'She's shaking something fierce, Bert. Can you pull a cloak or blanket out of that sleeve of yours to keep her warm?'

The Fae Lord conjured a soft wool cloak from the air and with Jack's help, wrapped me up tight. Some of the shivering eased away, but the chill in my bones was more than damp and cold air. All Will's shade needed to do was call and I'd follow him against all sense, even into the arms of the mer. He'd never have wanted that, nor wanted my need for him turned so fiercely against me. How Maddie knew, I couldn't begin to guess, but she'd left me no choice. I'd have to send Will's ghost away.

I buried my face in Jack's shoulder and fought to stop weeping. Pain, loss and fear held me tight.

Bert brushed a hand over my hair; his touch light as an Air sprite. 'We'll travel back a quicker way, Jack. No matter what you think you see, stay near and trust me. I'll keep track of the dog.'

'Lead the way. I'll keep up.' He whispered in my ear, 'Hold fast, Marian. You're safe with me.'

I burrowed deeper into the cloak, afraid that trying to speak would undo me completely. Whatever way Bert led us, Underhill or along Fae roads, I didn't want to see what might step from the shadows – just the thought of Will's shade beckoning me to join him in death set me to shuddering again.

Bert began to sing, the words drifting away before I caught the sense of them. Power held us tight, not leaving a gap for anything else to creep in; the song was all there was, cradling me as tenderly as Jack's arms and allowing me to let go of fear. I might have slept, though I remember nothing more than being safe and warm.

I opened my eyes to see the wagon canopy rippling over my head. Bert's amber and honey-gold wards were glowing softly, the glyphs hanging high in the air over the wagon warning anyone meaning us harm to turn aside. More wards were drawn on the uprights, edging the silk canopy overhead and the bottoms of kettles and pots. And now there were runes for healing, to bring peace and ease heartache, shining green on the sides of the wagon.

The chests were gone, the wagon-bed filled to bursting instead with the living. Julian slept tight against me on one side; Bridget was a ball of warmth on the other. The vixen whimpered and twitched in her sleep, lost in dreams of chasing down prey or the rough and tumble of playing with litter-mates. I touched her and she settled. Settling again wasn't as easy for me.

Jack slept on his side, blocking the open end of the wagon

with his body. He'd run hard to catch me and carried me back when I couldn't walk on my own. Now exhaustion lined his face. I knew those marks were my fault, all of them: each tiny crease and shadow under his eyes another shard of guilt laid at my feet. The true wonder was that I hadn't hurt him badly while forcing him away with magic and will. For that, I thanked the stars.

Wind tugged at the canopy, carrying the smell of burning herbs – thyme for courage, sage for strength and rosemary for faithfulness – overlaid with wood-smoke and damp earth. An owl called from deep in the trees, paused and called again, seeking an answer, hoping not to be alone in the dark. Bert's pipes echoed the owl's call, his melodies filling the quiet night.

My eyes grew heavy, all my worries falling away for the moment. I wasn't alone. If I called, someone would answer.

I woke sore and stiff, scratched everywhere and bruised in still more places. Jack fared little better. He'd had the advantage of boots and a leather tunic but sharp thorns and grasping branches had found skin nonetheless, and I'd hurt him more than he'd let on the night before. In his efforts to stop me, he'd landed badly, twisting one knee, and the side of his face was bruised purple, his eye swollen almost shut. The pain he couldn't quite hide filled me with regret.

Bert insisted I couldn't leave Cassie's gift behind, so Jack limped off with Julian and Bridget to search for where I'd discarded the blue woollen gown, dog and vixen following my scent without hesitation, leading him past the grazing horses and into the trees.

Robin stayed silently out of the way, fetching water and laying the fire with no complaint or need to be asked. I'd no idea what he'd seen, or where he was while Will's shade was leading me to the river, but the night had sobered him, that much was clear.

Bert's red-topped chest produced jars of salve this morning, as well as cheese and bread. He clucked his tongue like an old gram while smoothing it on my heel. 'Chucking your boots in the pond before chasing phantoms? A poor choice, Marian. You've been hurt beyond my power to heal with a touch. Still, you should be able to walk in a day or so if you take care.'

I pulled the warm cloak tight around me, doing my best not to flinch at the cold, sharp sting of the salve, but numbness started setting in once it had seeped into my skin. 'Truly, I can't remember taking my boots off, or throwing them into the pond – I know I still had them on when I fell asleep.'

He cocked his head to the side, studying me with the bird-bright stare that always left me thinking I'd no secrets. 'Tell me what you do remember. We need to puzzle out how I saw all your wards firmly in place when I returned, but still the Demisang found a way to bend you to her will.'

I tried not to show how much that frightened me and ran through my actions out loud. 'We had plenty of wood to last us until the morning, and in any case, you and Bridget come and go as you please regardless of my wards. But I set the wards after supper, as usual. Jack and Robin both fell asleep before me, but not by much, I don't think.'

I shivered, my trembling having little to do with the chill wind or the mist hugging the ground. 'I woke to the sound of Will calling for help – I didn't stop to think, or take time to pull off my boots; I just ran. The panicked need to find him – to save him – is all I remember, aside from slipping on wet grass in my bare feet – but I still don't know how I lost my boots . . .'

Bert frowned and went back to rubbing salve on my legs. 'Do me a service, sweet child. Stay where you are until I give you leave to come out of the wagon. Not that you'd be able to hobble far. Even the Archer would find you easy to catch. But I'd feel more at ease if you don't move.'

'You think she hid something here – a charm?' I looked at the rocks and the grassy meadow, trying so hard not to be afraid. For the life of me, I couldn't see how Maddie had managed to lay this trap for us – and that it wasn't for the first time was what was turning me cold.

The jars disappeared and with a wink, Bert pulled from his sleeve a set of pipes I hadn't seen before. These were beautiful, made of silver etched with leaves and vines which caught the light, sending silvery glints dancing across the front of his tunic. 'Try not to guess all the answers ahead. You'll take all the sport out of it for Old Uncle Bert.'

Robin's back stiffened the instant Bert began to play. He left off stropping his knife, looking not afraid, but wary and watchful, as if expecting the Fae Lord to summon serpents and monsters, but he surprised me by staying in his spot by the fire. I wondered if he recognised the pipes for what they were – after all, seven years Underhill could teach a man many things.

Bert pranced around the camp, playing the fool. I didn't know if he was aiming to make me smile or annoy Robin; he managed both. He sent the notes piling atop each other, sad and seeking one instant, joyful as a burbling stream the next, with hints of calling and summoning weaving and twisting through the melody as well. I found it difficult to keep my place inside the wagon as he'd asked – had it not been for the wards taking the brunt of the spell, I had little doubt I'd have been skipping along behind him.

A swarm of butterfly-bright sprites swept out of the woodlands, landing in his hair and perching on his shoulders, with more following in his wake, until Bert was trailing rainbows. Wings beat in time with the music as many rose in a spiral to dance above his head before settling again.

Some of the sprites broke away from the swarm to alight in my hair and hover close to my face. Tiny hands reached out to touch me, a few of the boldest even gifting me with soft kisses. I saw them through a haze of tears, a jewel-coloured blur moving so fast and so near they made me dizzy. Closing my eyes didn't lessen the wonder, nor the certainty that this feeling must be what Tuck meant by being blessed.

The little Fae were light as air itself and made no noise, but I knew when they left me. I opened my eyes to find them split into two shimmering clouds, one circling above the stack of firewood near Robin while the other shot off to the tumble of rock near the spring. They didn't settle, but they pointed the way.

Bert's tune changed, became softer, a lover saying a sad farewell. The small Fae came together, circled him once, twice, thrice, then streaked back into the trees. He slipped the pipe back into his sleeve, then walked over and kicked the pile of firewood apart, sending branches scattering everywhere, a few smaller pieces coming to rest at Robin's feet. Bert crouched down, frowning at what he'd found.

At first glance I couldn't make sense of the bundle of tattered rags lying there. 'What is it?'

'A pair of rag dolls.' He turned his body, keeping whatever he was holding from my sight. 'My guess is they're meant to look like you and your Will. They must be made of things that belonged to you both or the spell wouldn't be this strong. How she came by them is a question for later. Destroying this comes first.'

Bert took the charm to the fire, still carefully holding the dolls where I couldn't see them – and just as well he took extra care, for even safe inside his wards I could feel the tug of the foul thing, like a call to find the missing part of me. Singing softly, he dropped the poppets in the fire, flames flared as the figures caught, hissing and spitting, and smoke curled towards the sky. The stench was enough to make me gag.

Finally, Robin moved, scrambling back from the fire, staring at the cloth crumbling to ash, devoured by a sickly green flame. His hands trembled, as if one of the demons he feared so much watched him from the embers.

'Did you carry this with you, Archer?' Bert's voice coaxed Robin to speak, a patient father trying to get a child to tell secrets they shouldn't be keeping. 'Carrying Marian's death to her in your bundle of sticks isn't the part I saw you playing.'

'No! No – I've never seen that . . . that *thing* before.' Robin covered his face and sucked in a breath. 'No matter our differences, I've never wanted Marian dead. My soul is burdened with enough sin. I wouldn't add to my crimes, not willingly.'

I believed him, but the look Bert gave him made it plain he thought Robin a liar. The Fae Lord paced the distance to the rocks in grim silence, almost as if he knew what he'd find before he looked. I feared I knew too: the arrangement of rocks and water was almost twin to the place where Ethan died, although I hadn't noticed the likeness before now.

Spells break in different ways. Some fade like mist burning away when the sun climbs the sky, or crumble, whisper-quiet.

Other weavings come apart wailing like a new-born babe. Some are set as a hunter leaves snares, hidden and waiting to capture anyone who looks too close or tries to unmake them. It's not a spell that takes great craft; only a touch of skill for storing power in stone and earth and no care for who you might hurt.

Robin's daughter Maddie was long past caring who she hurt, if she ever had. I hoped Bert remembered that. Even the near-immortal Fae could die if the injury was great enough.

Bert stopped a few paces away from the rocks, looking to either side, then back at Robin. 'The wagon is a safer place to stand, Archer. Wait with Marian while I finish this.'

'No, I'm not getting inside your trice-cursed wagon.' Robin set his feet and crossed his arms over his chest. 'If you want me to move you'll have to force me.' His lip curled. 'You've had enough practise.'

'Given a choice, you always make the wrong one. Suit yourself.' He scowled and scraped the grass with the toe of his boot. The sharp crack of the spell sundering was loud enough to make my ears ring. Power lashed out at the Fae Lord, a viper striking from cover, making him stagger, then he fell, landing hard on his back, so motionless and quiet I wasn't sure he still breathed.

At last he moaned and rolled onto his stomach. I slithered off the back of the wagon, forgetting everything but the need to get to him, but my legs wouldn't hold me and the pain of my cut heel made it clear I'd not manage alone.

'Robin, help me!'

Robin turned to me, owl-eyed and staring, as if he needed to work out what I'd said. Maddie's spell had been aimed at Bert, or at me if I stumbled over it first, but it wasn't a surprise that being in the path of that much magic had left Robin dazed.

'Did you hear me, Robin?' I wrapped will and a touch of obedience around the words. 'I can't get to Bert on my own. I need your help.'

'I . . . I hear you.' He shook his head. The look of confusion left his face and he took my arm to help me hobble to Bert.

Power thrummed and crackled over the Fae Lord's skin, numbing my fingers when I touched him, but he was alive and breathing, his heartbeat strong and steady. Relief brought tears to my eyes. I couldn't say when he'd wake, only that he would.

'Is he dead?' Robin kept back, unwilling to come too near. He watched over my shoulder, raking his fingers through his hair again and again, nervous and fidgety.

Doubt whispered I should be careful of Robin, for all I'd known him once, known his heart as I knew my own. But he'd been gone from my life more than twelve years and that made him a stranger. I was able to believe almost anything of him now, even things that twisted my stomach.

'No, he's not dead. Not near dead.' I turned and looked him in the eye, searching for a spark of innocence, badly wanting to put those fears at least to rest. 'The wards on the wagon are still standing and strong. I'm hoping if we get him up inside he'll wake faster.'

He closed his eyes, but not before I caught a glimpse of fear, a kind of unreasoned panic, akin to a cornered animal, dangerous, looking for a way to break free. I silently gathered will and what power I could reach, ready to defend myself and Bert.

Robin groped for his cross, sighing as his fingers closed over the smooth wood. Holding the artefact calmed him and after a moment or two, he said, 'I can't shift him on my own, Marian, and you can't help. Jack will be back soon. The two of us should be able to manage him.' His fingers tightened around the cross. 'Maybe he'll wake before we have to try.'

'He might. I've no way of knowing.' I wove will and a scrap of power into a passing breeze and sent out a calling to Bridget and the dog. Jack would know something was wrong when they started herding him back towards the camp.

Robin went back to stropping his knife beside the fire as if nothing had happened. The firewood he'd stacked so carefully was scattered across the ground and green flame still flared in the embers, but he ignored it all. He'd swung from fear to calm in a breath and I couldn't find the sense in either. The strangeness of it all fed my growing unease, for I knew I couldn't lay the blame for the changes in Robin on faith in his God.

Staying wary as I waited for Jack to come back was all I could do for the moment.

Jack came back at a limping run, Julian leading the way and Bridget trotting at his side. He kept one hand on the blue wool gown slung over his shoulder to keep it from sliding off.

As soon as they caught sight of me, Julian and Bridget streaked towards the camp and immediately put themselves between me and Robin, their ears up, watching his every move. He ignored the dog and the vixen as he had everything else, not even greeting Jack until he'd been spoken to.

Jack and I managed to roll Bert onto a blanket, then with Robin's reluctant help, heaved him into the wagon. As I'd hoped, once inside the wards, the Fae Lord sighed and relaxed, the tension bleeding out of his muscles as I watched. The crackle of magic on his skin lessened, but sunset neared and he slept on.

I sent Bridget out to hunt down supper for us, for I wasn't

sure I trusted Robin out of my sight. Jack gathered the scattered firewood and quickly found a good deal more at the edge of the trees. Julian lay at the open end of the wagon, head on his paws, watching Robin.

The blue woollen gown was as clean and dry when Jack handed it back to me as if it had just come straight from Cassie's hand. Much as I longed to bathe before getting dressed, I knew I'd have to wait, but my pain faded once I put it on, healer's magic in the weave working as it touched my skin. That it stopped the wind chilling me to the bone was another blessing.

Bert's red-topped chest provided turnips and onions, as I'd expected, and a treat: a basket brim-full of bilberries. Robin silently ate his share before making his bed as far from the wagon as possible.

After supper Jack rooted through the rest of the chests piled up around the wagon, looking for salves and herbs, anything we might use to dress wounds and start them healing. Strips of clean linen he found in plenty, and among the dried herbs I recognised Saint John's wort by the scent. Mixed with honey, it was good for healing wounds and stopping them from turning sour, just what was needed.

Jack lifted me onto the back of the wagon and did his best to tend my wounded foot, washing the heel clean before smearing the paste on the cut. He wrapped a strip of linen snugly around it and tied it off. 'If that's too tight, say so now,' he said.

'No, not too tight. Thank you.' I put my back against the side of the wagon, suddenly bone-weary and fighting sleep. Julian and Bridget had curled up at the front, a hand-span from Bert's head. After a moment I said quietly, 'I've another favour to ask of you – to help me sleep. Stay in the wagon with me tonight?'

He nodded, then turned away, staring towards the pond where tiny waves were skittering across the water, running in front of the stiff breeze to lap at the stony bank on the far side. The ripples stirred the rising moon's reflection, keeping it from lying still and serene.

'I'd hope you know there's no need to remind me I'm bound to your service, Marian.' He rubbed a finger along the side of his nose, voice and expression serious and solemn. 'I've wondered when you'd get around to asking me to spend the night with you . . . and now you have. This isn't the place I'd pick, but we'll make do.'

I gaped at him, unable to believe he'd ever say such a thing. My voice breaking, I choked out, 'No . . . *no!* That's not what I meant . . . How could you *say* that?'

His face fell. 'Oh sweet Christ – I'm sorry, Marian, I didn't mean to hurt you. I'm such a bloody idiot. You're not finished mourning Will and me saying that – I'm sorry – you've every right to hate me.'

Every bruise and cut and scrape I'd taken was aching and each moment that passed without Bert waking worried me more. About the only thing that didn't make me want to cry was the thought of pulling my cloak over my head and sleeping for days.

'Oh stars, Jack, I don't hate you – but don't tease, please. I'm too tired – and in any case, it's not that simple.'

'I can't say I was teasing, not exactly, but we'll leave it there for now.' He brushed a finger down my cheek, the touch light and making me shiver. 'Things are never simple, Marian, and I am truly sorry. Tell me what you need me to do and I'll try my best.'

My heart was racing, but I looked away. I couldn't think about this now.

Robin was still wrapped in his cloak, his face turned away from the fire, towards the trees. Whether he pretended or truly slept, I could only guess. Lowering my voice, I told Jack all that happened, how Bert had been hurt, while he was off hunting for lost gowns.

As I spoke, Jack's expression grew grim. 'I wouldn't trust Locksley, not for a moment – I have a hard time believing he knew nothing of charms in the firewood or traps hidden in the rocks. It was his daughter who offered you up to the mer like a pig on a spit. We must be especially cautious until Bert is himself again and able to sort out this mess.'

He gathered our cloaks before hopping into the wagon and helping me settle nearer the front. The wards closed, sealing out harm. With Bridget's fur warm against my cheek and Jack's reassuring bulk at my feet, sleep pulled me under, plunging me into dreams as soon as I shut my eyes.

I dreamed of a pretty young Demisang with her mother's eyes and a cruel smile. Her hand rested on a lover's knot tied tight around Jack's sleeve.

Maddie looked at me and laughed.

Chapter 14

. . . I send the ghosts on their way,
and braid ribbons of memory into my hair . . .

ANON

Julian woke me not long after dawn, baying as if we were beset by raiders from the North. I sat up in time to see Bridget fading into the shadows under the rowans at the edge of the meadow. The dog, frantic to go after her, was lunging against the rope tethering him to the wagon's wheel.

Other than the horses grazing in the meadow, the camp was empty. The fire was cold, even the embers dead, with not the smallest hint of smoke curling skywards.

'Your Warrior hunts for breakfast, witchling.' Bert sat cross-legged against the side of the wagon bed, his face drawn. 'My supplies grow thin and I don't have the strength to call up more. The dog was supposed to act as our guard, not crow in the dawn like an overgrown cock.'

'He's not my Warrior, sly Lord. Giving him the name won't make it true.'

'So you've said before.' He played with his coins, rolling them across his knuckles and making them vanish into his palm. 'The Archer left some time during the night, but I feel no need to hurry or drag him back. My sight tells me that we'll catch him in Sheffield and that he'll know how to find the Demisang. The right time to catch all our cowards is almost upon us.'

I made myself comfortable leaning against the wagon side and watched Bert do his coin tricks. I couldn't deny the relief I felt knowing Robin was gone: a strange thing to feel, but there it was, filling my heart to bursting, and made even stronger by seeing Bert awake.

'We might be better off with Robin gone,' I said. 'He's scared witless one moment and carrying on as if nothing in the world bothers him the next. I don't know what to make of him.'

Bert didn't answer right off. Birdsong echoed in the clearing, the plaintive calls of mothers sitting on nests crying out to missing mates competing with Julian's whining: both sad sounds, out of place on such a bright day.

'Nor do I, Marian,' Bert said. . 'Robin is a question and a puzzle I've thought on without finding answers. The Archer abandoned my sister rather than face what their daughter had done and tried to hide behind his God.' He sat quietly for once, sleight-of-hand tricks put aside. 'Rather than tell you the truth or honour his marriage vows, he abandoned you in turn. Mayhap what he fears is his own heart.'

I couldn't say he was wrong, nor could I think of another answer. A world of misery lay at Robin's feet. 'It would be handy if your sight told you where Ma – well, where the Demisang is hiding, and what trouble she's thinking up. I'm weary of running after her and worrying about Kate and Robbie.'

He pulled five small silver balls from his sleeve and juggled them slowly. Sunbeams sought them out, the glitter and flash dazzling my eyes. 'My sight is a sword turned upon me, fair Marian, and if I reach wrong, the edges will cut me to ribbons. One edge shows me things I'd rather not see and the other not nearly enough of what I need to know. If I had a way to find the Demisang with confidence, I'd end things now, today.'

'End them how?' I asked.

The silver balls vanished. Aelfgifu's fan and a well-loved poppet took their place.

'There was a time I'd have taken the Demisang Underhill to live in my sister's court. The Lady of the Fae has the power to bind her own blood, a power no one else can wield. Robin's daughter could have lived out her days there and maybe found peace of a sort. That time is over.' Poppet and fan dropped to the wagon-bed and Bert slumped back, his eyes closed. 'I never believed she'd do so much harm in the world of mortals, nor that her spirit was so twisted she'd seek my death as well. There's only one end to this, Marian.'

I folded shaking hands in my lap. Speaking openly of killing Aelfgifu and Robin's child was making me feel ill, while the need to keep my own children alive was doing nothing to ease the sick feeling roiling in my middle.

Cassie told me I'd always have a choice. I'd just been forced to make mine. 'So we go on to Sheffield in our guise of pedlars, collecting Robin on the way.'

'The role of pedlar is an easy one to play. People see the wagon and clanging pots and our work is done. In truth, we've no need to pretend now. She knows where we are and that we're hunting her.' He opened his eyes and ran a hand through his hair, the weary gesture strangely human for one of the Fae. 'I'd give much to learn how the Demisang sets her snares ahead.'

I smiled, teasing myself as much as Bert. 'Knowing we'll blunder into them?'

A hint of the trickster shone in his eyes again, lifting more worry off my shoulders. 'You may blunder in unaware, sweet witch. I walk up boldly and stick my head in to keep my foot company.'

Julian's ears were up, his tail thumping the ground, just as I heard Jack's whistle, echoing the birds as he walked, exactly the way Bert did with his pipes.

'Your Warrior returns.' He stood, long limbs unfolding gracefully as a flower reaching for the sun. 'Sit quietly and let us wait on you. We'll bring you food as soon as it's ready.'

My fingers bunched in my skirts, clinging tight with frustration. 'Jack's not my Warrior,' I said. 'Meg's, maybe, but not mine.'

Bert stood over me, dark eyes magpie-bright. 'Is he not? Jack's willing to do battle for you and guards you in your sleep. What would you have me call him, Marian?'

I searched his face, at a loss. 'I don't know.'

'Then you should think about it and decide.' He leapt off the back of the wagon, and if the Fae Lord was a bit less steady than usual, I pretended not to take notice. Pipes appeared in his hand and with a liquid trill, he rekindled the fire.

Jack waved as I turned to watch him, grinning as he held up two pheasants in his other hand. I waved back, feeling a traitor at the unexpected lightness in my heart. My children were still in danger: I needed to finish what I'd started, make sure Kate and Robbie wouldn't spend the rest of their days fearing the

Demisang. There was no thought, no room, for anything else until then.

And Will's ghost haunted me still, shimmering in the corner of my eye, watching everything I did. I'd barely started grieving for him; I'd not had nearly enough time to grow used to his loss.

Bert stood next to the wagon. He rested a hand on my shoulder. 'It's not disloyal to live and keep on living, Marian. You learned that once but I'm told it's a lesson learned anew each time there's need.'

I swiped a hand over my eyes. 'And you've never had the need?'

'The Folk carry no ghosts to trouble them, sweet child,' he said. 'Our lives are overlong for regrets.'

He reached into his sleeve. I expected his pipes to appear, so the circlet of flowers he set on my head was a surprise – a pretty bauble to distract me, or so he hoped. He smiled, bright as a courtier's greeting. 'I must aid your Warrior if you're to be fed before nightfall. Food will speed your healing as fast as my craft.'

His step was near jaunty as ever, the tune he whistled designed to make toes tap. The master of masks wrapped himself in good cheer and carefree airs.

I didn't believe him. Not a whit.

We rested and healed four days and a night, warrior, witch and Fae trickster. Bruises faded under the Fae Lord's care, Jack's limp lessened and aided by the salves Bert pulled from his chest and the tunes he piped, my foot became less tender too. Without his magic, I knew I wouldn't have been able to walk for many weeks.

Bert needed that time to recover as much as we humans. He'd never admit how badly Maddie had hurt him, but that didn't mean it wasn't true. The Demisang had dug a hollow in his soul with her spell, draining away a portion of Bert's life and magic – a lesser Fae Lord, one with fewer scars and not as much stored power, would have died: the dark shadows under his eyes were proof of that.

We set on our way before dawn. Indigo, yellow and pink clouds streaked the sky, their colours fading as the light grew stronger. The air warmed early in the day, smelling of dust and sap oozing from split bark, and by mid-morning the meadow flowers were drooping in the sun. I was grateful the narrow road we followed was shaded.

Jack kept a sharp eye on the woods, his bow lying across his lap. The chance of Maddie and her Fae lover attacking us directly was slim, but he wasn't going to take the chance. Spells and traps weren't the only way to do us harm – firedrakes or even wolves might kill the horses if she sent them after us.

The clatter and bang of kettles was mercifully silenced now that Bert didn't have Robin to pester; instead, birdsong and the creak of the wagon wheels sang us down the road, accompanied by the trill of Bert's pipes. Bridget and the dog ranged ahead, flushing birds from cover. From time to time one of the lesser Fae ran out of a bush, dancing in the road until they'd tempted Julian into a loud, baying chase. Bridget followed, yipping at his heels. Fox and dog both thought tearing down the road after a leering goblin or brouny was a game, nothing more. They'd tire of playing soon enough.

Jack's long legs near spanned the width of the wagon bed as he unfolded them, missing only by the width of my hand or less. He glanced at the wagon seat where Bert lay sleeping, curled tight as a kitten on the hearth, while the horses found their own way.

'Is Bert all right? Never thought I'd find myself fretting over one of the Fae, but he's got me worried.'

'He says he's fine and just needs some rest,' I said. 'All I can do is trust his word.'

Jack rubbed his sore knee, his smile small, sheepish. 'We're a bit battered to be taking on rogue Demisang and Fae Lords, aren't we? I'd feel better if one of us weren't limping into battle.'

'I'll be ready when the time comes, Jack.' Bert blinked one eye open and peered at us. 'Rest will restore me, never fear. Watch the road, or entertain Marian with stories of the great battles you've fought, but don't concern yourself with me.' An instant later came a soft snore, a sign the Fae trickster truly slept this time.

Many warriors spent all their time bragging of their might in battle, but Jack hadn't said more than a word or two about the Crusades. Now I was curious. 'I'd love to hear your stories,' I said. 'Did you ever meet King Richard?'

Jack wiped a hand over his mouth and sighed. 'There weren't any great battles or any kind of glory in what they made us do – at least, I wouldn't call cutting the throats of prisoners glorious. I'll tell the story if you like, but it isn't pretty and ends badly. I deserted Richard's Crusade as soon as I could. No one took notice of having one less bowman trailing behind.'

Bert flipped to his back and flung an arm over his eyes, muttering like one deep in a nightmare, 'A king with a lion's stony heart . . . please . . . please, my children . . .'

The Fae Lord never set a foot down without having a reason, so no doubt he'd meant to lead me down this path, but nonetheless I was angry that I'd so willingly put my neck in the noose and in the process, likely hurt Jack. But there was no going back to fix that, not now.

Jack sat quietly, waiting for me to judge. I looked him in the eye, trying to imagine being forced to take a life, watching someone dying under your hand. 'Forgive me, Jack. I had no idea. I thought Bert was joking, so I went along. I don't have the right to ask you to tell stories you don't wish to tell. Your life is your own business.'

'No need to ask forgiveness. To be honest, I'm glad it's out in the open.' His eyes were full of memories and sorrow. 'It's a pitiful excuse for a friend who keeps such things secret. I mean to do better than that; I wouldn't have this hanging between us.'

Will was a friend from the first. Robin had been a lover but never a friend. I looked away, unable to hold any other thought, but when I looked up, Jack's face was stricken, lost. He expected me to hate him before we were done talking.

'Tell me the rest of the story, Jack.' I smiled. 'We'll sort it out.'

'You ever hear tell of a town called Pocklington?' he asked.

I shook my head.

'The town sits right at the foot of the hills up in the East Riding. The land between the town proper and the earl's keep doesn't do for farming – the ground's too full of chalk and rocks for a man to plough. But it's near-perfect sheep country and the earl made a right tidy living selling the wool. I was the earl's Sergeant of the Guard for his household.'

The vixen barked sharply, a warning call, I twisted around to see what was wrong and Jack stopped talking and sitting taller, craned his neck to look for whatever the trouble might be. A pair of lobs were teasing Julian from the safety of a tree, sitting just high enough that the dog's frantic leaps fell short.

Jack whistled for Julian, calling him away, and although he whined, repeatedly looking over his shoulder at the lobs, the dog trotted over to run down the centre of the road next to Bridget. I settled into my place again to coax the rest of the story from Jack. 'Why did this earl let you take the cross to follow Richard?'

He grimaced. 'The earl *made* me take the cross, Marian. All the lords from York to the sea were pledged to give the king men, and money to pay for his Crusade. The cardinal who delivered the decree told the earl adding another hundred men on top of what he owed was his tithe and duty to the Church.' I didn't think he was aware he was rubbing his hands over his knees, again and again. 'So off I went, with all the rest. We had a hard enough time of it at sea, but once we landed things grew worse. King Richard had captured a walled city three days' march away. We got there to find the rest of the army lined up in front of those walls. I was one of those ordered to march Richard's prisoners to a nearby hill – there were *thousands* of captives, Marian, both old and young men. When we got to the top of the hill, Richard ordered us to kill them all.'

In every corner of England, Richard was spoken of as a hero and a great man, fighting for a holy cause. There was nothing great or holy about murdering helpless people. 'Mother of us all . . . *why?*'

'The sultan failed to pay their ransom. Men who'd been there a long time said Richard got tired of waiting.' Jack sighed and ran a hand through his hair. 'But still, being told God wanted me to murder men tied hand and foot? That stripped away what faith I had. Don't believe the Moors can't speak English: men begged me, *In the name of Allah, spare me so I can see my children grow.* I heard those voices in my sleep long after coming home. The priest who took my confession afterwards said I'd done nothing wrong. He truly believed every word he said. I never did.'

He fell silent, lost in remembering.

'I'd been married for a few years. Allie was a smart woman with a temper hot enough to scorch the hide off a bull. Not many thought her pretty – she was a tall, strong woman – but to me she was beautiful. We had a boy, Simon.' Jack's mouth twisted, the words bitter-tasting. 'The lord's son and heir, Edwin, was Captain of the Manor Guard and not likely to march off to Jerusalem. He'd promised to look after Allie and my boy for me. I believed him.'

Dread coiled in my belly, for I knew that flinch as memory hit, that note of bone-deep grief behind calm words.

'What happened to your wife and son?'

'Depends on who you ask. It took us half a year to get to the Holy Land and longer still for me to work my way home again.' He looked up to watch a huge flock of starlings wheeling across a patch of open sky, his shoulders tense. 'The old earl was dead, Edwin lord in his place. He told me a tale, of raiders coming down from the North in midwinter, making off with the sheep and killing anyone who crossed their path. That's how he said Allie and my boy died.'

Bert came awake, sitting up suddenly and twisting on the wagon seat to face us. Tear tracks painted his face, sorrow pulling down the corners of his mouth. The Fae didn't grieve, he'd told me as much, and other sight showed me he was wearing a mask, but in that moment I was hard-pressed to tell flesh from glamour.

'Others told you a different story, Jack: one that tore your heart.' Bert's mask altered, becoming the face of a man I'd never seen before: one puffed up with pride, a face which had never known sorrow or want. 'Who did you believe?'

Jack's fist came down hard on the wagon bed, the sound sharp and full of rage, startling the horses and causing them to toss their heads and dance nervously in harness. With a wave of the Fae Lord's hand, they settled.

'You know the truth, Bert, and don't pretend you don't. Edwin was an earl, so no one was allowed to tell him he was wrong. Allie . . . my Allie couldn't stand idle while he beat a kitchen girl for spilling his soup. He killed her for that. Simon disappeared that same night. No one could tell me what happened to my son.'

Bert's face shimmered and blurred until it became his own again, weary and near human in sadness. 'You honoured her memory, Warrior. You faced this man with the truth.'

'Lords don't take kindly to truth. I knew Edwin would kill me for daring to speak, but I'd decided to force him to look me in the eye first.' Jack slumped back, not ashamed to wipe tears from his face. 'I didn't count on him letting me live. Edwin wouldn't dirty his hands, not with a man of low station, but he set his men on me. They beat me bloody before dumping me in the forest. Not killing me right away was a far crueller thing at the time.'

My own eyes burned. Sorrow calls to sorrow. 'Oh stars, Jack, I'm sorry.'

He brushed a tear off my cheek. 'Don't grieve for me, Marian. I lost my Allie and Simon more than eight years ago. I'll never forget them, nor how they died, but I won't let the memory haunt the rest of my days. I've no regrets about finding my way back to living.'

In the echo of Bert's words, almost as if I'd summoned him, Will's shade appeared between us, his smiling face blurred and wavering through a fog of tears.

'Sweet Jesus, Marian.' His gift of sight letting him see Will, Jack edged away. He knew better than to let a ghost touch him, opening the way inside. 'Has another of the Demisang's victims come looking to you for help in moving on?'

'No, Will's been here all along.' I wrapped my arms across my chest, fighting not to reach for a phantom.

Will smiled, the smile I'd lived for, and finally I understood.

The Demisang had found her way inside my wards through Will's shade, using his ghost to tangle me in spells without ever coming near me. Bert had known, yet he'd never said a word but waited for me to trip over the truth on my own.

'Go away, Will. Move on.' Putting power and belief behind the words was almost more than I could manage. Grief would choke me, I was sure of that, and equally certain that I'd never draw another breath without it catching on a sob. 'Nothing holds you here, Will Scarlet, not love nor memory nor need. Seek the next life and live again.'

I'd sent many ghosts on their way since leaving home, sad, weary work, and watching Will's ghost slowly falling to pieces, I wished nothing more than to never be forced to do it again. The edges tattered, then floated away until he was nothing more than ashes blown by the wind. Watching was the hardest thing I'd yet done, but I needed to make my peace with his going.

Bert clambered down from the driving seat, sure-footed as a goat, ignoring the jolt of wheels in deep ruts and the rocking of the wagon. He reached for my hand, but I batted him away. His serious expression didn't fool me, nor did it make me feel kindly towards him. I just saw another mask, one that hid how well-pleased he was, how clever he thought himself.

'Leave me be!' I pushed back against the wagon side, for all there was scant distance between us. My throat had closed, my voice was tight and raw and I couldn't stop sniffling. 'I'm less than fond of you at the moment, Bert. Touch me and . . . and . . . and I'm not sure what I'd do.'

Jack climbed up to the wagon seat, smart enough to stay silent, though I could see the sympathy on his face. He had said his own good-byes, sent his own ghosts on their way.

Bert rocked back on his heels, all Fae Lord again, studying me as if I'd sprouted horns and a forked tongue. 'What have I done to anger you so, Marian?'

'You tricked me again – don't even try to say it isn't so.' Crying and not being able to stop was making me mad enough to spit. I crossed my arms and held myself tightly to keep from lashing out at him. 'I'm tired of being pushed and pulled along the long twisted path just so I end up where you think I need be. I'm no child, needing trickery to swallow a bitter draught. Just tell me what I need to know, Bert.'

'No, not a child. Not near a child.' His hands rested on his thighs, long, graceful fingers spread wide. No magic or compulsion scented the air, but his gaze pinned me so that I couldn't look away. 'Answer me this, little witch. If I'd spoken plainly, told you from the start how the Demisang was using his shade to bind you, would the pain of sending Will on be any less?'

'No, it wouldn't hurt any less.' I shook my head, for all the movement made the pounding worse. 'But doing so would have been my choice, freely made. I'd give a lot to know I had that choice.'

The mask slipped, little by little, the dark circles under his eyes returning and joined now by sagging shoulders and a weary air to the way he held himself. 'Then I beg pardon, Marian. You have my promise: I'll speak when I can. But understand this: much of what my sight shows me can change just by the telling of it. A wrong word, too much revealed, and the path will alter under our feet.'

No guile shone in his eyes, his masks for once put aside in favour of truth. I looked at Jack, who shrugged; I took his faint smile to mean he'd no better plan.

'Tell me this, Uncle Bert, if you're able,' I said. 'Where has Robin gone off to?'

He brightened and offered me a nosegay of daisies pulled from his sleeve. More baubles. 'That's a riddle I can answer. The Archer is in Sheffield, searching for his daughter. He fancies he can persuade the Demisang to return Underhill, keeping her from doing more harm – and keeping us from harming her.'

Jack leaned over the back of the wagon seat. 'What makes Locksley think he can find her, or that she'd listen to anything he said?'

'Fathers always think their daughters will pay them heed. They forget a daughter will grow until she's no longer a child.' The Fae Lord hopped back onto the seat, sat next to Jack and took up the reins. He whistled sharply and was answered almost immediately by Bridget's yip and the noisy dog's bark as the two of them streaked out of the trees towards us. 'When the Archer finds his winter child he'll be no different.'

'We've chased after her through half the land.' Jack folded his arms, eyeing Bert. 'You make it sound like Locksley can lay hands on her whenever he wants.'

'Oh moon and stars, Jack ... he can!' I cursed myself for a thrice-named fool. 'Mother of us all, I should have thought of this from the beginning. Robin knows her name – her true name, not the nonsense she gave Tuck. He can summon her at need.'

Bert flicked the reins, truly driving the wagon for the first time. The horses moved from their normal plodding walk to a slow trot. He whistled again and this time fox and dog leaped into the back of the wagon and squeezed into a space between two chests. 'It's not that simple, witchling. The Archer has no craft of his own and he thinks magic, even summoning, an offence against his God. It would take a great deal to push him into trying to call her himself.'

'And you're saying he's been pushed?' Jack asked.

'That would be telling, Warrior.' Bert laughed and urged the horses to pick up speed. 'A swift journey will bring us an answer in good time – if fortune is kind, we'll find an answer we trust.'

The wagon jounced along, rattling my teeth and turning Jack's knuckles white where he was gripping the back of the seat. He hooked an arm around the narrow board and held on. At least the pots and kettles swinging over my head were banging together silently now. I braced myself between one of the chests and the side of the wagon, the half-moon handle on the side giving me something to cling to.

'There are swift journeys, Great Lord, and ones that come near to getting us killed . . . it would be a pity if we died on the road after the Demisang failed,' I said.

'I won't let you come to harm, sweet Marian, and there's a need for haste. We're close enough I can taste her scent on my tongue.' He slapped the reins down hard and grinned over his shoulder. 'We've three days' travel ahead and only six days until the next full moon. I'd have the Demisang in hand before that.'

Six days until power rode the light of a silver moon and filled the air to bursting. The Demisang and her Fae Lord would use any power they could find, but to what purpose didn't bear thinking about. She'd killed before when the moon was full and there was nothing to stop her from doing so again.

Nothing but a trickster, a witch and a warrior, a battered, ragtag group, but racing towards battle nonetheless. I held my tongue and held on.

Chapter 15

Will all great Neptune's ocean wash this blood
Clean from my hand?

WILLIAM SHAKESPEARE

The streets of Sheffield were still crowded, even this late in the day. Hand-carts clattered along, pulled by tired farmers who'd walked all day thinking of nothing but getting the best site for the next morning's trade. Wagons piled to the top with cabbages or baskets of beans and onions moved slowly, dodging women with strings of whining children in tow and dogs running underfoot, adding to the general chaos.

If you watched closely, you might think there was a touch of magic in the way people, animals and carts flowed together and came apart without ever tying themselves in knots. The first men settled the land surrounding Sheffield in the days when the Gods still took a hand in what people did. I'd heard tales of towns and hamlets built atop faerie rings and standing stones broken up to cobble the streets. That the dusty stone under our wheels held ancient power, however faded, was easy to believe.

Market didn't end until dusk in any of Sherwood's towns, shopkeepers and traders from the surrounding farms taking full advantage of the long summer days and the good weather. During the two weeks set aside for Sheffield's Summer Fayre, whole families roamed freely and bargained for goods and favours well into the evening. Thick beams set in the ground held oil-soaked torches; they gave off nearly as much smoke as light, but still burned bright enough that people could make their way comfortably around the stalls until closing time.

Bert guided the horses down a tight alley, the walls on either side so close that Jack could stretch out his arms and touch the sides as we passed. The place was a midden, the stench of rotten food, bones and chamber pots turning the air foul. Hobgoblins scrounged through the rubbish alongside the rats, though most of them were missing teeth and looking starved. Some were brave enough to hiss at Bert before running away.

Julian whined to be let free to chase them as they scrambled away from the horses and wagon. Given her own way, Bridget, perched in my lap, bright-eyed and nose twitching, would've run after them as quickly as the dog.

'Don't get any ideas, Bridget. You're staying put.' I tugged the vixen's muzzle around and looked her in the eye. 'People won't take kindly to a fox running loose in the town. You'll be the first accused if a bird or joint comes up missing and I am certain your own little head would be missing next.'

Bridget yipped softly, more a whining child sent to bed and missing all the fun than the hunter she fancied herself. She settled down to sulk, stretching out on my lap with her chin resting on my knee. I ran my fingers through her soft red fur, puzzled by hobgoblins bold enough that they ran the streets in daylight.

Sheffield stank of smoky fires and grease as the sun dipped low, the smell of scorched onions and rancid meat coming from the food stalls strong enough to kill any desire for food. Bert found his way to an empty spot on the south side of the market square. No houses stood here and the wind blowing off the water freshened the air somewhat. The wide swath of dry grass gave way to brown reeds growing along the River Sheaf, which twinkled silver and green in the last of the sunlight.

'This looks as good a spot as any.' Bert left the reins to dangle and hopped down. 'If fortune smiles we'll be on our way before we've had a chance to settle in.'

Jack helped me get my feet under me, holding my arm until we were both sure I wouldn't fall. The wound in my foot had healed, but my legs still wobbled, weak as a new-born fawn. 'Do you have an idea, or a plan to find Robin? I don't fancy walking the entire town hoping to catch sight of him.'

'No need of that. Your Warrior will find him for us.' He stroked the animals' heads. Both dog and vixen yawned wide, curled up together at the front of the wagon and were sound asleep an instant later. 'They won't stir till morning: one less worry for you until we get back. Jack's task is asking after the Archer in the taverns. I'll be doing the same for the Demisang.'

I stood alone, testing my balance. 'And what am I to do, Trickster?'

'Guard your virtue, fair Marian.' Bert clucked me under the chin, much like Tuck did with Kate. 'There are men in a town like this who would steal it away if they could.'

'There are those who'd say I've none to guard.' I smiled. Robin had claimed that very thing many times. Jack frowned and turned away. 'Set me a useful task closer to my talents, Bert.'

'Warding the horses fits your talents. Ward yourself as well while you're about it. The back of my neck prickles with the feel of eyes watching.' If I hadn't been watching as the glamour settled over him, turning his thick, curly dark hair a wispy fog-grey, I'd never have known him. The man before me, his back twisted with age, dressed in merchant's robes rich with embroidery, was a stranger. 'I've cast about searching for the one watching us and if I didn't know better, I'd say I'd imagined it all. But something is frightening the small Fae enough to drive them into the daylight. Best to be careful.'

I sought the reason for Bert's unease, looking towards the water with other sight. The old river slept, lazing between its muddy banks. Brief flashes of colour and dazzle were all I saw, flickers of life given off by fish and river animals. Wagtails and warblers settled in the reeds for the night while quiet flocks of mallard, moorhen and coot floated on the current, heads tucked under their wings to wait for morning.

Nothing spoke of magic strong enough to give the lesser Fae courage enough to walk openly, or to scare them from the shadows – nothing, but the shiver rippling my spine when I turned my back to the river. 'I can feel someone watching too, but I can't say who, or where they're hidden. I'll take care.'

'Two-legged monsters wander after dark in a place like Sheffield.' Jack put a knife in my hand. 'Drunken louts looking for a way to amuse themselves can come close to being as dangerous as anything Fae. At times a blade can serve better than craft, Marian. I'll feel better if you keep this one at hand.'

I thanked him for his care and watched the two of them wander towards the lights and the laughter, Bert with a hand on Jack's shoulder, leaning close to speak. I hefted the knife in my hand. Everything Jack said was true, but I'd try not to let defending myself come down to skill with a blade. I set the knife down.

Power rode the air: the moon was racing towards full, ripe for harvest. I drew the moonlight to me, savouring the feel of magic tingling over my skin until my ears buzzed and the power left me giddy. Pacing a circle around our camp, setting wards on the horses and wagon, took but a moment. Letting go of the magic I'd called took discipline.

Bert's wards were still shimmering with golden fire, out-lining the wagon and canopy. Now mine sprang to life from the boundary I'd paced, arching up in a dome of blue the colour of a winter sky. Those with other sight would see how his gold and my blue flowed together over the wagon, our power merging easily into a joyous rippling green: green, the colour of life, of healing and new growth. From the brief time I'd known Bert, that felt exactly right.

The horses danced in their harness as the protections closed over them, spooked and restless until I soothed them, petting their velvet noses and whispering calm words in their ears. They settled again, but I noticed their ears were still flicking and swiv-elling, listening, as they grazed every blade of grass within reach.

I listened too, but all I could hear was the laughter echoing from the taverns and stalls, getting louder and more raucous as the night wore on and men got deeper into their cups. When I turned to the river, there was silence, but too thick and heavy for a normal summer night. The over-abundance of quiet made me nearly as nervous as the horses.

My wards darkened on the riverside and other sight showed me a shadow in the shape of a woman. She stood almost as tall as Jack, reed-thin, clothed in dripping tatters. The wet cloth clung to the swell of her breasts and the slight curve of her hips. Shells and beads were knotted into her long ice-pale tresses, clattering with each step she took. Though far from the sea, she still smelled of kelp and salt. She touched fingertips to my wards, pulling back sharply as they sparked.

'Forest witch.' Her voice was the sound of waves sliding over sand. 'I've come for my children. Give them to me.'

My gram had taught me about Fae creatures who lurked in slow water and at the mouths of rivers, lying in wait for any who ventured too close. Mothers warned their children away from pools where others had drowned. These creatures earned a new name for each river or opening to the sea, and for the grief they left behind: Grindylow in the north, Peg Powler to the south, Jenny Greenteeth in the east, River Goblin or demon in the west. I didn't have a name for the river hag hunting for a way past my wards, but Grindylow would do.

I stepped closer to the wagon, planning to put Bert's wards between us if she broke through mine, when I caught sight of two of the small Fae I'd seen in the streets, huddled behind one of the wheels. They had been trapped inside my boundaries and were calling for their mother, their squeaking high and grating, and every time they cried, the demon pushed against the boundaries. They weren't hobgoblins after all, but spawn of the river demon.

She must have chosen her hunting grounds poorly, for it looked as if the Grindylow couldn't keep her young fed. They were thin to the point of starving, scraping for food with the rats – I wouldn't have been surprised to learn that she'd lost half the brood.

The small demons hissed, showing rows of teeth, some

already knife-sharp and pushing out the milk teeth. It was a poor bluff, coming from creatures who didn't top my knee, but I gave them room anyway. Their mother was the one who needed watching.

I tried a bluff of my own. 'I didn't take your children, Mother. They wandered in on their own, hungry and looking to steal what they could. My guardian will decide whether to send them back, or make them pay for their theft.'

She paced the edge of my wards, but never too far from the water behind her. I stood easy, my feet planted and arms crossed as if I'd not a care in the world. Pretending to calm was a lie, though: my hands shook each time she laid a palm against the wards and pushed, trying to break through. Sparks flew at her touch, reflected in eyes dark as river mud, and each failure had her hissing in pain and anger.

The gold of Bert's wards had spread across the top and down the walls of shimmering blue I'd built, melting into them until the whole was green as lily-pads. The Grindylow stepped back, eyeing me and the boundary in turn. Small dark shapes slunk out of the reed shadows near the river, moving forward a few paces, then stopping again: her children, driven from hiding by hunger and a need to be near her.

'This was made with High Fae magic, forest witch. You travel with a Lord of the Lady's court.' More of her brood gathered, milling at her feet, tugging at the ragged hem of her gown, their voices like wind keening under the eaves. She shooed them back, careful to stop any of them from touching the wall between us. 'To find one Lord walking openly among men was more than passing strange. To find a second in this place? That speaks of war in the Lady's court.'

'I only know what my guardian tells me.' I shrugged, still pretending to an ease I didn't feel. 'He seeks a young Demisang. If there's to be war over her, he hasn't spoken of it.'

The brood were clamouring for food, their howls growing louder. Some started climbing to perch on her shoulders; others dangled from her skirts while yet more crawled out of the shadows and roiled at her feet. I didn't want to think about how she'd managed to keep this many fed.

'You know more than you say.' The Grindylow picked up one of the smallest of the brood, cradling it in her arms. Panicked and squealing, her spawn struggled to get away. She petted her under-grown child for an instant before snapping its neck and tossing the dead pup away. The rest of the brood deserted her, chasing after the corpse.

'I can smell the lie on you, witch. Who is this Demisang that the Lady set hounds on her trail?'

My stomach twisted, but I wouldn't show fear; she too knew more than she'd said. 'The Lady has need of her. That's enough for the likes of you to know.'

I steeled myself and snatched up one of the small ones hiding behind the wheel. The poor starved thing dangled by an arm, impotently kicking its feet. Power came to my hand easily when called, blue flame and flashes dancing like will-o'-the-wisps in my palm.

'I can see the lie in you as well, demon. Leave now and let me deal with your spawn. I'll show them more mercy than you would, and more mercy than the Fae Lord will show you for sending them to spy for the Demisang.'

She flung herself against the boundary. I heard the sizzle of hair and skin over the howl of pain, smelled the stench of burning flesh over ocean salt. The Grindylow picked herself up and once again tried to force her way through the pulsing green wards.

They held.

She dropped to her knees, panting and shaking. 'No! Give me my children – the Demisang and her Lord are gone.'

'Another lie.' I brought the hand cupping power closer to the squirming water demon child, trying not to retch at the way it cried. Why she valued these two over the others was a puzzle, but I wouldn't question the gift. 'Give me truth or be gone.'

The Grindylow's voice became a viper's hiss as angry dark eyes reflected the glow of the wards. 'I haven't lied, witch. They commanded me to hunt for them, driving prey into their arms. The young pups they kept for themselves, but their mothers were mine. My children ate well. The Demisang told me you'd follow her – she said you would be easy prey. She said nothing of Fae Lords or guardians.'

My hand tightened on the arm of her young one, sick at the thought of what it had been feeding on. It might be small, but her child was as much a monster as its dam.

Air stirred next to me and Bert stepped out of nothing, followed an instant later by Jack, arrow nocked and sighted on the Grindylow.

His glamour discarded, Bert looked a true High Fae Lord again, in knee-high boots and tight black leather breeches, his scars gleaming with power on his dark skin. He grabbed the other demon child by the scruff of the neck, holding it high as it squealed and hissed. The smell of fear was growing strong as it kicked and twisted in a fruitless attempt to win free.

'How clever of you, sweet one, luring her from cover this way,'

Bert said. 'You were doubly wise to keep hold of these two until I got back. I'm proud of you for working that out.'

'What's special about these two pups?' Jack never shifted his gaze from the Grindylow and the young goblins at her feet. 'They've all got the look of vermin about them.'

Bert took the other demon child from me and dangling one from each hand, peered into their faces as if puzzling things out, but I knew he was doing it only to annoy the river demon. 'They're a mite bigger than the rest, probably getting close to a moult. Until the outer skin peels away, there's really little else to tell them from the others. Out of the whole lot, these two are the ones who'll fledge and leave the nest. The rest of the brood's only there to keep them fed.'

'The big pups eat the runts.' Jack's fingers flexed round the bow. 'So killing the pair of them is all that matters.'

The river demon hissed and spread claw-tipped fingers wide, stopping just short of touching the wards. 'Do not taunt me, Warrior.'

'It's not that simple. The Grindylow has a great deal to answer for.' I swallowed, trying to get rid of the sour taste in my mouth. 'She drove prey into the Demisang's arms – mothers and their children. They had a pact: anyone the Demisang didn't fancy, the demon fed to her brood.'

'Holy Mary, Mother of God!' Jack's eyes flicked to me and back to sight down the arrow. 'Bloody hell.'

'Are you certain, fair one?' The quiet rage in Bert's voice wasn't for me, but I too shrank from his anger.

I bowed my head and gave him the full tithe of respect he deserved. 'I'm sure, High Lord, for the Grindylow told me herself. The Demisang told the river demon to watch for us and promised I'd be easy prey. Once she'd told me the whole tale, I knew she hadn't lied.'

That air of age and burdens too great to carry came over Bert again and for an instant, I pitied him. Quick as I saw the weight settle on his shoulders, the weariness was gone again.

'I'll not let a threat to Marian go unanswered.' Proud and cold in his rage, the Fae Lord stepped between me and the river demon. 'You chose your allies as poorly as you did your hunting ground, beast.'

The Grindylow hissed, defiant and challenging.

He'd used my name, which told me enough. Bert began to sing, softly at first, harsh-sounding words with a sweet melody. The song didn't end so much as fade, leaving behind silence heavy enough to steal my breath.

He broke the quiet with one whispered word: 'Now.'

The sharp twang of the bowstring made my ears ring. Before I caught my breath the Grindylow screamed, the sound burbling in her throat. Red foam ran from the corners of her mouth, staining the rows of teeth in her wide-open maw. She clawed at the arrow in her chest, hissing and screaming with rage.

A second arrow thunked into her breast, a third into her throat. The stench of blood filled the air. Her young milled around her feet, keening, while smaller spawn, as timid as the one she'd killed, poured forth from the shadows to join the rest. The Grindylow stumbled backwards, her brood clinging to her skirts and ankles, pulling her down. They swarmed over her and I heard the river demon's screams change.

I turned away, trembling, unable to watch, but Bert faced me, the Grindylow's two children hanging wide-eyed and limp in his hands. 'This isn't finished, young witch. The rest of the brood will die. They were never meant to live. But it is for you to decide what's to become of these two.'

All I wanted to do was curl up next to Bridget and hide my face in her soft fur. The wards surrounding the wagon weren't keeping me from hearing the brood feeding on their dam. 'Why must it be me?' I whispered.

Pity sat in his eyes, and the sternness I remembered on my father's face when there was a hard lesson to be learned. 'You are the only one who can decide, Marian. Making the choice to offer mercy or to make a final end to one's enemies is no simple thing. These pups are small now and helpless-looking, but that won't always be true. Think on that before you decide.'

The river demon's children studied me with dark eyes, as if they knew they were waiting for me to pronounce judgement. They were so young – yet intelligence and cunning filled their gaze, the eyes of a hunter sizing up prey, and I found it hard not to think of them as helpless. If I set them free they'd likely starve without their dam to hunt for them, a cruel death by any measure.

Then one twisted in Bert's hand, hissing, wanting nothing more than to sink its teeth into our flesh. Their drive to survive was strong; I would be a fool to wager against the pair of them thriving. In time, they'd have broods of their own, feeding themselves and their own young by hunting the unwary and innocent.

I thought of Robbie and how he loved watching tadpoles in still water, the way he waded streams without a care. Marlow wouldn't allow Grindylow or other foul creatures inside Sherwood's borders, but other children didn't have a dragon's protection. The Grindylow's pups were enemies, no matter how I thought about their future, and not just to me and mine. I'd be an idiot to leave them at my back, or to set them loose to prey on others. I dreaded making this choice, but at least this was mine. I would put an end to the threat they posed quickly, mercifully, and hope in time to somehow cleanse the stain from my soul.

'Keep them still.' Shaping power to a dark purpose had a different feel; I feared the ease with which the weaving came together. I laid gentle hands on the Grindylow's young, thinking only of the spell and not what I did.

Mercy was a part of the weaving, to take away their fear. I wrapped them in thoughts of quiet, of breath slowing and the beat of a heart ending in stillness.

A small spell, but these were small hearts.

I'd lurched away once the pups' hearts stopped, falling to my hands and knees at the edge of the wards and retching for a long time, my body seeking to purge the feeling of willingly summoning death and ending lives. Bert left before I'd finished.

Somewhere in that time the noise of the Grindylow's spawn feeding on her disappeared as well. Moon trails rippled on the river, but not a glint of magic showed in other sight. Calm laid over Sheffield now, putting the thoughts of blood and death that were filling my head quite out of place.

Only then did I realise that no one had come to see what was going on, drawn by the brood's feeding frenzy or the Grindylow's agonising screams, even though the market square and surrounding alleys and lanes were full of people. Some slept soundly under carts or stalls and in makeshift tents; others danced around fires or sang loud and off-key in the taverns. It was as if nothing had happened. My ear was caught by a woman's high-pitched laugh which suddenly rose above the song and the men's good-natured shouting, their gaiety an enchantment laid on by too much beer and ale.

That none had heard the commotion coming from our camp I laid at Bert's feet. Placing blame for the ache in my stomach was harder.

My palms were itchy and prickly, though I couldn't say if that was caused by guilt or remnants of the spell. Wrapping my hands in the soft wool of my skirts helped, Cassie's healing spells woven into the cloth bleeding off the worst of the need to scratch, giving me another reason to be grateful for her generous gift.

Jack knew enough to leave me be, at least until I was done being sick, and made sure of his welcome by bringing a mug of water with him.

'Here, Marian, this will help. Go slow so it won't come back up.'

One sip stayed put, so I ventured another. Sweet and cool, the water washed the burning from my throat. 'Thank you. I haven't been that sick from working a spell in years.'

Tiny white flowers grew in the grass between us. Jack plucked them one by one, braiding the stems into a chain. He looked at me and smiled, light from the moon letting me see the sympathy in his eyes. 'You're a healer. Taking a life can't be an easy thing for you to do.'

'No, it wasn't easy.' I drained the mug, the sweet water turning sour on my tongue. 'But some things in life can't be healed and I'm well past old enough to know that.'

'That's true for both of us. But being forced into ending a life – having no choice? It isn't the same thing, Marian.' He took my hand, wrapping the chain of flowers around my wrist. 'Protecting those you love doesn't make killing any easier or put a gloss on what you've done. Doesn't matter if it's the hundredth time or the first, taking a life marks you.'

I'd thought of nothing but revenge on Will's killers since he'd died. Knowing what it felt like to feel a life end under your hand, even a river demon's spawn, cooled my hunger for vengeance. Those deaths were a sorrow and a burden I'd carry till the end of my days.

Jack understood that better than most, showing a strength and courage I could never hope to match. I twined my fingers with his. 'I'd never want to grow easy with death. It tells me far too much about the Demisang and her Lord that they enjoy killing.'

'No, it's not a feeling to grow used to.' Jack brushed fingers down my cheek, his touch shy, hesitant. 'Remember that and you'll be all right. I'll take the brunt when I can and Bert will bear his share. But if you're forced to defend yourself and can't see another way, you must do what you must. The Demisang won't show you any mercy.'

'I know – and I won't forget.' I toyed with the bracelet of flowers he'd made me. 'Did you find where Robin's taken himself off to?'

'People have seen him.' He stood, pulling me up with him. 'Robin Hood is a name all of Sheffield knows, even now. I met a farmer who'd tried to talk Locksley into proving who he was – wanted him to shoot the hat off a merchant's head or some such nonsense – but he said Robin was too busy quarrelling with a pretty young girl to pay him any mind.'

'The Demisang.' A winter child with a heart of ice. I worried that he'd waited much too late to try and talk to her. 'Did your farmer friend know where the two of them went?'

'There's no sign of the Demisang in Sheffield, gentle witch.' Bert stepped from shadow, clothed in glamour. The stooped merchant added, 'The Grindylow didn't lie about her leaving town. We'll find the Archer waiting for us in the abbey across the river.'

'Hiding in the shadow of God.' I couldn't look Bert in the face without remembering the feel of small hearts growing still under my hands; meeting Jack's gaze was easier. 'Robin believes we won't be able to drive him out.'

'We'll pry him loose.' Jack squeezed my fingers. 'But he'll have to wait until morning. I might be able to talk us past the porter, but they wouldn't dream of letting a woman in, not until the sun comes up.'

'The Archer will keep till morning.' Glamour shimmered and now Bert stood in his work-a-day clothes. 'In any case, I'd see Marian well rested before we bait the bear in his den.'

Jack swung me up into the wagon and I curled up between Bridget and Julian. With my head pillowed on my cloak, I watched the great washes of icy-white stars filling the sky, stretching as far as I could see. When I was small, my father would speak of stars as sapphires scattered at the feet of the old Gods, an offering from a prince seeking his lost love. So bright did the stars shine, I could well believe the old tale was true.

Falling asleep wasn't easy. I was more than half-afraid to give in to weariness and let dreams about the Grindylow and what I'd done to her children find me, but Bert perched on the wagon seat near my head and pulled out his pipes. A song about letting go of the day, of comfort, being safe, filled the night. He played the bad dreams away, chasing them off the way my mother had done with her cradle songs.

All my fears followed the nightmares into the dark. These were my mother's songs, the same ones I sang to my own children, and I half expected to hear her voice join the pipes. I listened as long as I could, tears burning my eyes.

My last waking thought was that I needed to ask Bert how he'd learned them.

Chapter 16

Like to a friar bold Robin Hood
Was accouter'd in his array;
With hood, gown, beads and crucifix,
He pass'd upon the way.

17TH CENTURY BALLAD

Morning came, but I never saw the sun, for clouds dipped low in the sky, grey billows that filled the air with cold rain. Water beaded in my hair and on the wool of my cloak, glistened in Jack's beard and shining like a coat of ice atop Bert's curved-topped chests. The only thing not wet to the point of dripping was Bert himself.

He sat on the wagon seat, the reins in hand, whistling a cheery tune. I wondered what he'd found to be so happy about: every person we passed was greeted with a nod and a cheerful wave. Bert smiled at each stranger as if they were long-time friends he hadn't seen since last market day. Most waved back, no doubt thinking they should know the tall, gangly man with the besotted smile.

Bridget huddled inside my cloak, almost as cross about being wet as she was about not being allowed to run free. One or two farmers we passed looked twice at the black nose peeking out, or caught the glitter of her eyes, but most travellers were sunk in their own wet misery, eyes downcast as they hurried to finish their business and find shelter.

Jack walked a short distance ahead, holding tight to Julian's rope. The dog trotted along happily, loving the rain, going so far as trying to find puddles to splash through. He showed no interest in chasing anything moving in the shadows or slinking down alleys, which I took as a sign that the Grindylow's brood was truly gone.

The bridge spanning the river near the abbey was just wide enough for two wagons to pass each other. The wood, slick with rain, was creaking under the weight and shifting and swaying as the wind hit, a strange feeling with the water rushing so fast underneath us, although the locals paid the swaying no mind, dodging between slow-moving carts as if the road always moved under their feet. Most were walking far too near the edge for my comfort.

The abbey was plainer on the outside than most big churches I'd seen, but the grounds were far larger than Tuck's abbey in Nottingham. In between the spread-out buildings were new saplings, for the place had been finished only a few years before. Grey stone towers rose at one end of the chapel, the wooden cross atop the tallest looking dull in the rain. High arched windows filled the chapel wall facing us, each window full of stained-glass scenes of angels and saints. Everything about the buildings and grounds still had the raw look of newness.

Thick black smoke spewed from a brick building sitting hard

up against the riverbank, separated from the church by a wide field. I guessed this must be where the monks worked their iron. Jack had told me they smelted it into rough bars, which they sold to weapons-makers and blacksmiths. It smelled worse than rotten goose eggs; both stench and smoke reminded me of the stories Robin told about fallen angels and the fiery pits imprisoning tormented souls. That the holy brothers tended such a place was more than passing strange to me.

A gate set in a low drystone wall stood open, hanging by one top hinge, with the bottom corner sunk in the grass. When our wagon rolled to a stop under a large, spreading oak, Bert hopped down from the seat and tied the horses to a branch – not that the horses would wander away without his leave, but seeing what they expected would stop anyone passing by from thinking too hard. No need to attract more notice than necessary.

Bridget wiggled in my arms, wanting to break free and run away. I made her look me in the eye. 'Fetch the dog some break-fast after you've found your own. Mind that you stay out of sight, and keep well away from the monks' poultry. I wouldn't want to see your hide stretched on the tanning frame. Now, off with you.'

She leapt off and ran towards the river, where she dived into the reeds to hunt while Jack helped me down, then tied Julian to a wheel.

Bert and Jack came to stand on either side of me at the gate. The ground beyond the gate was well kept, with a white stone path leading to the arched double door. I looked Bert in the eye. 'I can't imagine that God will take kindly to a witch and a Fae Lord entering his house, but that's where Robin will be.'

'Don't fret over our welcome, Marian. The Warrior has more to worry about than a kind witch and a wandering Lord of the

Lady's court.' Bert patted my shoulder and led the way down the path. 'Only those who hold faith and believe catch His eye. He'll pay no mind to the likes of us.'

Jack winked and took my hand. We followed the whistling Fae Lord as Bert pulled open one of the heavy arched doors and ushered us through. We stood just inside for a minute, letting our eyes adjust to the dim light and waiting to see if we'd be challenged.

'Luck's with us,' Jack said. 'Tierce is over and the monks have gone off to work. Next service is at midday. If Locksley is keeping vigil at the altar, he'll be alone.'

Bert hummed a quick tune, the notes soon lost in the high ceiling. 'I'll keep watch over the door. The two of you fetch the Archer out, quick as you can.'

The floor was laid in dressed stone. Our boot heels echoed no matter how soft we tried to step, Jack's long stride and my shorter one strangely in time with each other. There were only a few benches along one wall of the large, empty church, which had room for half the residents of Sheffield to attend services. There was a fenced-in area three steps up from the floor on either side of the altar, for the choir, I assumed.

Above the altar was a crucifix bearing an image of the Son, as new-looking and freshly made as everything else inside the sanctuary. Niches set in each wall displayed carved and brightly painted statues of saints and martyrs, nameless ghosts trapped in wood, lit with flickering candles set at their feet. Vivid paintings showed more angels, illustrating Bible stories. In the biggest niche, by the door, stood a marble statue of the Virgin Mary and her Child. Looking at those staring, lifeless eyes made me shiver.

Jack paid the statues no heed but made straight for the altar and Robin.

Shadows darkened the skin under Robin's tightly closed eyes. The tunic he wore was of the roughest wool, burrs and seed heads spun into the yarn and woven into the cloth. He muttered singsong prayers, repeating the same words over and over, stopping for a breath, crossing himself with shaking hands, then starting again.

'What's he saying?'

Robin's shoulders twitched at the sound of my voice.

Jack glanced at me, his forehead creased in a frown. 'I've heard enough priests praying to guess that he's asking Holy Mary to forgive his sins. From the looks of him, he's doing penance. My guess is that Locksley's been fasting and praying since the Demisang left.'

I touched Robin's shoulder and he shuddered, as if my touch caused him physical pain. Whether being near me hurt him or not, I couldn't leave him here.

'You're coming with us, Robin,' I said. 'No more hiding and pretending you're not a part of this. I need your help to find your daughter.'

Robin stopped praying and covered his face with his hands. He was trembling from head to foot; guilt might make a man tremble like that, or regret.

'I tried, Marian. Mother of God forgive me, I tried to talk to her. Nothing I said was enough.'

Jack hauled Robin to his feet. 'You'll try again, Locksley, and you'll do whatever Marian asks. Tell me where you left your clothes and bow. I'll fetch them so we can leave.'

'No!' Robin jerked away, stumbled and went sprawling face-first on the cold floor, hitting his head with a dull thud. He moaned and rolled onto his back. 'Leave me here. I've done enough harm.'

I stood over him, wondering how I could have thought I'd ever known this man. 'Nothing can change the past, Robin, but you can help us keep your daughter from destroying anyone else. Tell me what she said to you. Then give me her name.'

He threw an arm over his eyes, breathing hard and fast.

'Brother Robin? Is everything all right?'

I hadn't heard the small door behind the altar open, but two monks in white-hooded robes now stood there, watching us. The youngest stared, his eyes round as a barn owl's. He didn't move any closer, but he didn't bolt back the way he'd come to raise the alarm either. I was grateful for that small blessing.

The older monk moved out of the shadows and he didn't hesitate to confront us. He'd been a tall man once, but age had bent his back and stooped his shoulders and his right leg dragged enough to be noticed. Time played no favourites, taking its toll on holy men and farmers alike.

He took in the sight of Robin on the floor, with me and Jack standing over him, and came down on Robin's side, as fierce and fearless as any shepherd guarding new-born lambs.

'Are these people interfering with your prayers, Brother Robin? Say the word and I'll send Brother Edmund to fetch the others.'

A quavering voice answered from the back of the church, 'No need for that, Your Holiness.'

The white-robed monks turned to watch the old man struggling to hold open the heavy door, his arms shaking with the effort. 'No need at all. I'll be taking my boy home now.'

Without the sheen of magic clinging to him, I wouldn't have known Bert. Wrinkles and pockmarks covered his weatherworn face, and he looked to be missing nearly half his teeth. Wild dirty grey hair tumbled to his shoulders. He shambled down the aisle, Robin's clothes draped over one arm.

The older monk eyed Bert, distrust and disapproval clear in the set of his shoulders. 'Brother Robin is your boy?'

'Aye, Your Holiness. Robbie's m'boy.' Bert stopped short of bending the knee, but he did bob a bow to the old monk. He leaned in, as if to whisper, but his voice was louder than before. 'I beg pardon for the trouble he's put you all to. Robbie's not been right in the head since the cow kicked him. He wanders off when the fancy takes him, makes up such tales – I never know where he'll end up.'

Young Edmund stared, growing even more owl-eyed, and crossed himself. Unless I missed my guess, Edmund had a touch of other sight and saw through the glamour to the Fae Lord beneath. Bert looked Edmund's way and grinned, gap-toothed and simple-looking. 'His mam cries if he's gone too long. I keep fetching him home to stop her from fussing.'

Robin groaned, thrashing from side to side, his eyes screwed shut. 'Marian, I beg you, let me stay here and plead with God for forgiveness – don't let the demon take me away. I need to atone for my sins!'

Bert's fingers drummed a quick rhythm on his thigh before he patted Robin's shoulder. Robin stayed quiet, but when he lifted his head, I could see tears pooling in the corners of his eyes. 'Time to settle yourself, lad. Your mam's not cross with you, the cat came back all on her own.' He looked at the older monk. 'Jack and his wife's here to help me get the lad home where he belongs.'

'He came to us seeking help as a member of Father Tuck's abbey in Nottingham. Stories of Robin Hood joining Tuck's order are well known, even as far away as Sheffield.' The stern old monk slipped his hands into the wide sleeves of his robe, unyielding in his disbelief. 'The abbot himself heard Brother Robin's confession and offered him shelter as a brother in Christ. Why should I let you take him from us, Grandfather?'

Bert's fingers twitched, a movement easy to mistake for palsy in a man looking so old. He stared at the stone-faced monk for an instant, then burst out in a laugh that left him wheezing and coughing. 'Begging your pardon, Brother Monk, but take a good look at the lad, will you? It's a sad thing indeed to see a grown man grovelling on the floor like that. My poor boy's no Robin Hood, 'cept maybe in his own head.' Bert motioned to Jack. 'I've said I'm sorry for all the trouble he's been to you, but we'll be taking him home now. You've my promise he'll get a stern talking-to about telling such lies.'

Suspicion and doubt still creased the old monk's face, but he stepped back so Jack could get a hand under Robin's arm.

'Up with you now, Robbie,' Jack said, as if calming a skittish horse. 'Let's get your own clothes on you so as we can go home. Your mam's waiting on us.'

Jack was none too gentle stripping off the tunic and stuffing Robin into the one he'd worn before. All the while Robin stared at the floor, not making a sound, limp as a rag doll. Once dressed, we led him towards the doors, Bert following behind, humming a tune as if he'd not a care in the world.

At the door Robin came to himself, twisting in our grip to face the statue of the Virgin and her Child. 'Holy Mary, forgive me! I didn't know she'd cause such harm! I didn't know—'

He strained towards the statue, waiting for an answer, faith that he'd be forgiven shining in his eyes.

I watched the statue too, searching with other sight for the smallest glimmer that a piece of carved stone held life or spirit.

Painted eyes stared back, hollow and cold. Faith couldn't create life where life had never been.

'It's not that easy, lad.' Bert grabbed Robin's tunic and tugged him out of the door. 'Most folk have to work a long old time to earn forgiveness. The hour has come for you to start working for yours.'

Julian started to whine as he saw Jack, his long tail thumping loudly against the side of the wagon. Bridget's head popped up between two of the chests. Her muzzle was flecked with blood and a bit of rabbit fur stuck to the dog's whiskers, so I knew she'd done as I'd asked and fed him as well.

Jack lowered the back of the wagon. 'Get in, Locksley. I'm not giving you a chance to run again.'

'He won't run, Warrior.' Bert hopped onto the wagon seat, his glamour turning to dust and blowing away on the breeze. He offered me a hand up. 'Put the dog in the wagon and settle your-selves. We need to move quickly if we're to catch the Demisang.'

My dress caught on a protruding splinter but the soft wool didn't tear. I tucked the skirts under me and held tight. 'You know where she's going?'

Bert snapped the reins over the horses' backs for show and sang them into a trot. He grinned, his good humour out of place with my dark mood. 'No, fair one, the Demisang remains a puzzle and hidden from my sight. But the Archer knows where to find her.'

Robin's head came up and cunning replaced the fear in his eyes He knew he was cornered and likely staring death in the face, but this wasn't the first time and he'd always escaped in the past. I could see he still hoped there was room to run. 'She said many things – she never said where they were going.'

Jack watched Robin, sharp as a hawk, not prepared to give him an inch. 'You know her name, Locksley, and according to Marian, that's a sure way to find the girl. Best you start there.'

'Before the Archer speaks the Demisang's name and attracts notice, I've a question.' Bert twisted on the seat, hands busy juggling silver circlets. Jewels caught the sun, flashing rainbows. 'Does she travel with the Lady's Consort?'

'He wasn't the Lady's Consort while I was there. I knew him as a minstrel.' Robin rested his shaking hands on his knees. His voice was as ragged as a man with twice his years. 'The Lady talked of making me Consort when Aidan was a baby – mad talk, as if bearing my son could change things in court.'

I'd thought Robin lost for ever while he sojourned with the Lady. We weren't long gone from our outlaw days or completely free of men looking to settle a score with him. I'd searched almost the entire greenwood, seeking the place he'd fallen so I could at least bring his bones safe back. The seasons had turned before he'd wandered home again, telling tales of highwaymen and escorting a monk on pilgrimage to the sea, but I'd never pressed for another explanation. I took him back without question, as blind with love for him as he was blinded by faith now.

My life might have been very different had I insisted he tell me where he'd been, forced him to face me with the truth. Watching him now, I knew he would have left me no matter what – but at least I'd have known why. Tears stung my eyes and I looked away, not as far removed as I'd thought from the hurt of knowing he hadn't loved me as much as I'd thought.

Bert threw all three circlets high. I lost sight of them in sun-dazzle, but only one came down: all three plaited together in a crown as if it had been made that way. He plucked it from air and set it atop my head. His expression was solemn, all trace of the trickster masked by sadness. 'Keep this for now, little witch. It will be safe in your care until I've need for it.'

For the first time in my life I wished for a mirror. This desire to see jewels and silver nestled in my dark hair was vanity, nothing more, but knowing that didn't mean I wanted it any less. I brushed a fingertip along the cool metal, tracing the lines where the three joined to become one. 'Am I to go about finely crowned as King John's Queen, sly Lord?'

I'd grown accustomed to his sudden smiles, full of guile and glee, when sober words would suit better. The smiles I liked best, like the one he gave me now, had no mask attached: an unasked-for gift. 'No reason not, sweet Marian. I deem you twice as worthy as any in King John's court and you wear a crown with more grace. And none will see but me and your Warrior. I wager he'll not complain.'

'No, her Warrior won't complain.' Jack's gaze didn't waver. 'He won't complain at all.'

Heat burned in my cheeks. 'You can stop the flattery. Fools, both of you. I'll wear your bauble, but how will I know when you need the crown?'

Bert laughed and patted my hand. 'I'll ask. Don't fret.'

Jack crossed his arms and looked at Bert, squinting against the sun. 'I'll not deny that crown looks made for Marian. But what's a queen's circlet to do with Locksley giving us the girl's name?'

'Perhaps much, perhaps nothing at all. My sight is a fractured thing, crazed with cracks and gaps to be leapt.' Bert winked so only I'd see and picked up the dropped reins. 'I follow the path as it's given. Ask the Archer now and he'll provide the Demisang's name.'

The Fae Lord hummed under his breath, the melody calling up memories of my children's laughter. Robin shut his eyes for an instant, breathing hard and fighting Bert's compulsion. He'd brought this on himself, along with so much more, yet I pitied him nonetheless.

'Her mother and I both gave her names.' Robin stared at his hands. 'Maeve from her mother, Mary Magdalene from me. I meant it as a gift, to keep her safe.'

'Sweet Jesus, Locksley.' Jack shook his head and pulled the dog close, raking his fingers through Julian's fur, scratching behind the ears. 'You named the Lady's daughter after a Christian saint? I've no great knowledge of magic and the Fae, but even I can see that's daft. I'm surprised the Lady let it stand.'

'Once a child's name is spoken, the name belongs to them and can't be reclaimed.' Bert's shoulders drooped as if his burden were growing heavier again. 'Only death can change things now.'

'I wanted her to know God, Jack.' Life and passion came back to Robin's face. 'I taught her to pray and baptised her so she wouldn't die outside a state of grace. She loved stories from Holy Writ – she got so she knew them all as well as me. I'd no wish for my child to suffer for my sins. She was innocent. She deserved better.'

'And what of your summer child, Archer?' Bert peered down from the seat, his face expressionless. 'Did your son Aidan deserve less?'

Robin winced and slumped back. He didn't answer.

Jack looked at me and I saw my own thoughts mirrored in

his eyes. Ethan was an innocent, and so was Meg. They'd both deserved more than death and pain and fear. So much more.

'Time for you to join your Warrior, Marian.' Bert wrapped the reins tightly around his long-fingered hands. 'I've the scent of her now and the time has come to give chase. We've only two days before the full moon, so we'd best catch young Maeve up before then.'

The wagon halted long enough for Jack to hand me down. Magic closed in tight, thrumming with echoes of her name. The clop of hooves, the rustle of leaves stirred by the breeze, all whispered *Maeve, Maeve* . . .

Not far ahead, the road forked. One track went north along the river towards where Alan had died in York. The other went back the way we'd come. Bert whistled, three sharp notes, and he was done.

The horses turned towards Nottingham: towards home, and my children.

Chapter 17

Why should I be dismayed
Though flame had burned the whole
World, as it were a coal,
Now I have seen it weighed
Against a soul?

W. B. YEATS

Bert sang the hidden roads open, his voice strong and steady.

I hadn't travelled the Fae paths before, not while awake and aware, but I knew this was a place to be wary of. The woods on either side were the same, and yet not. The oak leaves were a shade darker than I knew them to be, but with edges sharp enough to draw blood. The sigh of branches and mutter of leaves wove a song on the breeze, bidding us rest, and ebon eyes opened in weathered tree boles to watch us pass. Hunger swam in those eyes, glittering with the hope we'd be reckless enough to come near.

Bright-feathered songbirds sang, but the notes were harsh and far from sweet, grating on the ears. Their songs all ended with a hiss.

Above the treetops the sky was equally strange, spider-webbed with clouds that were still one moment and roiling before an unfelt wind the next. Wraiths formed in the mist writhing between the trees and raced us along the path, turn by turn dipping down to brush their fingers over Bert's wards, filling the air with golden sparks.

Robin kept his eyes screwed shut and started praying as he'd done in the abbey, constantly repeating the words and crossing himself each time he reached the end of a phrase. I knew if I'd asked, he'd claim, as he'd always done, that prayer brought him comfort. I was equally sure his prayers acted as a shield, holding fear at bay.

The vixen slept, curled up next to me, paying no mind to whatever went on outside the wagon. Julian whined, wanting to chase each flash of magic, every creature pacing us. Jack was struggling to keep him from running off until I whispered sleep in the dog's ear.

'I really wish I'd the knack for doing that.' He eased the dog half onto his lap, keeping Julian's head from bouncing over every rut and bump. 'My thanks. This isn't the place for him to run after everything he sees.'

'He'd not last a minute, Warrior. There's plenty in these woods would lure him away and take him for their supper.' Bert was humming under his breath, his face set and grim. 'Sweet witch, do your Uncle Bert a service and put an end to Robin's wailing. I'd not ask you if there wasn't real need. This isn't the place for him to be raising power of his own. He's making it hard to keep the way open.'

Jack steadied me so as I could lean across and put a hand on Robin's face. My fingers and arm tingled as I touched him, fear giving his chant power the words shouldn't otherwise hold. I gathered my will and turned the power back on him. Robin let out a breath, half surprise and half relief, and crumpled into sleep like an overtired child.

Time had turned as strange as everything else I saw. If I trusted to mortal sight, counting the shifts from day to night and back, we'd been travelling Fae roads without pause for more than four days before we came to the end. Bert's song hung in the air – and suddenly was gone, closing the way.

Leaving the road was akin to waking after a troubled sleep, unsure where the border between dream and the real world ran. Sunlight brightened slowly, bringing midday warmth and comfort. Oak and rowan leaves took on their proper colours, once again rustling in the wind as they should. Clouds were just that and nothing more, wafting high and thin over a summer-blue sky.

'Here we are, safe in the world of mortals – and with hours to spare before moonrise.' The Fae Lord hauled hard on the reins, pulling the horses up short. They hung their heads, breathing hard, but I saw no sign they'd laboured to the point of harm. 'Wake the Archer. We'll need him to flush the Demisang from cover.'

Bridget uncoiled, stretching and yawning so wide I thought her jaw would unhinge. She sniffed the air and leapt from the wagon, vanishing into the greenwood. Julian tried to follow her, but Jack was quicker. The dog whined as the vixen disappeared between the trees.

Given the choice, I'd have left Robin, but Bert said we needed him, so I put my hand to his cheek, intending to wake him gently. Sparks snapped between us before skin touched skin.

'Mother of us all!' I snatched my hand back, wrapping my

tingling fingers in my skirts. Cassie's healing spells soon took the sting away from my fingertips, but numbness still froze my hand. I found it more than passing strange how much power surrounded Robin.

Robin himself sat up with a gasp, wild-eyed and sucking air. Before he'd more than opened his eyes he'd crossed himself, habit and talisman both, to ward off evil.

Jack hauled him to his feet. 'Up with you, Locksley. We walk from here.'

'You drag me through Lucifer's hell and then expect me to meekly follow on?' Robin wobbled, but he swatted Jack's hand aside, refusing aid. 'But I'd expect no better from ruffians and demons.'

'It's less than half a league to Nottingham.' Bert hopped over the seat, flipped open a small, green-topped chest I'd not noticed before and pulled longbows and quivers from inside, drawing stares and yet more muttered prayers from Robin. 'Take hold of these, Warrior. Pass one to the Archer when he's got his feet under him.'

'You're sure she's here?' When I searched with other sight for signs of Maeve's passage, stillness and the feel of waiting hung over Sherwood. Birds called tree to tree, but they were mournful cries, not the bright joy of high summer. Small creatures, squirrels, stoats and rabbits, rustled in bush and bramble, but stayed oddly quiet, avoiding notice. I couldn't find one thing to point at to say this was done with Maeve's hand, but I knew nonetheless. *I knew*.

'Young Maeve is near.' Bert sniffed the air, a hound catching the scent. 'She's retraced her steps. We need to be quick before she slips away.'

'I'll be quicker if you tell me where to go.' Jack slung his bow over one shoulder, the quiver over the other. 'Are we searching wood or town?'

'She'll go to Tuck.'

We turned as one to stare at Robin, who turned aside rather than look me in the eye. 'He's heard her confession since she first came to find me. That's the first place she'll go.'

'Stars, Robin . . .' The circlet in my hair suddenly grew heavy, less a shiny bauble and more of a burden. I didn't understand what I carried yet, but the way of burdens was always to grow heavier. 'Will she hurt him?'

He leaned on his longbow, staring at mud on the toe of his boot. 'It's more than seven years since she asked for me at the chapel door and began coming to mass. She never told Tuck she was my daughter, but he was always more than kind to her. I'd like to think she'd not hurt him.'

Robin stood straight and finally gathered himself. 'But I never thought she'd hurt her brother, or anyone else. I can't say what she'll do.'

Bert clapped his hands, making me jump. The horses and wagon full of bright-topped chests vanished, not even tracks in the dirt showing where they'd been. 'Lead the way, Archer, and step quick now. The sharp-eyed dog and I will be at your heels.'

Jack and I followed behind. We'd not gone more than a dozen steps when he offered me his hand. I smiled and took it for an instant, squeezing his fingers in thanks before letting go.

I didn't need help to keep up or find the way, but it was good to have a friend near. There was always a need for friends.

*

The strangeness and the feel of things being *not quite right* stayed with me, growing stronger with every farmer and goodwife heading home we passed on the road. A few nodded, faces I recognised and could put names to, and one woman, clutching her child to her breast, turned round after passing us, as if wanting to cry out a warning but immediately forgetting why. No one smiled, nor spoke a greeting; they all looked too far sunk in grim thoughts.

One countrysider, even a couple, so struggling with a weight of troubles they'd pass in silence – that, I'd believe. Not a score or more.

'Bert . . .'

'I feel it too, sweet Marian. The forest is a coin balanced on a knife-edge, waiting to see which way it falls.' He whistled, calling a robin to his hand. Bert cocked his own head, one eye meeting the bird's bright gaze as the robin spoke, trilling replies from time to time until the bird spread its wings and took flight. 'Beast and bird sense something amiss as well. They don't know the cause any more than you or I, but I fear we'll find the reason soon enough.'

When I wasn't much bigger than Rose, summer evenings were quiet in Nottingham. Market ended early so farmers could get home in time to tend to their animals before dark, leaving townsfolk and those who had other business there to eat and drink and talk away the long evenings. In those days our king dwelt far from our sleepy county.

John Lackland ruled now and because he'd brought his court to hunt stag and boar in the greenwood, nobles, soldiers, weapon-masters and scribes, blacksmiths, cooks and dozens more servants, all busy on the king's business, walked the streets of Nottingham from the sun's first rays to long after moonset. Many always stayed on after he'd gone back to London to ensure the palace was always ready for the king's return. The sleepy town of my childhood was nothing but a memory.

That was a blessing now. We threaded our way towards St Mary's Abbey, dodging weary merchants bent on reaching a favoured tavern, women shepherding their children home and soldiers patrolling three abreast. No one gave us more than a passing glance before hurrying on their way. We didn't need magic or glamour; people saw what they expected to see in Nottingham on a summer's eve: three foresters, one with a foot-sore wife, and their ragged hound.

Bert winked at me over his shoulder, false cheer writ large on his face. 'Take heart, sweet Marian, the deed's near done. You'll be home soon, your children safe in your arms.'

A chill brushed the back of my neck, icy as a shade's kiss. This time I reached for Jack's hand. He gave it willingly, the warm, solid feel driving away the cold rooted in my heart. 'Don't call ill luck down on us, sly one. We haven't faced her yet.'

I'd never before gone beyond the gates of St Mary's, for all I passed it each time I visited Nottingham. Folk went to mass in the chapel, but that was all most saw of the abbey. A high wall surrounding the buildings and gardens, separating the abbey from the town which now surrounded it. Some of the brothers spent their entire life there, praying or working as scribes, existing apart from the world, but others, like Brother Timothy and Tuck, went abroad to do God's work among the townsfolk and countrysiders, shepherds to a far-flung flock.

Robin tugged at the iron handle on the gate, which rattled against the frame. 'This entrance is for the monks to come and go. I've never seen it locked before, but it's shut tight – barred from the inside, looks like.'

'Is there another way in?' Jack stepped back, searching the length of the wall for another gate. 'Can we get in through the chapel?'

'There's no need, Warrior.' Bert shouldered Robin aside, his long fingers drummed on weathered old wood, the rhythm a match to the tune he hummed, then he spun on his toes, playing the fool, and blew on the handle. The gate swung open without making a sound. Bert strolled in, a pleased smile on his face, but Robin near trod on his heels in his rush to get inside.

Jack bowed and waved me in. 'After you, Lady Marian.'

The garden beyond the wall was much like my own, with stone paths winding between well-tended beds full of vegetables, fruit and herbs. Fat black and yellow bees buzzed among the blossoms, drunk on nectar and the scent of summer flowers. Butterflies danced everywhere, painted beauties outshining even the lush flowers gracing the edge of each pebbled path and surrounding stone benches set to best catch the sun.

While Sheffield's abbey was raw and new and near-empty of life, Tuck's gardens were rich with green and growing things, giving it an ancient, peaceful feel, as if the ground the church stood on had roots sunk deep in Sherwood. Tuck's faith ran deep, but he'd clearly found a different way to worship God, one that took joy in beauty and simple things.

Bert led Julian to the shade of an apple tree and rubbed the dog's ears. 'You're best out of this, brave one. Sleep. You've my promise we'll return for you.'

'Shouldn't there be monks about, Locksley?' Jack nocked an arrow, readying the bow. 'This isn't the hour for service.'

'Summer's a busy time. They could be in the cellars turning the casks. And there's the cheese-making ...' Robin swallowed and crossed himself. 'But Brother Henry should be out weeding. He likes getting that done before supper.'

'Right then.' Bert hitched up his breeches. 'Lead the way, Robin. We won't find your brethren watching the flowers grow.'

I called power to me, drawing what I could from the growing things around me and the faint outline of the moon in late afternoon skies. The spell to protect us all was made of life, easier to craft than the one I'd used on the Grindylow's spawn.

The door from the gardens into the monks' quarters stood propped open by a broken crock. It was hard to see in the unlit passage until Bert and I called blue witch-light to bob ahead of us. Robin crossed himself again, but held his tongue. He had as much need to see as the rest of us.

The silence weighing on me grew heavier with each closed door we passed. I knew little of life in a monastery, but this lack of life and movement surely wasn't right. Jack kept me close and I didn't pull away. I didn't feel easy here.

We rounded a corner and stopped before two heavy doors with a cross hanging over the lintel, flanked by carved figures of women. Jack, seeing me staring, leaned to whisper in my ear, 'Angels, guarding the way into the chapel.'

'Stars and moon.' I sent my ball of witch-light closer. The faces were meant to be beautiful, but the eyes looked hard and the set of their mouths cruel. 'Rose's angel ...'

Robin reached to open the door, but I grabbed his hand. 'Hold a moment.'

Other sight showed the trace of wards criss-crossing the door: a web meant to catch the unwary. The angels' eyes gleamed, full of power and ready to pounce. More power wrapped the latches. For all my troubles with Robin, I'd hate to see that spell triggered by his touch.

'She's set a nasty trap for us. You're twice as clever for finding it beforehand.' Bert passed a hand just above the wards, humming a light tune, stopping every few breaths to whistle. 'Even so, I've doubts how much is Maeve's doing and how much Mikal's work.'

Jack frowned. 'Mikal? Is that the Lord travelling with her?'

'Just so, Warrior, just so.' Pipes came to Bert's hand. The notes he played went rising so high I couldn't hear them; they would surely have set Julian to howling. One long trill climbed until I wondered how he had breath to go on, but at the end of that run of melody, the web on the door shattered, falling like shards of broken ice. The pieces didn't wink away as I'd have expected of a broken spell but remained solid, pulsing on the stone flags.

'I'd thought the Lord travelling with her might be Mikal when the Archer called him a minstrel, but I needed to see craft done with his hand to be sure.' Bert's smile was as brittle as the bits of wards crunching underfoot. 'Mikal is brother to the Lady's Consort. All the court knew he thought himself better suited to that high position, but I wouldn't have thought him bitter enough to plot against the Lady. It does explain much of how young Maeve has achieved all her mischief.'

'Mother of God.' Jack kicked at the floor, sending a shard from the wards spinning. 'Are you saying all this misery was caused by a jilted suitor?'

A fair question, one without a fair answer.

'Games within games, circles within circles.' I wiped my face on a sleeve. 'This is about power, Jack: a struggle for the crown and who will rule the Fae. They usually keep their quarrels to themselves, but Maeve has clearly changed the game.'

Robin looked to Bert, waiting for a nod before yanking the door open. We crowded through on his heels.

The inside of the chapel was plain. There were no fancy statues in niches, nor stained-glass windows shining like jewels in the walls. An altar covered in a spotless cloth of fine white linen stood at the front, flanked on the left by a shelf of candles, all of them burned low and close to going out. Benches for the old and infirm sat along the back and side walls; the rest of the chapel was open for people to stand. Above the altar hung a crucifix, the body of Jesus nailed through wrists and feet. The maker had felt the need to splash red over the wounds, presumably to show God's Son bled the same as any man. An angel hovered over the Son, hands raised in blessing, her painted face gazing out over the chapel.

Robin staggered past the benches at the back and dropped to his knees, raising his hands to cover his face. Rocking back and forth, he moaned, 'In the name of God, Maeve, why? Why? You'd no cause, no reason . . .'

The monk kneeling in front of the altar had his face turned up towards the cross, his hands folded in prayer. He had the look of someone who'd been quite unaware Death was standing at his side until his breath stopped and his heartbeat stilled.

There were more monks kneeling behind him, their eyes wide, and some had their hands raised as if to ward off a blow. My relief that Tuck and Tim weren't among them was short-lived – even if they had escaped, a great many people had fallen prey to the spell, for there were merchants and minor court officials and their families in the chapel too, and even some farmers. Small bodies leaned on fathers or huddled tight against their mothers.

I clutched Jack's sleeve. 'There are so many little ones . . .' My voice caught.

He turned me around so I was looking away from death and into his eyes. 'Stand here, Marian. I'll go.'

I must have been imagining the circlet was feeling heavier. I took a breath, then shook my head. 'No, Jack. This is my task too. I can't turn away now.'

'We all go, gentle witch. And those with the most guilt will share the burden.' Bert was wearing the harlequin mask now, covering his true face and hiding his feelings. He yanked Robin up by the back of his tunic. 'Come, Archer. It's your job to see if the Demisang spared any of your brothers.'

Anger gives strength, lets a man do what otherwise seems impossible. Jack was angry; I'd no doubt of that, and yet he moved from one still form to the next on the far side of the chapel, searching for life, while I did the same on the other side. I couldn't think about Will, or all the long years of Ethan's life stolen away, or that Midge would never see Meg holding their child, not and do what I had to do, so instead, I thought about anger, nursing that flame to get me through.

Going from woman to child, from child to man, pausing each time to look for a stir of breath, listening for the flutter of a heart, was hard, and harder yet as hope that any had escaped the Demisang's madness died early on. Only stubbornness and a need to be certain kept me searching.

I nearly passed the empty bench, but my skirts caught on a poorly set nail, yanking me back – and setting my heart to racing. I turned, thinking to find a shade desperate to draw my attention.

No ripple of air or glimmer of a wandering spirit greeted me, but something did shift in the shadows under the bench. I knelt and pulled out two baskets I hadn't before noticed.

'Oh stars and moon above – thank you, Mother, *thank you*.' Breath caught in my throat and my hand trembled as I brushed baby hair soft as thistledown off sleepy faces. I whispered urgently, 'Jack! Bert – here!'

They reached me at the same time. The Fae Lord dropped to his knees and touched each of the babes, humming under his breath. He rocked back on his heels and the mask was gone; that he let relief show, even for an instant, told me much. 'The little ones are unharmed, Marian. A boy and a girl, unless my craft failed me. They're fortunate you found them.'

The shades of two women, one rowan-tall and dark-eyed, the other acorn-round and fair, now peered at me over Bert's shoulder. They were watching everything we did, guarding their children even in death. If Bert knew they crowded his back, he gave no sign.

Jack sucked in a breath. 'Two – out of more than sixty people. Where did you find them?'

The youngest babe, fair-haired and rosy with health, began to fuss, wakened by our voices. I picked her up and cuddled her under my chin, breathing in the scent of milk on her breath, until she quieted under my hand, once again going limp in sleep. 'The baskets were pushed under the bench – my guess is they were out of the Demisang's sight, sleeping quiet enough to go unnoticed.'

'Oh bloody sweet Jesus . . . *the baskets*.' Jack loped to the side of the chapel and started scrambling under the other benches. He came off the floor with a baby boy near a year old, I thought, in his arms. The little one yawned and rubbed his eyes, lip quivering, looking for someone he knew.

'Well done, Warrior. Well done.' Bert took the baby and started gurning until the threat of tears turned to smiles. 'He too is unharmed. Three times lucky on an ill-fated day: three young souls destined to go through life bonded one to another. We need to find care for them swiftly. The Demisang is on the move. Come, Archer, we're leaving.'

Robin made the sign of the cross over a monk. 'You'll go without me. My brothers died because I failed. I'd see them on their way to God.'

'The living come before the dead, Locksley.' Jack held the tiny dark-haired boy in the crook of his arm. 'I won't stand idle while you say prayers and let Maeve and her Lord bring death to more innocents. We have to find them, so if Bert wants you with us, you're coming if I have to drag you.'

'I'm leaving him no choice in the matter, Jack. He'll come.' Bert made faces at the fussy babe, but power and the compulsion to obey filled his voice. 'You've a moment or two, Archer, no more. Make your peace with what is. We'll await you in the gardens.'

The sun was over-bright after the dimness of the chapel and unlit halls. I shaded the baby's eyes. 'Care for one child this young is hard to come by. I'm waiting to hear how we'll manage three, and quickly at that.'

'Have a bit of faith, fair one. Your Uncle Bert knows what he's about.' He sat the older boy on a patch of soft grass and set balls of blue, silver and red dancing in the air to keep him happy. Pipes appeared in his hand next, but after a quick run of notes, he tucked them away again. 'Help is on the way, as quick as it can.'

I'd barely set my babe down next to Bert's when the gate from the street creaked open and three women slipped through. At first glance little set them apart from the goodwives abroad on the streets of Nottingham; only when I looked closer did I mark a slant to green-eyes, an odd shape to their faces. The way they moved marked them as Fae, yet I'd be hard-pressed to pin them to the Lady's court. But High Fae or something other, they each took a poor orphan babe and cradled them with tenderness.

Bert kissed each child in turn. 'Guard them well, little sisters. Tell anyone who'd think to take these children from you that they're under my protection.'

I watched them go, fiercely missing Kate and Robbie. I was so near home, but I couldn't dare go to them, not with the Demisang about.

Robin came into the gardens, each step grudging, looking sad and bewildered. He'd never reminded me so much of Robbie. 'I looked in all the places Tuck might be other than the chapel – his quarters and the kitchens, the cellars, the library. He's not here.'

'Be glad he escaped the massacre, Locksley. Hold up, Bert.' Jack jerked his head towards the chapel. 'Is it safe to leave things as we found them? I'd hate to think of anyone else falling into the girl's traps.'

Bert was halfway out the gate, Julian's rope in hand, but he turned back and squinting against the late afternoon sun, let his gaze roam over the chapel walls and roof. 'A good lesson in why you're a warrior, Jack, and I'm the fool. You've more wisdom by far than I in the ways of war. Take the dog and the Archer to the street and wait for us.'

The gate closed and he held a hand out. 'Can you call fire, clever witch?'

Not all versed in craft can call fire beyond lighting candles or putting a spark to tinder; that was a true test, one that required force of will, control and a core of power within. Tapping that inner power came with a price.

I put my hand in his, knowing why Bert asked. 'There's no other way? This place means everything to Tuck.'

'None that would let me rest easy and not take days in the doing. Fire will cleanse the ground and destroy the rest of young Maeve's scheming.' He squinted at the rooftop again. 'So much death in one place raises a power of its own. Look close, Marian: the Demisang's spells feast on misery every moment we delay.'

He was right. Other sight showed me the shadows boiling at the base of the chimneys over the kitchens, writhing over all the windows and doorways. The spell-weave was growing ever larger, swallowing ghosts and wrapping all of St Mary's in murk. Haunts were struggling to escape, wailing in terror before sinking into darkness.

I set the first flame to the roof, another to the shutters, set more to wooden doors and left Bert to sing them higher, coaxing the fire to seek ways inside and trapping it there. Heat filled each breath, sent sweat drowning my face and soaking down my back. I heard Robin's shouts and Jack's sharp answer, heard other cries in the distance, and still I sent more fire.

When smoke curled thick and oily and flame shone in every window, Bert tucked me under an arm and tugged me through the gate. He kept going down the road, pushing our way through the gathering crowd, trusting Jack to follow.

We stopped under an oak at the edge of the greenwood. Breathing through my mouth was just about keeping me from retching, but the shadows dancing at the edge of my vision were making my head spin. I felt Bert start to let go and scrabbled to hang on, knowing I'd pitch onto my face without him.

He tightened his arm round me. 'Don't fret, little one. I won't let you fall.' Bert conjured a blanket, Jack spread it, then the two of them eased me down. I was shaking head to foot, cold nestling tight in my bones and feeling weak as a new-born foal. The Fae Lord brushed my hair off my face and whispered, 'Rest, Marian. Your Warrior will guard you while I seek word of the Demisang.'

Robin fingered the knife on his belt. He kept his face turned from me, but for once he straightened his shoulders and looked Bert in the eye. Tears slipping down his face, he said, 'A favour, if you would. Seek word of Tuck if you're able. He's a good man, better than I deserve to call friend. I'd save him if I can.'

Bert put on his brightest smile, clapped Robin on the shoulder, stepped back, spun in a circle and vanished.

I wrapped myself in the blanket and shut my eyes. Robin had the right of it: Tuck was a good man. That wouldn't save him.

Chapter 18

. . . let us sit upon the ground
And tell sad stories of the death of kings.

WILLIAM SHAKESPEARE

I slept for a short time, restless sleep, full of fire and spirits crying out in pain.

Jack was sitting next to me when I woke, his back against the tree, a hand resting on my shoulder. He smiled. 'The vixen came back, sniffed you and ran off again. You started yelling right afterwards, but got quiet soon as I touched you. Seemed best to let you sleep.'

'Where's Robin?' I sat up, relieved I was no longer shivering and dizzy. The light under the trees was little changed, the sun not much further in its slide down the sky. I'd hold it there if I could, but not even the Lady of the Fae had such power. We still had time until moonrise, though, and I had to be content with that.

'Not far.' He pulled his knees up and wrapped his arms round. 'Bert's got him spelled or some such. He set Julian to follow. If

Robin wanders too far, his tether jerks him right back. I'm close to feeling sorry for him.'

I saw the shimmer a heartbeat before Bert stepped from air. That he didn't try to mask his worry was more than enough reason for the sudden feel of eyes on my back. 'Now isn't the time for the Archer to vanish,' the Fae Lord said. 'Finding young Maeve is enough of a test.'

'Has she gone Underhill?' The wood was still too quiet, the birdsong muffled and the leaves rustling right overhead sounding far off. Many things sprang to mind as to the cause. None gave me joy.

'If she'd gone home, my sister would know.' He juggled absently, small balls of unpainted wood making a slow circuit. 'I've asked the Lady, but she knows no more than her fool of a brother. It's as if Maeve has stepped behind a wall and I've no way to see over it.'

'Maybe you'd be able to set Julian on her trail.' Jack stood and offered me a hand up. My knees wobbled, but held. 'He tracked for the king's foresters before he found the firedrake.'

Birds, nearly silent a breath before, screeched as one, fleeing the treetops and bushes, whirling in confused circles before winging away in panic. That was all the warning allowed us.

Sound reached us first: wind keening through the trees, a bean sidhe heralding death. A whirling gale followed, whipping the leaves back and forth until the air was full of green shreds. Jack pulled me close and curled over me, turning his back to the branches and brambles torn loose. He grunted in pain as splintered wood slammed his arm, but held fast, his heart beating hard and fast, his breath a rasp in my ear.

As suddenly as the maelstrom started, it stopped.

'You can let her go, Warrior. I think it's over.' Bert rested a hand on my head for an instant. 'You've my thanks. Now let Marian tend to your arm.'

He held me for a few breaths more before pulling away. 'The arm will do for the moment. I've had worse.'

'You're bleeding. I need to see how badly you're hurt. Hold still.' I ripped his sleeve, which was already dark with blood, jarring his arm. Jack couldn't stop himself hissing with pain as I pulled the cloth away from the wound. The gash wasn't as deep as I'd feared, but it was long and weeping blood the entire length. 'I don't have any of the things I need to clean away the dirt properly, nor the herbs to keep the wound from going bad, so staunching the blood and wrapping it is best I can do for now. Unless Bert decides to pull what I need from air.'

'I fear not this time, fair one. I don't think it wise. Enough magic's been unleashed and run wild this evening.' He picked broken twigs and scraps of leaves from his hair, his sharp eyes scanning trees and road. 'Your cottage isn't far and we're nearer still to the old dragon's meadow. You can tend to Jack at your hearth. We'll gather the Archer and leave straight away.'

'Hold a moment. Let me do what I can to stop the bleeding.' I took Jack's knife, cut a strip from the bottom of my gown and bandaged his arm while Jack, like Bert, watched the greenwood. They were Warriors both, no matter that Bert claimed to be nothing but a jester and a fool.

'My thanks, Marian.' Jack flexed his fingers and bent the arm. 'It's not too tight. I can use a bow easily.'

'Tell me what just happened, trickster.' The press of quiet and the feel of eyes on my back was still threatening to push me to my knees. 'Faith in the Lady's charm stretches only so far: I don't feel easy going near Kate and Robbie – I don't wish to lead the Demisang to my door.'

Bert turned towards me, genuine surprise on his face. 'The Lady gave you a charm? She said naught of that.'

The earth suddenly shifted beneath us and I grabbed for Jack, but neither of us kept our feet. All the giants left this land long before men arrived and yet I turned first to those old tales. The ground was rolling in waves, sending trees toppling and opening cracks a hand-span or more wide. Even Bert was thrown, landing on his back. I lay still, even after the wayward earth settled again, afraid of being knocked back down.

I'd thought this was the worst, being tossed about like a child's toy, watching giant oaks and stately elms and slim rowans swaying and crashing to the ground, knowing that if they fell towards me, I couldn't move in time.

I was wrong. There were things worse by far.

In his sun-drenched meadow, Marlow began to bellow. Sky-shattering roars full of pain and grief rang through the green-wood, every one reverberating, on and on, until the dragon lost his breath. Each time my heart nearly burst. I was wondering if he'd start again, or if each cry of agony would be the last. I was terrified of hearing him die and equally afraid of not knowing death when it came.

Bert grabbed my hands and pulled me up. 'Come, Marian, we've little time now. Hold tight to my hand and don't let go. Jack, find the Archer and follow us.'

I lifted my skirts to my knees with my free hand and ran at Bert's side as he began to sing, willing the Fae paths open.

Jack called after us, 'Where will I find you?'

'With the dragon!' I stumbled and Bert put an arm round my

waist. 'Robin knows where the dragon's meadow is,' I gasped, having breath enough only for running, as the way opened and closed around us.

We stepped back into the world of mortals at the edge of the meadow to see the dragon hunched in the midst of ruined grass and shredded flowers, panting and wheezing. No trace of glamour clung to him, which dismayed me more. I started to go to him, but Bert held me back.

'Have a care, Marian. The old dragon is half-mad with pain. He'll crush you and never know you've come.' He pulled me into the shelter of two silver birches, where we could see, but stay safely out of reach of lashing tail and lethally sharp claws.

Marlow stretched his neck to its full length, threw back his head and roared in agony.

I clutched at anger and held it close: being angry held off the helpless feeling. 'I can't stand by and watch him suffer, Bert. Tell me how to help him.'

The Fae Lord watched Marlow for a moment, then turned back to me. There was no trace of trickery or riddles in his eyes when he told me, 'Look around, gentle Marian. Look – but don't let your heart colour what you see.'

I did as he asked, and found yet more reason to grieve.

Uprooted grasses and flowers lay all across the meadow, petals and seedpods shredded, the smell of crushed greenery heavy in the air. Deep furrows scarred the ground, crossing one over the other all around the dragon. Marlow's wings were tattered widow's lace, the flesh eaten away to nothing but weeping holes surrounded by thin threads attached to bone. He spread them wide, trying to catch air, revealing more wounds shining red on his neck and belly. The sour scent of dragon-blood mingled with dying flowers.

The wyrm threw his head back and labouring for breath, screamed rage at the sky, then retched up pieces of bone and chunks of flesh in foaming yellow bile that soaked into the churned mud at his feet, staining his chipped claws.

'Oh stars, stars . . .' I could see the head of a stag and a half-eaten body a few paces away, a fresh kill. Blood congealed around the gaping wound where the stag's belly had been. Marlow had gorged himself on tender flesh, thinking nothing amiss.

Only one poison could kill a dragon. I'd have given all I owned to know how the scent and taste of iron had been masked from one so canny.

I fell to my knees, my hands clasped tight together, unable to breathe as Marlow continued to roar. He was still pawing at the ground, but his cries were growing weaker, his body sinking lower into the blood- and bile-soaked mud. His tail rose and slammed down, sending churned soil and grass into the air to rain down on him. New wounds ripped open on his back, oozing blood and pus. The skin flaked away around his eyes. At last the roars stopped, each wheezing breath saved to flail at the earth.

I searched with other sight, desperate to find a way to help him, but the iron was running in the dragon's blood, deep in his bones, even his heart. Wounds were bleeding as freely inside Marlow as out. If I'd possessed the powers of the Lady herself, still I wouldn't be able to save the guardian of Sherwood. I couldn't even ease his suffering.

I turned away. I hadn't the strength to watch Marlow dig his own grave.

Tears choked me, but I had to know. 'What of the dragon, Fae Lord? Did your sight show you any of this?'

'No, sweet child, no.' Bert wrapped me in his arms. 'This I didn't see.'

When the dragon grew too weak to do more than gasp for breath, I went to him and sat at his head, rubbing his soft jowls. He'd opened one eye when I drew near, sighing as if worry and pain had eased at the sight of me. Perhaps they did – if so, I was glad.

'Sleep, old wyrm, and join your brothers. You haven't hunted with them in far too long.' I tried to keep my voice light; he didn't need my pain to add to his own. 'They're waiting for you.'

I felt the rumble of his laugh under my hand. The tremor that followed told what that had cost. 'Would you have me cede this fight, fair witch?'

'You can't win, noble dragon, and you've earned your rest.' I wiped my face on a sleeve. 'Let others battle in your place.'

He didn't answer. He'd fight to the end, that I knew.

Bert was prowling the edge of the meadow, poking around rocks, trees and bushes. He'd waded across the stream, tucking something small he'd found on the far bank into his sleeve along the way. A ball of witch-light bounced at his shoulder, aiding his search, for dusk came quicker under the trees.

I was starting to fret that Jack and Robin hadn't arrived yet, and worried still more that they'd run into Maeve on the way, but they couldn't have travelled the way I'd come, running down Fae roads that brought me to the dragon's side in a moment, and walking the forest's human paths took longer.

'Marian.' Marlow stirred and I leaned closer to hear. 'I need a pledge from you. This is important.'

Bert whistled three long notes. Julian's bark answered, then Jack's voice, calling the dog back.

'You have it.' I rubbed his face, crying again and nearly blind with tears. 'Anything you ask.'

Small tremors rippled over Marlow's ravaged skin. He sighed. 'Forgive him . . .'

He grew cold quickly.

Mud squidged underfoot as I scrambled away from Marlow's body. My toe caught on my skirts and sent me pitching onto my face. I spat mud, but that did little good; the stench of bile and death was already coating my throat. I crawled away on hands and knees, sliding on the ripped-up grass, wanting nothing more than to be far away.

Jack caught me under the arms and lifted me to my feet. He wiped mud and tears from my face, not shying away from my grief. 'Come over to the stream with me, Marian. We'll see about getting you cleaned up.'

I nodded, for I wasn't sure I could pry words loose without breaking apart. Jack pulled me close, holding me tight and fierce, not uttering a sound. A tiny speck of warmth seeped back into me, a reminder there was more to life than grief. I found I wanted to stay in his arms until the edge of overwhelming pain was blunted, but the moon rose higher and time wouldn't hold still for me.

Stepping away from him was hard, but he kept an arm around my shoulders and walked me to the stream, staying quiet, but there if I needed him. I liked him all the more for that.

The water ran clear and cold, but still I struggled to rid myself of the taste of death, no matter how often I rinsed my mouth.

Getting my face and hands clean would have to do for now; the rest would wait. There were more important things by far to worry about than muddy skin and wool.

Robin sat with his back to the meadow. I'd no way to know what he was feeling or thinking, and in truth, I found I no longer cared. He'd known where to find Marlow in all our long years of roaming Sherwood, but he'd never dared to face the dragon. I'd always suspected it was fear kept him away, no matter how he went on about demons and offences against God, for he knew the old tales as well as I did. I guessed Robin was afraid the dragon would read all the dark secrets of his heart.

The moon crawled slowly up the sky, but still moving too swiftly for my liking, until the top edge peeked over the tallest rowan trees like a round-faced child spying from the loft. Power crowded the air, itching over my skin and filling my chest. Strong as I was in craft, I kept a tight rein on the temptation to drink in all I could hold: the strongest were often the first to fall prey to madness.

Maeve was already mad. The Lady's child would command all she could from the moon and still keep reaching for more. Robin had good reason to pray for his daughter's soul.

I wiped my face and went to stand with Bert and Jack. The Fae Lord stepped aside, making room for me between them. Dusk might deepen and blur the lines of the old wyrm's body, but it didn't change what was lying in the midst of the meadow.

'Long ages have come and gone since the world last saw the passing of a great dragon. It's been longer still since one as powerful as Sherwood's guardian crossed to the other lands.' Bert paced out a ways, grim-faced and no longer the trickster, spun and came back. 'None of the Lady's court has slain a dragon before. The Demisang will be cursed by all the Fae for this foul deed. If she'd done nothing else, killing the dragon would seal her fate. She must think there's much to gain.'

'The Demisang has what she wanted, Bert. And new ways to wound me. The dragon – Marlow – wouldn't allow her to harm me or my children, or anyone in Sherwood. He kept the forest free of evil and darkness. With him gone, there's nothing to stop her.'

'The moon is rising.' Robin stood, brushing leaves and loam from his breeches. He snatched up his bow and quiver. 'Maeve won't wait for us to puzzle out riddles. We need to find her, Marian.'

Bert turned from studying the dragon to studying Robin. He closed his eyes for an instant, the look of sorrow on his face come and gone in a breath. 'There's many a place to hide in the greenwood. Find your daughter if you can, Archer, and we too will seek young Maeve.'

After keeping so tight a rein, I was surprised when the Fae Lord sent him off on his own. Bert watched him go, his mouth set and hands balled tight, and only turned back to me once the shadows under the trees had swallowed Robin. How much Bert had changed, dropping his masks and letting me see his true face, made me shiver. The Fae trickster I'd first met would never have let me see the grief in his eyes, or the torment. He'd never have touched my cheek in passing before walking to the centre of the meadow.

I kept hold of Jack's hand and followed. Bert had seen some new thing. That he didn't hide it frightened me beyond measure.

Bert pulled his pipes from his sleeve and craned his neck to squint at the moon. 'We're out of time, Marian. You know these woods. Where would you seek young Maeve?'

Sounds filled the night: owls calling one to another, small creatures darted from shadow to shadow, rustling leaves in their wake. A rabbit screamed its dying cries, the sound near enough to a child's to set my heart racing.

Far from the meadow a fox barked and after a moment I listened closer, thinking it might be Bridget. The barking went on, sharp and insistent, pointing me towards a deep silence: a stillness that didn't belong in a summer forest.

'She's not at the cottage.'

The fox stopped barking.

'The standing stones – she's there.'

Bert whistled, calling Julian to him. He spoke in the dog's ear and sent him streaking into the trees. 'We need to run now, or we risk being too late. Hold tight to your Warrior's hand, Marian. I don't want to lose either of you.'

He took my other hand. 'No Fae paths run from Marlow's meadow to the standing stones, at least none we could risk taking.' Bert began to sing, weaving a different spell, one that would let us cover ground quickly as a galloping horse, neither tiring, nor stumbling. His spell bore us up and kept us strong, and if my heart was pounding hard as the stones came into view, that was not the Fae Lord's failing.

Chapter 19

Angels are bright still, though the brightest fell.
WILLIAM SHAKESPEARE

Not all rings hosted the Lady's court or saw high-ranking Fae entice maidens to dance under the moon, but those still in use seldom went empty. On a full-moon night the lesser Fae always came out in great numbers, the lobs and goblins, greenmen and brounys holding their own sort of revels, making music with pipes carved from bone and drums fashioned from hollow logs and bits of skin. The small ones mimicked their High Fae rulers, dancing until sunrise. The Fae nobles knew, but they let the lesser Folk be.

The standing stones were dark and lifeless, a rare thing with the moon's power at its peak. We hid just inside the tree line and watched for signs of the Demisang, though no glimmer of magic showed in other sight, nor any flash of spell-casting. Long talons of shadow slithered away from the tall stones, leaving dark twins on the grass. A hare burst from beneath a nearby bush and raced off, but nothing else moved.

If any of the lesser Fae were out, they were staying well hidden. Sudden terror that I'd chosen the wrong place filled me.

Jack touched my shoulder and leaned close to whisper, 'Do you hear that, Marian?'

I didn't at first. The sound was very faint, easily missed in the moan of wind through the stones ... then the small whimper came again and I knew.

'Kate ...'

Bert looked at me, we both flung balls of witch-light to blaze atop the standing stones and as the spell used to conceal the inside of the faerie ring was stripped away by the light, I saw my daughter, lying inside a salt circle paced out by the Demisang. Her hands and feet were bound, but she was tearing at the bindings with her teeth and twisting her hands, trying to loosen them. Blood wept into the cords and ran down her arms and her skin was rubbed raw where she'd fought to win free.

She whimpered with every movement: a small sound, but full of fear and pain.

The Fae Lord, Mikal, stood outside the salt circle near Kate's head, stripped to the waist. The scars marking his high rank gleamed on chest and arms. His skin was lighter, but the shape of his chin and long, sharp nose branded him as the Consort's brother. His mouth was thin-lipped and even from a distance, his eyes looked flat and cold. I knew there'd be none of Bert's brightness in his smile.

At a guess, the Lady's Consort was sired by a different father. A bend in Mikal's spine cocked one shoulder above the other, perhaps explaining something of why the Lady had passed him over in favour of his brother. He might have won top ranking, but in the Fae a twisted body was a sign of mixed blood, most often true goblin or greenmen. I was surprised that Maeve had tied her fate to Mikal; surely the court would never let them rule.

Only now did I spot Robbie as he came out of the shadow of one of the standing stones. He was pacing the circle drawn around his sister, struggling to carry a large silver basin as he trailed behind Maeve. His mouth was set in that puzzled frown I knew so well, but he never once looked towards Kate and that panicked me.

More light flared, racing from stone to stone and filled the spaces between with the amber curtain of Bert's wards. He meant to seal the Demisang and her Fae Lord away from escape, that much was clear, but he'd trapped my children as well.

'Stay hidden, Warrior,' Bert said softly. 'Creep closer when you may, your bow at the ready. Do whatever you must to keep the young ones from harm.'

I watched Robbie paying no heed to his sister's cries of pain. He was close enough to me now that I could see his eyes were as dream-clouded as the yeoman Maeve had bound in Nottingham. He was senseless to everything but what she willed him to see. That she'd bound my son made me sick to my stomach. Knowing I couldn't free him yet made it worse.

Bert took my shaking hand, his touch drawing my gaze to his face, until calm began to crowd out the panic coiled in my gut, letting me think straight again.

'Hold tight to anger, Marian,' he said. 'Anger will serve you better than fear.'

'Anger is an easy thing to ask of me.' Rage took root, grew and blossomed. 'But don't ask me to grant mercy for I can't.'

'The time for mercy is long past.' He glanced at me, his face set in anger that matched mine. 'Keep the circlet hidden till I say otherwise. We tread a path I didn't see.'

We strode towards the stone circle, hand in hand. Maeve ceased her slow pacing and stood behind my son, watching us come. She leaned to whisper in his ear, he set the basin on the ground and buried his face in her skirts.

'You should have stayed away, Uncle, and not leapt to do my mother's bidding. I'd have let you live.'

Bert stopped just short of his wards and gave her one of his bright smiles, poisonous as a viper's bite. 'What harm can an old fool do, Maeve? You'd be wiser to worry about the Lady's anger. And you'd be well to be wary of the witch of Sherwood as well. Those are her children you threaten.'

She'd clearly thought her name safe: there was a flinch, almost a step back before she mastered herself, that told me as much. Maeve put out a hand and Mikal stepped up to take it, looking to her for an answer. No lover's ribbons graced his arm, but I'd wager that Mikal was bound to her. No Fae Lord would defer to a Demisang, not unless she held him in thrall.

'I don't need to fear you or a mortal witch, Uncle. The Lady's power dwindles and she won't rule long.' Maeve ran a hand over Robbie's hair. 'More of the court begin to question why she hasn't produced an heir who lived. Some even whisper of a curse.'

'The Lady's child? Her baby is dead?' Anger grew until I was shaking with it.

Maeve glanced at Kate, then back to me. 'Not yet, but her spawn will be dead before the night is out. Why concern yourself with my mother's bastards, witch? God will take him into heaven when his time comes.'

'You play a dangerous game, Demisang.' Bert's expression

stayed the same, amused and watchful, but I could hear both insult and threat in his voice. 'The Folk won't be ruled by a child-killer.'

'Won't they? You'd be surprised how many are willing.' Maeve smiled, knotted her fingers in Robbie's hair and pulled his head back so he was looking her full in the face. He didn't resist or cry out but stood limp as a poppet. 'My mother will be content to let me rule with my father back Underhill. Robbie and Kate are the last ones to hold Da here. He'll come with me once I send them to God.'

I began to tremble, the need to do something almost more than I could hold, but Bert tightened his grip on my hand, offering comfort and keeping me from charging in to rip Robbie from the Demisang's arms. He knew the path we walked, or most of it, but I was following him on blind trust and hope. It chafed that Bert held back, but it was well and good that he remembered caution when I'd lost all memory of it.

'Do you truly think to bind the Archer to you with the deaths of his children?' He tipped his head, watching her the way a raven eyes a carcase before he feasts. 'You're twice wrong to think more murder will bring him to your side. The death of the summer child is what drove him away. Your father couldn't bring himself to hate you, Maeve, so he left.'

She flinched again. 'I'd only meant to scare Aidan – but he threatened to tell the Lady. I got angry and the game ... the game went too far. Da didn't understand that was a mistake. But I prayed to the Holy Mother, asking what to do to bring Da back to me and God sent me an answer. It's people who hold him here, or he'd have come home with me years ago. He'll stay Underhill this time.'

Kate began to roll, over and over, but before I could yell a warning she fetched up against the edge of the circle Maeve had paced. Power reached for Kate, lapping over her skin until she was covered with sparks and rippling will-o'-the-wisps. She screamed, the sound climbing higher with each ragged breath.

I lurched forward – and Bert yanked me off my feet, pinning my arms, holding me so my kicks landed on empty air. 'Let me go!' I screamed, 'let me go to her!'

Bert whispered in my ear, 'Be strong, Marian, and grant me a measure of trust. I won't fail you, I promise. This is not yet the time for us to act.'

I slumped in his arms, weeping from anger and frustration, but I would put my faith in Bert and his sight as he asked. His wards were keeping me from reaching Maeve, just as they kept the Demisang from fleeing the faerie ring. I might be able to pull enough power to me and break them, but I'd be a fool to try with Kate and Robbie so near, when a broken spell could lash out, the power under no one's control, catching them in the middle.

The moon was at the top of the sky now. Power came to me easily and I pulled in all I could hold. The Demisang might think me weak, but she was badly mistaken. I'd bide my time, doing as Bert asked and waiting on his word.

Scowling, Maeve dragged Robbie with her to the edge of the circle, scattered the salt with a toe and released the power. She turned to Bert, the coolness of her smile showing the truth in calling her the winter child. 'You think us trapped, Uncle. You think to wait us out? Remember which of us is the fool.'

She gestured to Mikal. 'Pick up the girl. We're leaving.'

Kate lay curled on her side, panting. Mikal stared at her for an instant, as if a human child was a new thing, then, confused, the Fae Lord looked to Maeve.

'I said, pick her up.' She poked Kate with her toe. 'Do it – we're going.'

With her attention spread among all of us, the Demisang's control slipped and Robbie came to himself for a few moments. Crying, he struggled to win free, until Maeve started soothing him, patting his back and murmuring in his ear until he drooped against her.

I realised that she'd never learned to juggle and I began to see part of the trickster's scheme: the more things we gave Maeve to keep in the air, the more likely she was to drop them all.

My trust came easier.

Bert let me slide from his grip, winking in a way that only I could see. 'You'd be foolish to leave now. Best to stay and barter for what you want, Maeve Mary.'

Her breath came faster and this time she did step back, her fingers opening and closing as if she were grasping to hold onto something – control of Mikal and Robbie, I guessed. Kate was still struggling to escape, which suggested the Demisang lacked the power to bring my daughter to hand.

'You've nothing I want, Uncle,' she rasped. 'I've no interest in your bargains.'

'You wouldn't stay to barter for a crown? For your life?' Bert looked to me, his voice soft. 'I've a need for what you carry, brave witch.'

He'd told me the time for mercy was past, but he still meant to offer Maeve a last chance to turn aside. The Fae cherished the few children born to them. They took abandoned Demisang children Underhill to raise when their mortal mothers couldn't keep them. Remembered fondness was in Bert's eyes, and more: the memory of a small girl before winter claimed her heart, for all he'd never speak openly of affection. It wasn't the way of the Fae to admit love.

I took the circlet from my hair. Foxfire played along the silver, lit the jewels like stars. Knowing what I carried made the crown all the heavier. Reluctance stayed my hand an instant, followed by the utter certainty that I had the right to claim the crown as my own.

He'd not tell me no, nor make me give up the crown; the truth of that sat in Bert's eyes. Knowing a kingdom was mine for the asking terrified me. I laid the circlet in his hand and turned away from regret.

Bert threw the crown high. It came down with Aelfgifu's fan, the carved fox and frog that Tuck had bought in Nottingham's market, and Maeve's poppet. He juggled them in a slow circuit, each one easy to see in the glow of his amber wards. 'There are other kingdoms, Maeve Mary, lands under the Lady's sway and away from the world of men. I've the power to take you there, along with any who wish to follow you. No one will question your right to rule.' He plucked the carved frog from the air and held it out for her to see. The rest continued to circle. 'By the Lady's command, death waits for any who bind a child. I have that power as well.'

Maeve pulled Robbie closer, stroking his hair: a shield to stay her uncle's hand, and mine, if she thought of me at all. I needed Bert to make an end to this now – or I would.

'You offer me exile, not a kingdom. Exile is close kin to death, but slow in arriving. Any land the Lady cedes me will be barren.' She looked up at that, the tilt of her head and the twist of her mouth reminding me far too much of Robin. 'Will my father follow me?'

'The Archer makes his own choices.' Bert waved a hand and the circlet balanced on his palm. 'Choose your path, Maeve Mary Magdalene. The witch of Sherwood has little patience left, and I've less still.'

He didn't bind her, but the weight of her name pulled down the corners of Maeve's mouth, turning the haughty young maid into a tired, sullen child. She sought Mikal's gaze and held it. 'I need to finish this now that I've started. Bring the girl.'

This time Mikal did pick Kate up – and she twisted her head and sank her teeth deep into his arm. He howled and dropped her, rubbing at the wounds, smearing blood everywhere. More blood dripped down his arm.

Disgust and anger replaced empty obedience. Mikal raised a booted foot to kick Kate in the face. 'You fawning piece of pig-shit – you'll not bite me again—'

Bridget and Julian streaked through Bert's wards, charging through the opening he'd made as if the curtain of light was nothing but harmless glitter and dazzle, an illusion meant to keep Maeve in hand so Bert could work his wiles. Dog and vixen darted in side by side, sank their teeth in Mikal's leg, danced back out of reach, then shot back in to bite him again. He screamed and spun away from Kate, gathered power sparking in his raised hands.

Puzzlement replaced rage before he'd taken a step. The Fae Lord fingered the arrow in his belly. He dipped his fingers in blood and stared at the sticky red stain. A second arrow took root in the Fae Lord's chest. Hands already slippery with blood pawed at the fletching, fumbling until he managed to break off the shaft. His eyes fluttering closed, Mikal pitched forward onto his face and lay still.

Julian and Bridget were standing over Kate, growling at Maeve with their teeth bared. The Demisang backed away, but my son was still held firm. She cried out, though not with grief for a dead lover: this was the wail of an angry child seeing her toy broken.

The Fae trickster's fingers twitched and Jack stepped out of the darkness and through the wards gleaming between two standing stones, his arrow nocked and ready. He took aim at Maeve and waited.

'Now, patient witch, now!' Bert threw the carved frog into the faerie ring. It charred to ash and the amber curtain blinked out, leaving our blue-white witch-lights blazing atop the stones.

Robbie began to cry and started pounding Maeve with his fists, trying to win free. She tangled her fingers in his hair, spun him to face away from her and wrapped an arm across his throat to keep him still. He clawed at her forearm, then stood on tiptoes, stretching back to try to reach her face, until she yanked his hair and tightened her grip on his throat. She was all but choking him before he stopped fighting.

I shoved will and the need to let him go at her on a strand of moonlight, a hard thing to craft with Robbie so close, done too quickly. Maeve gave me a sharp look and the spell shattered on her own surge of power, blue sparks raining to the ground, as if she'd effortlessly brushed aside the magic with a mere thought. She was left untouched. I feared she was beyond heeding anything but her own madness.

'You lied to me, Uncle.' She was weeping, but each word was sharp and bitter. 'You never planned to let us leave unharmed.'

'He didn't lie, Maeve. He'd have taken you and let you live in peace.' Robin slipped from the shadows between stones, his bow held loosely in one hand. 'The Fae don't break a pledge once given. But men make pledges too, and Jack is sworn not to let Kate come to harm. Now let Robbie go.'

'I did everything you asked of me, Da.' Tears ran down her face, but Maeve straightened her shoulders and looked Robin full in the face. 'I remembered all you taught me about Holy Mary and angels taking souls to heaven. I confessed my sins to God, asking him to forgive me for what happened to Aidan. And I waited for you – I waited and waited, but you never came back.'

Robin bowed his head and crossed himself, his lips moving in prayer, then he looked at her. 'I couldn't come back, Maeve. I'd duties here, and my own sins to atone for. That wasn't your fault.'

'No, *they* kept you here.' She stroked Robbie's hair, but she was paying him no more mind than a hound under her hand. 'They bound you to this place and wouldn't let you leave. God showed me the way to free you.'

'Locksley . . .' Jack held his bow steady. 'Say the word.'

Robin turned and held Jack's gaze for a breath or two, then returned his gaze to Maeve and nocked an arrow to his own bowstring. 'There's no need, Jack. Stand easy.'

The harlequin mask covered Bert's face and a jester's cap sat on his head. He leaned to whisper in my ear, the fool's bells ringing softly, 'This I've seen and know the working of. We've no part to play here, unless the Archer can't find the heart for his. Watch closely. You'll know if we need to act.'

'No one bound me, Maeve,' Robin said. The words were quiet, but I could hear the truth in every one. He stepped closer. 'Not the brothers at St Mary's, nor my friends, nor my brother

Will. And if any mortal had the power, Robbie and Kate are innocent of it.'

Her head came up sharply and for the first time the madness was stark in her eyes. 'Not so innocent, Da: the girl's a witch like her mother. And the boy – he poisoned the dragon.'

Robbie's eyes sought mine, over-large and dark in his too-pale face. Marlow's last words sounded sinister now . . .

Forgive him.

'God will forgive him. He forgives much if we turn away from sin.' Echoing tears tracked down Robin's face. He moved closer still, then took a pace to one side. 'You've sin enough on your soul, Maeve. Let your brother go.'

Jack moved with Robin, keeping his bowstring taut and his shot clear. Both fox and hound continued to growl through bared teeth, the sound full of menace, and while Bridget went slinking towards Maeve on her belly, Julian stood firm over Kate, guarding her. My daughter lay still and quiet, watching everything with wide eyes.

For an instant I thought Maeve would do as Robin asked, and I knew then that even so, I'd not let her walk away. She'd bound one innocent and hurt my own children in ways I wasn't sure would ever heal. As long as Maeve walked this world, they would know fear, and so would I. Whatever part Bert thought I was meant to play, there would be more.

'You've forgotten, Da. My brother was the summer child, most beloved of the Lady. She mourned him seven years before she left her chambers and sought the sun again.' Maeve kissed Robbie's cheek and tightened her arm on his throat. 'I used to dream of the sound Aidan made while he was dying – such a small sound, to cause so much grief.'

Bert put a hand on my arm to hold me, but I used my gathered power to push him aside and ran—

Robin's arrow took Maeve in the throat before I'd covered even half the distance. She tried to speak, dropped her arm from Robbie's throat to stretch her hand towards her father, took a stumbling step.

'May God forgive you, Maeve Mary.' Robin choked on a sob and steadied his fingers on the bowstring. 'I can't.'

The second arrow found her heart.

I snatched up my son, running hands gently over his throat, listening to his wheezing, rasping coughing and choked sobs. He'd no open wounds and for that I was deeply thankful, but I'd no way to tell how badly he was hurt. The nonsense I murmured in his ear was less than useful for staunching tears, his or mine, but I couldn't bring myself to stop.

'Marian, let me see to the boy. Just for a moment.' The mask was gone; Bert's face was set in kind lines, the fond uncle once again. He smiled at Robbie as he slid his long fingers down the boy's neck, taking care to move slowly, not to startle him, all the while humming a bright, merry tune.

When the song ended, Robbie was breathing easy, but still I clung to my son, rocking him as I had when he was a babe in arms. I looked around for my daughter and found her in Jack and Bridget's care. The vixen was washing Kate's face with her tongue, cleaning away dirt and tears, while Jack cut the cords binding her. He was speaking calmly all the while, explaining everything he was doing, even warning Kate to be ready for the pain when he eased the rope away from the bloody wounds on her wrists.

Julian was sitting near Jack, still for once. He whined softly, deep in his throat, but somehow the dog knew to stay out of the way while Jack worked. I heard Kate asking questions about the odd-looking, scarred hound and I worried about her a little less.

Moonlight picked out the tears slipping down Robin's face as he knelt next to Maeve, chanting blessings for the dead to send her on the way to God. I'd once watched Tuck do the same for an old farmer and knew that each cross marked on forehead, hands and feet carried deep meaning.

Bert waited until the prayers were finished and Robin stood up before he lifted Maeve into his arms and cradled her close. His face was marked with grief he didn't attempt to mask. The Fae did love their children.

'I'll see that she's buried as befits a child of the Lady and her spirit sung to the other land. You're welcome to come with me, Archer. None will deny you the right, you have my pledge on it.'

'Underhill isn't the place for me.' Robin wiped his face on a sleeve. 'Lay her to rest with her brother, if you would. I'll pray she finds peace now.'

Bert bowed his head. 'As you wish, Archer. And may you too find peace.'

When he turned to me, I knew the sadness in his eyes was real. 'I'll see you again, sweet Marian. Make your Uncle Bert happy before our paths cross again: find your way back to life.'

The air behind him shimmered, a door opening to another place. I caught sight of bright sunlight, hills green with new spring grass. He settled Maeve in his arms, spun on his heel and was gone.

I blinked away tears, already missing him. But my children

needed me and I wouldn't rest easy until I saw them sleeping safe in their own beds. There would be time to come to think of all the days past, of all the things I'd seen and learned.

For now, we were going home. I found joy in that.

Chapter 20

Grey and ghostly shadows are gliding through the brake;
Shadows of the dappled deer, dreaming of the morn,
Dreaming of a shadowy man that winds a shadowy horn.

ALFRED NOYES

The cottage was sitting silent in the shadow of the oak. I'd seldom seen home looking empty and abandoned, with no fire in the hearth or a single candle-flicker showing past the shutters. But after my children were born I'd not travelled far afield, so a homecoming such as this was a rare thing. The vixen ran ahead, sniffing the doorstep first, then circling the entire cottage. She came back to the front, nudged the door open. Julian followed her inside, tail wagging.

After a moment, Bridget came back to the step and yipped. All was well.

Jack carried Kate inside, followed by Julian, who insisted on licking her toes, making her giggle. The dog leapt on the bed as soon as Jack had laid her down and stretched out, his head near her shoulder, his tail slung over her legs. She snuggled up to him and was fast asleep within seconds. My Kate was strong, a fearless girl at times, but what Maeve had done to her and Robbie would leave its mark. If having the dog close let her rest easy and feel safe, I was grateful for the gift.

Robin hesitated on the threshold, watching me light candles and call fire to the hearth. Robbie was asleep on his shoulder, looking small and much younger in his father's arms. He'd never held his son before. I knew I wasn't imagining the regret in Robin's eyes.

'Put Robbie next to Kate for me if you would, Robin.' I hunted in the chest at the foot of the bed for the spare blanket. 'It will be easier for me to take care of them down here tonight. You and Jack can take the pallets in the loft.'

'I won't be staying, Marian. But if you'll allow it, I'd like to visit Kate and Robbie soon. I've a lot to make up for.' Robin gently brushed the hair back from Robbie's face. As he watched our son sleep, I wasn't sure which child he was seeing, the one here or the one long lost. 'Someone in town might have word of Tuck by now. I am praying he's safe and that Maeve ... I need to know what happened to him.'

'They're your children too, Robin. I won't stop you from visiting. And you know Tuck is as much my friend. I'd be grateful if you'd send word when you can, and if you get word of Tim, too.' I hugged the blanket in my arms, suddenly reminded that I wasn't yet finished mourning myself. Tomorrow I'd try to find where Beth fell and lay her ghost to rest. 'I'll hope for good news.'

Robin turned back at the door. 'Mari ... I'm sorry. Truly. I never should have lied to you. I don't expect you to forgive me and it won't make things right, but ... I'm sorry for all of it.'

With that, he walked away. Night swallowed him two strides

from the door as completely as if he'd never been here. This time I wouldn't weep over his leaving.

Jack put his arms around me, resting his chin on the top of my head and trapping the blanket between us. 'I've a favour to ask, Marian, if you think Kate would be willing. Do you think she'd look after Julian for me? I need to leave myself—' At my flinch, he said quickly, 'Just for long enough to sell the mill for Meg, or find someone to run it for her if she wants to stay. I'll be back once Meg is settled somewhere safe.'

'It's clear Kate's taken to the dog already. She won't say no to Julian being around as long as you like.' I pulled back so as I could see his face. 'Are you sure you're coming back for the dog?'

'Not just for the dog. I'm hoping you won't say no to keeping me around too.' He brushed his fingers down my cheek and didn't look away. 'Watch for me when the leaves begin to fall. I don't expect you to stop mourning Will that quickly, but I want to give you some time to think things through.'

I took a breath. My heart was pounding, my mouth dry. Bert had asked me to find my way back to life. For just an instant, I wished for his sight to see the road ahead, knowing that was one wish I'd not be granted. 'Then it's settled. When will you leave?'

'Tomorrow morning,' he said. 'The sooner gone, the sooner back again, and leaving will be harder if I stay over-long.'

'At least let me tend to your arm before you go!'

'No need. I'm guessing Cassie wove a bit of herself into that scrap of wool, for the wound's nearly healed.' He cupped my face in his hands and kissed my forehead. 'Sleep well till we meet again, fair Marian.'

Jack climbed the ladder into the loft. I wrapped the blanket around my shoulders and settled myself at Kate and Robbie's feet. Sleep came easier than I'd expected.

I woke just after dawn. Buttercups and meadowsweet covered the top of my small table, tied in bunches and nosegays with thin strips of damp blue wool.

A promise. I'd take it, and be glad.

Acknowledgements

Like most writers, I'm always afraid I'll forget to thank someone when it comes time to write the acknowledgements. I'm going to beg forgiveness in advance, because it's inevitable I'll leave someone out.

A huge thank you to Steve Mancino for the mediaeval era research help and encouraging me to write this book, and to Dennis Wright for confirming I had the history straight. More thanks to all the denizens of the Zoo, past and present, especially Rae Carson, Charlie Finlay, Elizabeth Bear, Amanda Downum, Kat Allen, Fran Wilde and Celia Marsh for their friendship and encouragement, to Stephanie Burgis for being my shining example of not ever giving up, to Susan Jett for being willing to read anything I write, no matter how rough, to my poetry group, The Musers, Marcy Mariotte, Mikal Trimm, Marcie Tentchoff, John Borneman and David Kopaska-Merkel, who tolerate my absence and encourage me to chase my dreams, and to all the writers and readers cheering me on. I see you all and I won't forget. Finally, my deepest thanks and gratitude go to my agent, Michael Carr, for seeing this novel the way I did, and being willing to take me and this book on.

Jaime